KEEP YOUR
ENEMIES CLOSER

KEEP YOUR ENEMIES CLOSER

SHARON OLIVER

URBAN
CHRISTIAN

www.urbanchristianonline.net

Urban Books
1199 Straight Path
West Babylon, NY 11704

ISBN-13: 978-1-60162-965-4
ISBN-10: 1-60162-965-6

First Printing July 2008
Printed in the United States of America

10   9   8   7   6   5   4   3   2   1

*This is a work of fiction. Any references or similarities to actual events,
real people, living, or dead, or to real locales are intended to give the
novel a sense of reality. Any similarity in other names, characters,
places, and incidents is entirely coincidental.*

Distributed by Kensington Publishing Corp.
Submit Wholesale Orders to:
Kensington Publishing Corp.
C/O Penguin Group (USA) Inc.
Attention: Order Processing
405 Murray Hill Parkway
East Rutherford, NJ 07073-2316
Phone: 1-800-526-0275
Fax: 1-800-227-9604

DEDICATION

This book is dedicated to the memory of my mother, Charlotte M. Oliver (1936-1998), whom I sorely miss and whose death was like that of a grain of wheat which fell to the ground to produce a harvest. 'Til we meet again . . .

ACKNOWLEDGMENTS

First and foremost, I would like to acknowledge my Lord and Savior, Jesus Christ, who reminded me that He knew the plans He had for me, and they were plans for my good, not disaster (Jeremiah 29:11).

To my sister and brother-in-law, Esma and Johnny Dennis: there is no greater love than what we have for each other. I thank God that He answered my prayer as a child for a little sister. To my father, Ben Oliver: thank you for not being an absentee father. You surprised me with your support. I love you so much.

To my cousins *in the know*: Teresa M. Oliver and Ernestine Johnson. You encouraged me from the beginning.

Those who knew: Carla Aveirls, Sharon D. Davis, Parrish Williams, Prophet Dallas Williams, Kathy Richardson Caw, Ertha and Debra Bowman, Natalie Favors, Christa Oliver, Charlisa Hinson, Alphonso and Daisy Black, Kim and Phyllis Johnson, Angela Taylor, and Sharniece Moore. Thank you all for believing in and pushing me.

And last but not least, to my former supervisor, Nikki Flowers, Esquire, my mentor and friend, who helped me recognize the seed for what it was. You truly were the catalyst that propelled me in this direction to challenge my God-given abilities. I love you. You have stuck by me with encouragement and would not allow me to dash water on my dream. You deserve praises for your loyalty.

To Joylynn Jossel and the UC family: thank you for embracing me. May the favor of God rest upon you.

PART ONE

*And call upon me in the day of trouble; I will
deliver you, and you will honor me.*

Psalm 50:15

1

"Mash it! You gotta mash down hard on the lock," Mattie Mae said to her granddaughter, Charlotte. They were ten minutes late, and Mattie Mae Morley did not like being late for church, especially when it was her turn to read the announcements and welcome visitors. Mattie Mae's husband, Edmund, was already several paces ahead of them.

With beads of perspiration threatening to ruin her makeup, Charlotte stood under the hot August morning sun, struggling with the door lock of Edmund's old, beat-up truck and trying to understand his reason for locking the truck in the first place. After all, this was the country, the deep South. Charlotte loved coming to the small coastal town of Turtle Island, South Carolina. It was a refreshing change from her hometown of Washington, D.C. The biggest crime that local authorities had to contend with, as far as she knew, was the frequent disorderly conduct of the town drunk, Otis Moss.

Aside from that, there had only been occasional reports of grand theft chicken, also compliments of Otis

Moss. Apparently, Otis had a fondness for stealing Nora Jones's hens from her chicken coop. Sista, as Nora was affectionately called, was Mattie Mae's oldest and closest friend, but Sista and Otis were far from being friends. In fact, the two fought worse than cats and dogs. "It seems to me that the only thing that needs locking around here is Miss Sista's chicken coop," Charlotte mumbled to herself as she kept fumbling with the lock.

Charlotte checked herself out in the driver's side mirror. With her ring finger, she smoothed over the smoky gray eyeshadow she chose for her eyelids then smacked and puckered her lips for an even blend of the frosted lip gloss. Satisfied with her skillfully applied makeup, Charlotte returned to the duty at hand. Finally, she got the lock to snap in place and made a mental note to take her grandfather's truck to a mechanic for repairs as she made her way up the old brick steps leading to the entrance of Greener Pastures AME Church.

As soon as Charlotte took a seat on one of the back row pews, childhood memories of summer visits on the island made her smile. She and her cousins were dragged to church every Sunday by their grandparents. It was a Morley family tradition to send the grandkids to Edmund and Mattie Mae, saving money that would have otherwise been spent on babysitting and/or summer camp fees. Charlotte's parents had trusted her enough to travel on the Trailways bus to South Carolina alone since she was twelve years old. Her mother, Betty, would dutifully pack her lunch in a greasy brown paper bag. It consisted of fried chicken sandwiches, thick slices of jelly-layered coconut cake, and a large mason jar filled with iced water, which would turn into warm, tasteless liquid by the time Charlotte got to her destination.

Even though things had changed in the years since her own childhood, Betty still insisted on preparing lunches whenever they traveled. Packed lunches had been a must for African-American travelers for many years. They weren't allowed to eat in most of the white establishments back in the day, and if they were allowed, they usually didn't trust the person who slipped their meals to them through a back door.

Now that Charlotte and her cousins were all adults, they no longer needed looking after by their grandparents. However, she still enjoyed visiting her grandparents on the island whenever she got the chance. Spending summer vacations on Turtle Island was still one of her favorite pastimes. Life there was so simple. It was an oasis, an escapism that took her away from the pressures and disappointments of adulthood. The air was fresh and free of smog. Turtle Island was a charming town. Many of the hundred-year-old oak trees were draped in Spanish moss, and the cypress, willow, banana, and palm trees added character to the tiny town. Although she often found the Southern dialect of the island residents to be comical, every word came from the heart and was honestly stated. They were a warm and friendly lot who greeted strangers as if they were longtime friends.

However, up North was an entirely different story. If a stranger dared to speak or gazed at you for too long, it was a sure bet that there would be repercussions. Turtle Island seemed void of the stress typically caused by heavy rush-hour traffic, schedules, and meeting deadlines. The deafening shrills from sirens blasting from patrol cars, ambulances, or fire trucks sounded like air raids, and it felt good to get away.

The time spent with kinfolk during her childhood was what she considered real family reunions, before black folks coined the phrase, picked the site, and scheduled the events. Going down South and getting together with loved ones used to mean spontaneous fun and family unity. Now, whenever anyone tried to coordinate a family reunion, it would turn out to be nothing more than a stressful formality resulting in a few arguments and hurt feelings.

Charlotte fought hard to keep from falling asleep during church service. But she began dozing off anyway as soon as the preacher started reading from the New Testament, Book of St. Luke. The Greener Pastures's Senior Choir's singing beforehand hadn't helped matters either. They might as well have selected a lullaby instead of "I Know It Was The Blood." Their monotone voices sent Charlotte flying toward la-la-land.

Before drifting into her shameful slumber, Charlotte had been totally turned off by Reverend Holiday's ranting and ravings about how the religious leaders used to question Jesus' authority. The reverend vehemently compared it to how the congregation of Greener Pastures challenged his own authority and leadership, hinting at taking action against usurpers.

If it weren't for an annoying fly that kept buzzing around her ear like an alarm clock, Charlotte probably would have slept, not only through the mind-numbing sermon, but past the benediction as well. However, she woke up just in time to see the congregation scampering out the front door like racehorses, and she followed suit after snuffing out the life of the fly with a Martin Luther King fan. Charlotte was embarrassed and ashamed of herself for sleeping through service, especially since she, too, was an ordained minister.

Suddenly, a strange feeling came over her as she walked down the brick steps. She found herself feeling sad and depressed. This was not the first time that sadness came for no apparent reason. As a child, neighbors used to speculate that she had ESP, while some analyzed her as being overly sensitive. But like Mattie Mae, Charlotte knew that it was the Holy Spirit.

"I don't think I can take one more Sunday of that man shamin' God like that!" Charlotte heard her grandmother telling Sista. Mattie Mae, who was somewhat portly, and Sista, who was almost as thin as a sheet of paper, were standing near Edmund's truck expressing their opinions. Charlotte tiptoed over to the truck, careful not to break one or both of her stiletto heels, opened the door, and sat inside. It was just too hot to be standing outside in the sun.

"Reverend Holiday talking 'bout he called to preach. Ain't nobody call him to preach. He just went, wit' his big-doin' self. I get sick of him tryin' to scare folk. That man ain't nothin' but Satan wearin' a black robe," Sista said defiantly, with one hand on her hip and the other hand thrashing in the air.

"And have you ever noticed his hands? He's got soft hands. I bet he ain't never worked hard a day in his life. You and me, we worked hard all of our lives. Just look at our hands." Sista stretched out her hands, layered and rough with calluses and thirsty for lotion. "The back of our hands look like we've been walkin' on 'em. I think a person's hands say a lot about 'em. Don't you?"

Charlotte chuckled at the comment as she searched in the rearview mirror for her twenty-four-year-old twin cousins, Tina and Terry, who were nowhere in sight. Tina and Terry were her Uncle Charles's bourgeois daughters, who were also down for a visit. Charlotte wondered why they even came. Although they'd been in town less than a week, neither one of them liked Turtle Island.

Edmund and Mattie Mae had raised Terry since she was thirteen years old, while Tina remained with her parents. Terry did, however, spend her school breaks with her parents and sister in Washington, D.C. After the twins graduated from college in Atlanta, they both moved back to Washington, D.C. to live.

"I don't know what those two are up to, but I know they're up to no good," Charlotte said to herself. She remembered seeing a pretentious Tina acting as if she was filled with the Holy Ghost during church service. "My poor cousin is filled with a spirit all right." Charlotte sighed and shook her head. "Something wicked this way comes."

2

Charlotte had come to Turtle Island to get some rest before starting her job as a staff counselor at her new church home. Charlotte had joined Greater Faith Center a year earlier, after months of searching for a new church. She had left one that frowned upon female preachers. She didn't appreciate being treated as some sort of she-devil just because she wore her hair in twists. Many staff members at her former church, Truth in Love Tabernacle, frowned upon her hairstyle. Members of the ministerial staff, particularly the men, looked at her hair as if it represented the devil's horns, and treated her as such. The fact that she was going through an ugly divorce at the time had also earned her looks of disapproval.

As soon as Charlotte found out that her husband, Anthony, was "fellowshipping" with one of the "sisters" from the church, she had filed for a divorce. Throughout their entire four-year marriage, rumors and evidence of Anthony's bed hopping had been surfacing. The entire church, including children, knew of his blatant affair with the young usher. And as if the pain and embarrassment caused by this illicit affair weren't enough, the pastor pulled Charlotte, not Anthony, aside for "a little talk." Pastor Brown emphatically told Charlotte that she should concentrate more on being a virtuous woman instead of bucking so hard for a place in the pulpit. He suggested she curtail the amount of time she spent at church, advising that she should spend more time ministering to her husband.

Point well taken, and she agreed it was applicable and sound advice. However, after informing Pastor Brown that Anthony was never home for her to minister to in the first place, Charlotte suggested that perhaps he should have "a little talk" with her husband as well, right after he took his religious foot off of her neck. She politely pointed out that if Anthony controlled his roving eye and strong urges to unzip his pants, the divorce would not be happening.

Furthermore, she wanted Pastor Brown to know that she *was* a virtuous woman and she was not bucking for a position on the pulpit. Although she longed for a chance to teach, she did not wish to take over his position as leader. She only came to church to learn, worship, and serve. Anthony, on the other hand, attended church to lust, conquer, and be served some human flesh. Charlotte also pointed out that she was insulted by Anthony's decision to add salt to the wound by sleeping with a member of her church. The scandalizing scoundrel didn't even try to go undercover with his mess.

Once Charlotte and Anthony officially separated, he and his girlfriend stopped attending Truth in Love Tabernacle. Two months after the divorce, Anthony phoned Charlotte to express his regrets. He told her that he had made a mistake and wanted her to give him another chance. Charlotte poured out her regrets also, calmly informing her cheating ex that she regretted marrying him in the first place, and he could squash the idea of a second chance. The relationship between Charlotte and her pastor also deteriorated after their finger-pointing conversation, and she left Truth in Love not long after that. Sadly, because of Pastor Brown's dry and repetitive sermons, half of the parishioners also exited.

Charlotte looked in the rearview mirror again to see if her cousins were nearby, but saw no sight of them or their rental car. It would be just like them not to go straight to the house, in order to get out of helping with dinner. Despite theories that most twins are kindred spirits, everyone in the Morley family knew that Tina and Terry were not. In fact, the two had a nasty habit of competing against one another, and now they were on the island acting as if they were soul sisters? Whenever the two siblings did act as if they were of one accord, history proved otherwise. The last known stunt that Tina and Terry pulled had the entire Morley family talking for months.

A few years ago, Tina somehow managed to convince Terry that they should celebrate their high school graduation by taking a trip to Hawaii, unbeknownst to and at the expense of their well-to-do parents. One day, their mother, Francine, received a bill for purchases made at a trendy boutique in Maui, a place she had not visited. Tina and Terry had nearly bought out the store with one of Francine's cherished platinum credit cards. Francine was livid! She didn't even know the two had gone to Hawaii. In fact, Francine was under the impression that the twins had celebrated their graduation in Virginia Beach that particular weekend. Tina would later claim that the whole idea of going to Hawaii and going on a shopping frenzy was Terry's.

Charlotte was growing more and more suspicious

ıt the presence of Typhoon Tina and Tropical Storm ry. She had briefly considered spending her summer vacation relaxing on the white sands of St. Croix, but for some reason, the pull to go to Turtle Island had been stronger. It was almost as if there was some sort of urgency that required her presence. Charlotte forced herself to stop thinking about her cousins and turned her focus back to her grandmother's conversation with Sista.

"You know, Sista," Mattie Mae began, "I was just thinkin' the other day about how Esau and Betty done such a good job raisin' Charlotte. Look at how she turned out. I'm so proud of her. She got rid of that husband the devil sent her and now she's a minister. I sho' do hope I get to hear her preach some day. Now, as for Tina and Terry, I don't know what to say about them two wit' they little fast behinds. Ever since they've been here, they been stickin' to each other like glue and always whisperin' about somethin'. They hardly say anythin' to me and Edmund, or even Charlotte, since they been here. And *we raised* Terry! And raisin' Terry was like tryin' to break in a mule, let me tell ya. That gal is so stubborn and downright stiff! I just don't know, Sista." Mattie Mae sounded exasperated. "Me and Edmund done all we could, but it seems as though every time Terry is around Tina, she act like she ain't got no sense."

"Mattie Mae, I know they is yo' grandchi'ren, but I used to always tell you them two is as crack as a sidewalk, 'specially that Terry. Tina don't half speak to nobody, and Terry talk so proper, I don't half know what she be tryin' to say."

"I know it, but Terry didn't act so crack until she left from here," Mattie Mae defended.

"Mattie Mae! Terry been crack ever since she first come here as a chile," Sista corrected.

Charlotte struggled not to laugh out loud at Sista. She

had always admired Sista for her bluntness. No matter who you were or what you thought about her opinions, she was going to let you have it, like it or not.

"It ain't their fault, Sista," Mattie Mae began to explain. "And it sho' didn't help that Charles and Francine was half-raisin' them gals, lettin' all kinds of folk in their house like that. Maybe if I had both of 'em here wit' me, things would've turned out different. I tell you one thing, though: God sho' got His hands on Charlotte. I can see that. And she can pray up a storm, too."

"I can remember when she was just a little bitty thing runnin' around here," Sista said, opening her eyes wide, as if she just remembered something. "Oh yeah, I forgot to ask you if you heard 'bout Lucille's chile bein' on drugs. Just throwin' her life away. These chi'ren sho' know how to put a hole in a mother's heart."

"I did hear about that. It's such a shame."

"I don't know why that gal got herself hooked on that stuff. I tell ya the truth. She ought to know better. You know they buryin' Annie Nettles's son tomorrow afternoon over at Macedonia. He wasn't but twenty-two years old, and they tell me he was on that stuff too! These young people droppin' off like flies. They don't realize they can leave here just as quick as us old folk can. Anyhow, I'll talk to ya later on today." Sista spotted her son, John Edward, arriving to pick her up, and walked over to his car. "We gotta keep prayin' for the chutch too," Sista shouted back as she opened the passenger door. John Edward waved at Mattie Mae before driving off in his turbo-charged Mustang.

By this time, Edmund was seated inside the truck and had asked Charlotte what she thought of today's sermon. Charlotte shifted to the middle of the seat to make room for Mattie Mae. She dreaded admitting to her grandfather that she slept through most of the service, and was saved from doing so when Mattie Mae instructed Edmund to hurry up and drive, prompting a minor road trip spat. Edmund drove off of the gravel-covered parking lot muttering about Mattie Mae's bossiness. After all, it was she who kept them waiting in the first place. Then like bats out of Hades, Charlotte could see Tina and Terry tailgating them in Tina's rented BMW.

Edmund and Mattie Mae argued up until the time they arrived at the house. Edmund parked his truck on the side of the wood-frame house, running over a gardenia bush loaded with flowers. This careless act cost him a stern tongue-lashing from Mattie Mae as she squirmed and wiggled out of the truck.

"Didn't we just leave the church? Apparently there wasn't anything in the message about keeping peace," Charlotte said to herself as she slid out of her seat. Sensing Mattie Mae's irritation had little to do with Edmund, Charlotte asked the Lord for insight, and in a still, small voice, she heard the words "watch and pray."

3

"Grandma, what's going on with your church?" Charlotte asked as she followed Mattie Mae inside the house. Edmund remained outside struggling to revive the flattened gardenia bush.

"Why do you ask that?" Mattie Mae asked, tossing her crocheted purse on the sofa.

"I just sense that something there isn't right. And when I heard you and Miss Sista talking . . ."

"First of all, how would you know if something is not right? You slept through the whole service," Terry interrupted, surprising Charlotte, who was unaware of Terry's presence.

Slithering like a snake, Tina came sauntering behind Terry, wearing a smirk worthy of being slapped off her face. However, Terry's attempt to get a rise out of Charlotte failed. Not feeling quite so holy, Charlotte wisely chose to ignore the comment and went upstairs to her room to change clothes, skipping the chance to hear her grandmother's answer to her question.

Mattie Mae went into her spacious kitchen, thinking

about her expected dinner guest as she called out to her granddaughters to set the table. Since she was on the Willing Workers Committee, it was her turn to feed Reverend Holiday, and she was not too happy about it. Mattie Mae did as most women in the South did when it came to preparing Sunday dinners: she fixed most of the meal the night before. She had, however, gotten up early to fry the chicken before going to church, and kept it warm in the oven.

Mattie Mae was grateful for her blessings, but she did have one topic of complaint: Reverend Holiday. He was a definite thorn in her side. "He really thinks we don't have any sense, but I got plenty of sense," she fumed to herself. "That is one well-fed, fat-behind man." She stirred the collard greens that had been picked fresh from the garden. "He's got his feet planted at somebody's table every day of the week, and I don't care if he ain't married! He usin' Lois like he's married. Over there eatin' up all her food. That gal sho' is fool!" Poor Lois Watkins was the church's homely-but-has-money-in-the-bank secretary. Allegedly, she was also the reverend's girlfriend. Lois was the daughter of Busta, one of Edmund's closest friends.

Mattie Mae began to ponder Charlotte's question concerning the church. Charlotte was correct in discerning that something was not right. Confusion had been birthed in the church, causing a riff. Half of the members were threatening to boot Reverend Holiday out of the church, and the other half promised to follow him if he left. "Folk busy threatening this and busy threatening that, and here he is wit' his greedy self comin' to my house for Sunday dinner," Mattie Mae mumbled as she checked on her bubbling macaroni and cheese.

On one occasion, a member who wanted the reverend

hog-tied and railroaded out of Greener Pastures told Mattie Mae, "I wouldn't throw that no-count preacher my hog slop, much less let him in my house and feed him." But one of the mothers from the church convinced Mattie Mae to go ahead and serve the reverend, pointing out that, "It's the Christian thing to do."

Meanwhile, Edmund had given up on trying to salvage the downed gardenia bush and was in the living room resting comfortably in his recliner, savoring some of the aromas of this Sunday's dinner. The scent of candied yams, peach cobbler, and the mouth-watering ham covered with a mustard, cloves, and brown sugar glaze had him excited. Edmund could withstand any tongue-lashing Mattie Mae gave him, but he just couldn't live without her cooking. He loosened his tie and watched a cable news network while rehearsing in his mind what he was going to say to the jackleg preacher once he arrived.

"Reverend Holiday needs to be somewhere askin' for forgiveness instead of comin' over here parking at my table and gorgin' down food!" Edmund huffed to himself.

Twenty-seven-year-old Reverend John Cedric Holiday came from a small fishing town in South Georgia. He had recently graduated from seminary school in Memphis and was now the senior pastor of his first church. Reverend Holiday had only been at Greener Pastures for about six months and had already earned a not-so-nice reputation. He was a short, dark-skinned, pudgy, bald-headed man whose favorite pastime was eating. Some locals considered him to be kind of cute, in an odd sort of way. Sista thought he looked like an overgrown toddler.

Immediately after church service, Reverend Holiday

rushed over to the parsonage and changed from his brown pinstriped suit into a navy blue polo shirt and a pair of navy blue elastic waistband pants. He then drove hastily to the Morleys's home with aluminum foil in tow and visions of leaving with leftovers. Many people on the island, including the reverend, viewed Mattie Mae as the best cook in the community, maybe even in the whole county. Driving way above the speed limit, it took the famished preacher no time to reach the Morleys's modest home.

Once Charlotte returned downstairs, she noticed Tina practically charging out the front door with a tomcat grin on her face. That's when Charlotte saw Reverend Holiday parking his brand new Cadillac Escalade behind Edmund's truck.

Charlotte had been in South Carolina for only three weeks, and had spent the past three Sunday mornings at church. Reverend Holiday failed to plant a Word in her spirit, and she had become extremely agitated by his whooping and hollering.

What in God's name is he talking about? she had asked herself the previous Sunday. *And for God's sake, what is with his screaming? Is he going to just scream his way through, or is he going to say something?* Yet, with every whoop and every holler, he got an "Amen" from the congregation, as if they really understood what he was rambling about.

Edmund muttered something as he walked by to take his place at the head of the dining room table.

Charlotte removed the blue velvet case that contained the silverware from the china cabinet, and heard Tina inviting Reverend Holiday in. "Grandma and I slaved in that kitchen all night for you, Reverend Holiday," Tina lied.

Charlotte couldn't believe Tina had said that. She wondered why she was lying. *Grandma might have put her foot in it*, Charlotte thought, *but God knows Tina wouldn't sea-*

son a piece of chicken if she thought it would break one of her fake nails.

"Sho' was good preachin' today, Reverend," Mattie Mae fibbed as she entered the dining room.

Charlotte was appalled by her grandmother's statement. "Has everybody around here gone mad? Is there a lying spirit in this house, or did he actually preach a good message?" she questioned softly. Unbeknownst to Charlotte, Mattie Mae was merely buttering up the unsuspecting preacher for the kill, and she had no intention of being still before the Lord and letting Him fight this battle. The Lord was going to get a little help from her today.

Suddenly, Terry made her grand entrance into the room wearing a form-fitting Ann Taylor pantsuit and an attitude like she was the second coming of Christ.

"Yes, ma'am. Thank you, Sister Morley," Reverend Holiday remarked as he pulled out a chair for Terry. By this time, Charlotte was halfway in the kitchen to retrieve the remaining side dishes. "I ask God every Saturday night during my studies to give me a Word for His people." After popping a few Tums in his mouth, Reverend Holiday continued. "And every Saturday, God is faithful in giving me a Word for the congregation on Sunday." Reverend Holiday was too busy ogling the spread set out before him to even notice the searing glares coming from Edmund and Mattie Mae.

As soon as everyone finished piling their plates with food, Reverend Holiday appointed himself to say grace. No one realized he had run through grace like a marathon until they heard him smacking on his meal like a cow on crack. Charlotte chewed her food slowly, feeling the hair on her neck rise because of the tension in the room. To her, it felt as if a dam were about to break. And after everyone had almost finished their meal, it did.

Surprisingly, it was the normally reserved Edmund
Morley who opened the floodgates with, "Reverend Holiday, I'm sorry to have to do this, but I just can't wait
until Tuesday's board meeting to say what I gotta say."

"Go right ahead, Brother Morley. This is your home.
Speak your mind. By the way, Sister Morley, I must com-
mend you for this mighty fine meal. I don't know how
you do it," Reverend Holiday replied through his pink
lips.

Mattie Mae grimaced. Although he was well aware of
the fact that some of the church members disliked him,
Reverend Holiday was too arrogant to believe that this
included Edmund and Mattie Mae Morley. He continued
to aggressively shove food down his throat, absolutely
clueless as to what Edmund had on his mind. As a matter
of fact, no one was prepared for what Edmund had to
say.

Edmund folded and rested his arms on the table.
"Reverend, my family has been paying dues at Greener
Pastures way befo' you was even born, and I think it's
only fair for you to know that those of us on the trustee
board done had a meeting of our own."

Reverend Holiday did not skip a beat in his fork-to-
mouth action, so Edmund wasn't sure that he was even
listening. However, Edmund continued. "Those of us in
favor of yo' leavin' has outvoted those who want to give
you a chance and let you stay on. We got proof of yo'
spendin' the chutch money on things the board didn't
approve of, like the house you bought over in Clark. It
wasn't right and you know it."

"How'd you find out about that?" the horrified
preacher asked, dropping his fork and splattering food
across the table. Now Edmund was convinced that he
had Reverend Holiday's undivided attention.

"Never mind how we found out, and please don't interrupt me again. It's a shame how you used poor ole Lois too. I know you near 'bout dried out her bank account. You best be thankful that I talked Busta out of comin' over here today and fillin' you wit' bullet holes."

Reverend Holiday's mouth fell open.

4

For a moment, the dining room was so silent that the slightest bit of noise could have easily caused any one of them to jump like a scared rabbit.

"Son, I may be old, but I ain't no fool." Edmund's voice raised. "I thank God Almighty that He gave me *some* wisdom. Being a minister, you should know this, but the Lawd can lift the covers up and expose things, and He don't just show everything to a preacha, either! Now, some of us know about everythin' you been doin' wit' our money, and we *should* have you arrested for it. What Lois sees in you, I don't know, but I *do* know that you *are* leaving Greener Pastures. We hope to be able to stop foreclosure proceedings on the chutch. Thanks to you, we got *that* to deal wit'."

Terry glared angrily through teary eyes at her grandfather. Tina's mouth was opened wide enough to put a fist in it. Charlotte could understand Tina's shock. She was shocked herself, but what puzzled Charlotte the most were Terry's crocodile tears. Surely, it wasn't because she was feeling any empathy for someone who just got called on the carpet for wrongdoing. Charlotte pushed back a ringlet of hair that had been dangling in her face.

Mattie Mae, who was nervously wringing her hands, also sat wide-eyed and speechless. Reverend Holiday looked like a deer caught in car headlights and too frozen to run. After regaining his composure, Reverend Holiday managed to thank Mattie Mae for the delicious dinner then politely excused himself from the table to go home. He left with no explanation, no apology, and no leftovers to go in his aluminum foil, and for some odd reason, it was the twins who accompanied the disgraced pastor outside to his vehicle.

Mattie Mae leaped from the dining room table, went over to her husband of over fifty years, and planted a big, wet kiss on his forehead. Charlotte felt something was wrong concerning the church, but she hadn't seen that coming. Still, she felt like there was more to it than just Reverend Holiday's stealing. Charlotte grew even more suspicious of Tina and Terry. They were awfully friendly with a man they'd just met.

"Edmund, most of us had an idea that he was a rogue," Mattie Mae said. "But I had no idea he was takin' Lois's money too. Lawd, have mercy! Busta could have hurt that man. You know how he is about his chi'ren, especially Lois. Tell me. Are we about to lose the chutch?"

"Mattie Mae, you know I speak when I have to and say only what I need to say. There is a lot 'bout that man you don't know, and it's best left alone, so long as he leaves from around here. He left behind a big mess for us to clean up, and like I said, we hope to stop the foreclosure. I don't wanna go into that right now. The least he coulda done was own up to it and say he's sorry. Well, pride prevents a *boy* from admittin' when he's wrong, but only a man has the guts to say he's sorry, I suppose. The Lawd, in His time, always has a way of makin' you deal wit' yo' pride." With that said, Edmund got up from the table and left the house as he usually did on Sunday afternoons to sit with his friends, Joe Green and Busta Watkins.

Charlotte helped her grandmother tidy up the kitchen while Tina and Terry remained outside whispering, plotting, and scheming as usual. She and her grandmother didn't say much to each other while doing their chores. They were too preoccupied with their own thoughts. Mattie Mae thought about how the Lord had her to be still and then showed her that He knew how to handle Reverend Holiday through her normally mild-mannered husband.

"Lawd, thank you," she said softly, not wanting Charlotte to hear her. "I'm glad you stepped in, 'cause I would have acted like a plum fool and messed it up. Look like Edmund know more about what is goin' on than I do anyhow."

Charlotte was also thinking about her grandfather and how he confronted Reverend Holiday. As she stood in the kitchen drying the blue willow dishes, Charlotte thought she heard Mattie Mae saying something about Terry. "I'm sorry, Grandma. Did you say something?" she asked.

"No, baby, I'm just talkin' to myself," Mattie Mae answered.

Suddenly, Charlotte felt that overwhelming sense of sadness and dread again. If what happened today at dinner was in any way like a dam break, then she hated to think of what could be coming up next. She started wiping down the kitchen countertops and prayed silently. *All right, Lord. Since that wasn't my grandmother talking, it had to have been you who said something about Terry, but I'm asking you to give me a little bit more than just her name.*

What are you trying to tell me? Charlotte opened the cupboard doors to place the water goblets back.

She thought about how Tina and Terry were both such beautiful girls, with their flawless caramel complexions and long, reddish-brown hair. They were petite, athletic, intelligent, and articulate, but unfortunately, they gave a whole new meaning to the term "terrible twos." They could be overly ambitious, jealous, conniving, and downright nasty when they wanted to. Tina and Terry had so much going for them, yet they had so many disturbing issues working against them.

The way her cousins were behaving only increased her suspicions about them, and now, somehow, this Reverend Holiday seemed to be involved. Charlotte placed the heavy crystal water pitcher inside the refrigerator and said, "Grandma, I think I'll go upstairs and take a nap."

"Okay, but it's so early. You'll wake up in the middle of the night if you go to bed this early, and then you'll have a hard time going back to sleep."

"That's all right. I'll just get up and read if that happens. I need to study anyway." Charlotte kissed Mattie Mae on the cheek and left the kitchen. However, before going upstairs, she peeked through the front door screen. Tina, Terry, and the rented BMW were gone.

As soon as Charlotte got inside her room, she stripped down to her lacy underwear, slipped on a Redskins cotton T-shirt, and plopped down on the bed. Her "short afternoon nap" lasted through the night.

5

The piercing howl of a nearby hound dog woke Charlotte from a very strange dream. She struggled to remember all of the details but couldn't. She got out of bed and stood in front of her bedroom window to bask in the sun's warm rays and toyed with the idea of writing a play for her church's drama ministry based on the lives of the people of Turtle Island. God knows the town was filled with enough colorful characters. She didn't know a whole lot about the town's history, but was willing to do the research. Charlotte figured if she wanted to know anything about Turtle Island, Mattie Mae and Sista would be the two people to ask.

As for her family, Charlotte knew that her grandparents came from a long line of sharecroppers. Edmund's ancestors had inherited land from their childless plantation owners. Edmund and Mattie Mae were well-respected in the community, and many people confided in them, especially Edmund. Together they raised four professionally successful children. Edmund was a well-to-do farmer, and Mattie Mae was always called upon for her cooking skills, especially during the holidays. "Folk 'round here act like they don't know how to boil water. I got a family of my own to feed during the holidays," Mattie Mae would often fuss. In reality, Mattie Mae loved every minute of cooking for people.

Edmund and Mattie Mae married when they were very young, and while neither of them had finished school, both had a wealth of common sense. Edmund liked the fact that Mattie Mae was deeply rooted in her Christian beliefs, and her cooking rivaled that of his own mother's. The couple believed in praying about everything, and they made a practice of having family prayer together each morning. Mattie Mae consistently prayed for protection, health, and happiness for her children and grandchildren, but most of all, she wanted them to know the Lord.

Their oldest daughter, Willa Belle, had been divorced for a number of years from her ex-husband, Thomas, who left her because, according to him, she spent too much time in church. He was so fixated on crooked ministers and backsliding members until he couldn't see or appreciate the godly wife he had at home setting the example for their family. Edmund once told Willa Belle that Thomas was just looking for an excuse not to accept God in his life. He told her to just let Thomas go, and she did. She was heartbroken over her divorce, but managed to successfully raise their three children on her own. Willa Belle had always held on to the hope that her Thomas would change someday and come back home. Unfortunately, that never happened. Thomas was killed during a barroom brawl on the fifth anniversary of their divorce.

Mattie Lee and Charles were another story entirely. Although they grew up in the church, they pretty much drifted away from the church scene once they became adults. Mattie Lee went to church once in a while in Philadelphia, but Charles and his wife, Francine, were more interested in becoming social butterflies than being holy rollers. Unbeknownst to many, Charles had his own reasons for running away from God.

Mattie Lee had never married. However, she did have two sons, Sean and Tony, who were fathered by the same man . . . a married man. Their father occasionally came around to visit them while they were growing up, and he did provide Mattie Lee with financial support. Even though Tony did not really accept his father in his life because he resented being sired out of wedlock by a married man, Tony followed his father's exact footsteps. He too fathered children outside of his own marriage.

Charlotte walked slowly over to the bedroom closet, which was filled with mothballs and cedar blocks, feeling disappointed in the amount of false prophets out there. People were being deceived, and she could not understand why God wasn't intervening, at least in the way that she thought He should. Charlotte was also disturbed by the number of backbiting ministers crawling out of the woodwork, whose sole purpose seemed to be putting other ministers down. "Sign of the times," she surmised.

As Charlotte continued sifting through the rack for something to wear, she reflected back to the time when she was ten years old and she and her mother had gone to the hospital to visit one of her mother's friends. Charlotte vividly remembered the image of the woman so heavily bandaged that it frightened her. She thought the woman was a mummy, and the startled look on Betty's face did nothing to calm her fears. When Betty and Charlotte left the woman's hospital room, she heard the words "once appointed to die" and then she heard the word "husband." But who said it? Being a child and not knowing that a child could actually hear the voice of God, Charlotte dismissed it as crazy thinking on her part. Looking back, she realized that the Lord had been talking to her for a very long time.

Charlotte learned later that her mother's friend had not been hospitalized due to any illness, but because the woman's husband had severely beaten her. There had been a warrant out for his arrest, but the police could not find him. A few days after their visit, the woman died from her head injuries. Her husband was eventually found in a condemned house five blocks from where they lived, dead from a self-inflicted gunshot wound to the head.

Charlotte stood in front of the closet, no longer searching for something to wear, but standing as if she were in a trance. Now she was remembering another tragic incident, when she and her cousins spent one summer at Camp Liberty in western Pennsylvania. Edmund and Mattie Mae were in New Orleans visiting Edmund's relatives and could not keep the grandchildren that year. Near the camp was a wooded area with a fishing pond. It was private property and had a NO TRESPASSING sign posted on a gate.

There were two boys at Camp Liberty who wanted to ignore the sign and climb over the fence to go exploring, but Charlotte felt a strong sense of danger in that area and adamantly warned her cousins not to follow the two boys. She even threatened to tell one of the camp counselors if the boys did go over the fence. Fortunately, she was able to persuade her cousins, but the other two boys ventured off in the prohibited area anyway. Later that evening, the boys were reported missing.

Sadly, the boys were found the next day, strangled with nylon stockings tied around their necks. They had been sexually assaulted with some sort of object. They were among several victims murdered in western Pennsylvania within one week. The police soon realized that all the murdered victims were young boys who were sexually assaulted and strangled with nylon stockings. It became clear to them that a serial killer was on the loose.

One month and eleven victims later, the killer was apprehended—ironically, in the City of Brotherly Love, Philadelphia. The last victim, who miraculously survived, was found gagged and tied up in an old refrigerator that someone threw out in an alley. That child had been a classmate of one of Willa Belle's sons, and the serial killer turned out to be an emotionally disturbed eighteen-year-old female who had been abused and neglected by her mother, who never wanted a daughter, so she doted on and adored only her sons.

Stunned family members were grateful yet baffled by Charlotte's insight. At the time, Charlotte could give no answer other than she was just convinced that there was danger on the other side of that fence. No longer a stranger to dreams and visions, by the time Charlotte reached young adulthood, she had noticed an increase in them. At first she didn't know what to make of them.

During the early stages of her spiritual growth, Charlotte had tried talking to someone about her visions. The first person she approached for help was a fellow member of Truth in Love, and the woman looked at her as if she were crazy. Charlotte concluded that the woman did not understand enough about God-given dreams and visions to help her.

Charlotte again tried to find someone to confide in, only to learn that this person pretended to understand and would later claim to have had visions that were eerily similar to hers. Charlotte soon discovered that *this* woman had a serious problem with covetousness, especially when it came to people possessing spiritual gifts. Since that time, Charlotte had learned how to pray about her dreams and visions.

6

Charlotte finally chose a sheer, sleeveless beige dress with ruffles around the neck and a matching beige slip to wear. "Oh Lord, please forgive me. I forgot to pray," Charlotte said out loud as she went to kneel at the foot of her bed. During the middle of her prayer, Charlotte heard the word "storm," and she was completely caught off guard by God's interruption of her flow. She kept quiet for a second.

After waiting for a minute and not hearing anything else, Charlotte prayed, "Father, I don't know what you're trying to tell me. If you're saying that someone in my family is in trouble, then I ask for your guidance and protection. But, if at all possible . . . I'm sorry, I know all things are possible through you, but I come against this storm if it is not a part of your will, and I plead the blood of Jesus over every situation right now. I plead for divine intervention in the name of Jesus. Amen." Still, Charlotte had a sinking feeling that whatever this storm was, her prayer was not going to stop it, and she and her family were going to need the strength not only to brace for it, but to get through it as well.

Charlotte got up from her knees and sat on the side of the bed. She reached in the drawer of the nightstand for her address book to look up Elder Theodore King. She was thoroughly convinced that the Lord was trying to warn her about something, and some of it, if not all of it, had to do with this Reverend Holiday and her cousins. Elder King was the mentor assigned to her at church, and she wanted his advice, along with his prayers. Charlotte dialed the church phone number then the extension, and got his voicemail. She left a message asking Elder King to call her back whenever he got the chance. After hanging up the phone, she grabbed her toiletries from the dresser and went into the bathroom to brush her teeth and shower.

After Charlotte was dressed, she brushed her hair and pulled it back into a neat ponytail then went downstairs to the kitchen, where she knew her grandmother would be. One didn't have to be prophetic to know that Mattie Mae could usually be found either in her kitchen or at Sista's house.

Mattie Mae informed Charlotte that Edmund had gone fishing with his faithful buddies, Joe and Busta, and that she had already prepared a banquet of a breakfast that included homemade biscuits with molasses syrup, grits, fresh fruit, and leftover ham from yesterday. Mattie Mae placed an empty cup in the sink. Knowing that not even a forklift could get them up this early in the morning, she didn't bother to ask Charlotte if Tina or Terry were out of bed.

"Charlotte, I'm goin' over to Sista's house for a while to help her shell a bushel of peas. Don't worry 'bout keeping breakfast warm. Just put some water in the grits pot when you're done. Let it soak. Tina and Terry ain't no babies. They know how to get somethin' to eat when they get ready. You can come on over to Sista's house after ya finish eatin' if ya want to." Mattie Mae grabbed her wide-brimmed straw hat from a hook nailed in the wall and left through the back door.

Charlotte wished her grandmother a good time with her friend. She then settled down with a plate of ham and grits with a side dish of biscuits soaked in molasses and a half cup of cream with just a smidgen of coffee.

Sista and Mattie Mae had one of the most admired friendships on Turtle Island. The two women had been neighbors since childhood, and when they married, they married men who had properties adjacent to each other. It was almost as if they were destined to stay neighbors. Sista had been a widow for nearly twenty years now, and only John Edward, one of her twelve children, still lived in South Carolina.

John Edward, who was thirty years old, was Sista's last-born child and had never lived anywhere on his own. He'd had a few problems with the law in the past, but had since turned his life around. Sista's other children lived in various parts of the United States, and they all made sure that at least one of them came home to visit their mother on holidays. Sista made sure that she was seen with her children whenever they came home. She particularly enjoyed showing off her brood in church.

Sista's children would march in behind her as she strolled down the aisle of the church like a supermodel on a showroom runway, showing off her latest outfit. She would proudly usher her children to a seat on the front row as she twirled around in the aisle for all the congregation to see, before sitting her own behind down.

"Hey there, Sista," Mattie Mae greeted as she approached her friend. Sista was watering her prized flower garden of jumbo roses, huge sunflowers, daisies, and lilies. Hydrangeas had been strategically planted and framed neatly around the house. A barren pecan tree stood firmly in front of the house, providing an abundance of shade for the newly screened-in front porch.

"Hey," Sista greeted back. "Go on up. I got everything set up on the porch. I meant to tell you to bring some freezer bags, but we might have enough. Just let me finish watering these flowers befo' the sun get too hot. Looks like it's gonna be a burner today too." Sista ran the water hose over her flowers one last time. Then she dragged the tangled hose behind her and turned off the water before joining Mattie Mae on the front porch.

"Sista, Edmund sho' told that ole scoundrel Reverend Holiday off yesterday," Mattie Mae said gleefully as she bent forward to grab a handful of field peas from the crate.

"Hush up! I wish I had been there when Edmund told him off. I always say 'let God use ya.' I meant to call you to find out how things went, but I got so busy. John Edward told me some things he heard, and I tell you the truth, that preacha is something else!"

"I know he is. What did John Edward have to say?" Mattie Mae asked, knowing that aside from her husband, John Edward knew as much, or perhaps even more, about the latest gossip around town, since he spent most of his time in town collecting and spreading news. Sista leaned over in her chair, eager to talk.

"Lawd, forgive me for talkin' about folk, but the other

day, John Edward was outside ole man Johnson's bank, and he heard ole man Johnson and Edmund talkin'. John Edward was parked in front of the bank 'cause he had to drop off Essie Mae Parker so she could cash her check befo' the bank closed. She'd been pullin' double shifts at the Sleep and Slumber Motel lately. That Essie Mae, now, she gonna find herself a job and work. That gal ever did work hard. Her ole lazy, good-for-nothin' husband ought to try workin' sometimes. Don't make no darn sense. Anyway, while Essie Mae was in the bank, John Edward was waitin' for her in his car, and you know how loud ole man Johnson can talk. I think he talks loud on purpose.

"Anyway, he was tellin' Edmund that Lois Watkins had just been in the bank all upset 'cause she was missin' some money from her account. It turned out that Reverend Holiday's name is on her account, and he nearly took out every penny she had in the bank. She had around ten thousand dollars in the bank and that rascal left her wit' only fifty dollars. She in there talkin' 'bout she gonna sue Reverend Holiday. She ain't suin' him and she know it! If Reverend Holiday showed up at her doorstep today wit' a glass ring from a Cracker Jack box, she'd forgive him.

"Ole man Johnson said that Lois was so upset that he had to call Busta to come and get her, and you *know* Busta don't go nowhere without his pistol. Edmund was the one who calmed Busta down. Good thing too, 'cause Busta will shoot ya in a minute."

"Lawd, have mercy! No wonder I didn't see Busta or Lois in chutch yesterday," Mattie Mae said, swirling the peas around in the pan.

"They say Busta went to the parsonage lookin' for Reverend Holiday, too, but Reverend Holiday wasn't home. I betcha somebody told Reverend Holiday Busta was lookin' for him. I'm surprised Reverend Holiday had the nerve to show up and preach yesterday. I guess he figure Busta won't shoot up the chutch. I heard that Reverend Holiday got a big fine home over in Clark somewhere and paid for it wit' the money from the chutch account. I also heard that he got a big stash of money up North somewhere too."

"I'll be doggone! Well, ain't nothin' wrong wit' people havin' money stashed somewhere."

"No, ain't nothin' wrong wit' it, so long as it's *yo'* money and not the chutch money. He got Lois thinkin' he gonna marry her. You remember the time when Reverend Holiday hired Petey Moss to come over and fix the chutch roof? Don't you know he ain't paid Petey a dime for that work yet? Reverend Holiday ain't never contracted nobody to do the plumbin' like he said he was either. And he had the nerve to ask the chutch to put extra money in the plate to help out wit' gettin' the plumbin' fixed.

"I'm glad the board members are taking back control of the finances. I can't stand a crook! If Reverend Holiday was one of my chi'ren, I'd strap him to a tree and beat him like a slave. That don't make no darn sense! Did Edmund tell you that the chutch mortgage note hadn't been paid in months?"

Mattie Mae nodded her head.

Sista continued. "The bank had been good to us 'cause they know most of us, but now they talkin' 'bout us losin' the chutch if somebody don't come up wit' the money."

"It's a shame befo' God. Reverend Holiday was the one who said that he'd make sho' the mortgage was paid."

"He *did* make sho' the mortgage was paid . . . *his mortgage!*" Sista shouted.

The two women saw Charlotte approaching them.

"Good morning, Miss Sista," Charlotte greeted.

"Hey, Charlotte."

"Excuse me for one second, but Grandma, did you know that Tina and Terry were leaving today?" Charlotte asked.

"No. They ain't said nothin' to me 'bout leavin' today!" Mattie Mae answered. Creases formed in her forehead and she looked confused.

"I knew it, I knew it!" Sista announced hysterically, startling Mattie Mae and Charlotte. "I seen the way one of 'em been eyeing the preacha and I said then somethin' wasn't right."

Ignoring Sista's remark, Mattie Mae placed her pan of peas in the chair as she got up and walked down the four concrete steps to face Charlotte.

"Grandma, I saw Terry, at least I think it was Terry, get inside John Edward's car with her luggage," Charlotte said, wiping away small beads of perspiration from her forehead.

"Them gals ridin' wit' my boy?" Sista asked, now laying down her pan. "Oh Lawd Jesus! What that boy done got himself mixed up in now? I thought I heard his car a little while ago, but Sam Carter got one of them ole loud cars too. You sho' it was my John Edward?"

"Yes, ma'am, I'm sure it was your son," Charlotte replied. "They drove off before I could ask where she was going. I was upstairs cleaning my room and just happened to look out the window to see Tina's BMW speeding down the road. I didn't pay too much attention to it at first. I just thought that one of them was going to the store or something, but soon after that, I went into their room to get the vacuum cleaner. That's when I noticed their luggage was gone. Nothing of theirs is in the house."

"Sista, let's go home and find out what's goin' on," Mattie Mae said as she started to briskly walk away.

"Go ahead, Mattie Mae. I'll try to find out where John Edward is totin' that gal, but Mattie Mae, I bet you on my Johnny's grave that the other grandchile of yours is wit' Reverend Holiday," Sista stated.

7

Without looking back, Mattie Mae shuddered at the thought and kept walking. She and Charlotte arrived at the house and found no trace of Tina, Terry, or their belongings. Not even a note. It was as if they had never been there. Mattie Mae picked up the telephone and dialed the number to Joe Green's shop. She asked Joe's wife, Lilly, to send someone over to Turtle Creek to tell Edmund to come home. Mattie Mae didn't know whether to call Charles and Francine now or to wait. Normally, she was not at a loss for what to do in a strange circumstance, and to her, this was strange. Tina and Terry left without telling anyone a thing, and she didn't appreciate it. And to top it all off, Sista was throwing Reverend Holiday in the mix.

Mattie Mae wasn't blind to the twins cozying up to Reverend Holiday. After yesterday's dinner, she had a funny feeling about it herself. If Tina or Terry had run off with Reverend Holiday and the church money, then that meant scandal. The gossip grinders at the rumor mill

would smear the Morleys's good name all up and down
the island. Mattie Mae finally decided to just pray and
wait. By the time she finished praying, Charlotte had
made her a hot cup of sassafras tea and told her about the
Lord placing the word "storm" in her spirit.

Mattie Mae sat quietly for a moment, listening intently
to Charlotte and sipping her tea. After much thought,
Mattie Mae said, "Somethin' is fixin' to happen and we
just gonna have to trust the Lawd through it."

Shortly afterwards, Edmund came inside the house
swinging his arms as he walked. The two women quickly
filled him in on what little they knew, and Edmund
calmly told Mattie Mae to call their son, Charles.

"Those two hadn't been here a hot minute and I could
tell they were up to no good the whole time. I know they
is grown and everythin', but you don't just up and leave
like that and don't tell nobody. I hadn't talked to Charles
in a long time now anyhow," Edmund said somewhat
angrily.

Mattie Mae could only stare blankly at her husband,
and although she dearly loved Edmund, normally he
would frustrate her with his laid back ways. Now, after
years of praying for her husband to be more aggressive,
the Lord had finally answered her prayers. Before Mattie
Mae could reach over to pick up the phone to dial Charles'
number, the telephone started ringing.

"Hello," Mattie Mae answered.

"Hey, Mattie Mae," Sista called out, sounding as if she
were out of breath. "I found out that John Edward drove
one of yo' grands to the airport. I called over to Joe
Green's shop and you know that gal who calls herself
likin' John Edward, Mary? Well, Mary said that this was
something that was planned ever since Tina and Terry
been here. John Edward was to take Tina to the airport,

but he was told not to say anythin' to you or Edmund or Charlotte about it. How he kept that a secret, God only knows! Everybody knows that boy can't hold water."

"Did Mary say where they was goin'?" Mattie Mae looked disgusted.

"Mary said she didn't know. She might be tellin' the truth. You know how scary Mary is when somebody confronts her," Sista replied. "You wait until I see him."

"Sista, I'll have to call you back later. I need to call their father," Mattie Mae said, lowering the telephone receiver until it settled down on its cradle. She hurriedly relayed Sista's message to Edmund and Charlotte. All the while, Charlotte could not shake the feeling that Tina and Terry were in some sort of danger.

"Edmund, where do you think they could be going? You think they went back home to Washington? Somethin' don't add up. Why would one ride wit' John Edward to the airport?"

"I don't know," Edmund said.

"I mean, I'm assuming they were takin' the rental car back to the airport. They came here together. Why aren't they leavin' together?" Mattie Mae pondered, wringing her hands.

Edmund paced up and down the floor with both hands in his pockets. "I don't know. They ain't got sense enough to let somebody know they leavin' town. After we talk to Charles, I'm goin' over to the parsonage," Edmund said, walking toward the front door.

"Whatcha goin' over there for? Edmund, please don't go startin' no trouble," Mattie Mae pleaded.

Edmund released his hand from the door handle, allowing the screen door to slam. "Trouble done started. Go ahead and call Charles for me. I'll wait. Mattie Mae, I never told you this 'cause I was hopin' it wasn't true, but I was told that one of the twins was seen a couple of days ago wit' the reverend, all hugged up. Since Tina and Terry look so much alike, this person didn't know which one it was. This is all we need; one of our granddaughters to be hooked up wit' Reverend Holiday, especially when stolen money is involved."

"No! That can't be true! Who in God's name is the person who told you that?" Mattie Mae shouted, jumping up from her seat. Edmond didn't answer. The thought of one her grandchildren being involved with Reverend Holiday made Mattie Mae sick to her stomach.

Charlotte watched helplessly as her grandparents displayed their anguish, and thoughts of the previous day's dinner fiasco came drifting back. "No wonder they acted so funny yesterday when you told Reverend Holiday off," she mumbled as she composed herself.

Instead of Mattie Mae pressing for an answer from Edmund, she simply started dialing Charles's number at the hospital. The receptionist informed Mattie Mae that Dr. Morley had not come in yet, but he was expected at any moment, and promptly transferred Mattie Mae to Charles's answering service. Mattie Mae left a curt message for her son to call her. She then dialed his home phone number, hoping to at least reach his wife. After the third ring, Francine answered the telephone sounding as if she was one apple martini away from being drunk.

By this time, Edmund's patience was running short. "Let me have the phone," he demanded while reaching for the receiver, only to have Mattie Mae push away his hand.

"Hey, Francine. This is Mattie Mae. You doin' all right?"

"Yes, I can't complain. How are you?"

"Fair to middlin'. Francine, it's a shame we hadn't talked to you in so long, but I have to ask you a question. Have you talked to Tina and Terry lately? You see, we didn't know they was leavin' today, and we was won-

derin' if they were on their way back up there," Mattie
Mae said.

"They left?" Francine said through the phone receiver.
"You mean they left Turtle Island already? No, I didn't
know they were leaving today. They told me they were
staying for a month to help out one of Terry's high school
friends. Terry said the girl was terminally ill and needed
somebody to help around the house and help take care of
her son."

"I know good and darn well that chile ain't tell you
nothin' like that!" Mattie Mae protested. "Ain't nobody
'round here that bad off sick. At least not no young person, and Terry only had three close friends in school. I
know all three of those girls, and I know their people.
Two of them girls live off somewhere in another state,
and the other girl is right here and doin' just fine. Plus,
Tina and Terry hadn't been anywhere long enough to
help anybody out. They sho' ain't said nothin' to me
about it," Mattie Mae responded, looking even more disgusted.

"I should have known better. They act as if they can't
even bring me a glass of water," Francine stated.

"Let me have the phone," Edmund said, successfully
taking the receiver from Mattie Mae's grip. "Francine, I
don't want to page Charles at the hospital, but will you
do me a favor when you see him and tell him to call us
right away? I want to talk with him."

"You know what, Edmund? I think talking is an excellent idea. I'm sick and tired of the lies and secrets. I don't
know what Tina and Terry are up to, but I did notice yesterday that all of their things are gone from the house.
Normally, I don't go in their rooms, but I was looking for
a blouse of mine and couldn't find it. So, thinking that
one of them borrowed it, I went to Tina's room first, since
she's notorious for taking my things without asking.

Long story short, the closets and dresser drawers were empty. If they are on their way back to D.C., I don't think they're on their way back here. It looks like they have moved out. I'm curious as to what is going on."

Francine paused. "Edmund, there is something else you and Mattie Mae should know."

8

Edmund pressed the receiver close to his ear.

"Charles and I are no longer together," Francine nearly blurted out. "We've been separated for a year and divorced since last month. Why he wanted to keep it a secret from you guys and why I honored that secret, I don't know. But I think you should know. So from now on, I will stop covering for him.

"Remember in the past when I would tell you or Mattie Mae that Charles wasn't home? In a manner of speaking, that really was the truth. I used to give Charles your messages and he would call you back from wherever he was staying. As for Tina and Terry, I wouldn't worry too much about them. They are adults, and they sure do know how to call you when they need something. Edmund, if you have a pen, I'll give you the number where you can reach Charles."

Edmund wrote the number as she recited it.

Francine sighed into the receiver. "Edmund, I'm sorry for being the one to tell you this, but I think you and Mattie Mae deserve to know the reason why Charles and I have divorced. Charles prefers to sleep with men and sometimes other women, rather than with his own wife."

Edmund was so stunned that he just hung up the phone without saying goodbye. Then he thought back to "the incident." No wonder such a disgraceful thing happened.

"What happened, Edmund? What did Francine say?" Mattie Mae asked.

"I'll tell ya later, Mattie Mae." Raising his eyebrow, which caused his hairline to recede even farther, Edmund said, "If Charles don't call back here soon, I want you to go ahead and make arrangements for me to fly to Washington." He pulled a platinum credit card from his wallet and said, "Here's my card just in case I'm not back in about four hours. Give Charles four hours to call here. That's it! Four hours. Then go ahead and make the arrangements for me."

"What! Why?" Mattie Mae cried out after just imagining rumors about her granddaughters. She couldn't remember the last time she saw Edmund this angry, and she wondered if Tina and Terry had stooped so low as to be involved in some money-stealing scheme.

"I need to talk to Charles. I don't know what Tina and Terry are up to. I don't expect much from Tina, but I expected better from Terry. Terry acts like she was raised by wolves." Edmund flung the screen door open and drove off in his truck.

Mattie Mae looked at Charlotte, who was just as perplexed as she, and said, "I wonder if there is something Edmund is not telling us."

The black rotary telephone, now considered to be a family heirloom, started ringing again. Charlotte answered to the soothing voice of Elder King on the other end. Once she finished updating Elder King on the recent drama, Elder King sighed and said in the most serious tone,

"Reverend Morley, I believe you are right. I believe the Lord is trying to tell you that your family is about to go through a storm. There is something going on, and if one or even both of your cousins are involved with this Reverend Holiday and the mishandling of church funds, it could cause very hard feelings from the church members toward your grandparents."

"I know, Elder King. But what I don't understand is how my cousins could possibly know this man. My grandmother's friend, Miss Sista, was real adamant this morning about some sort of connection between them. She seems to believe that at least one of my cousins is involved with Reverend Holiday, and then my grandfather comes home and says that Reverend Holiday had been seen with one of them. Granddaddy didn't say who told him, but whoever it was insinuated that it looked romantic. I don't get it. Reverend Holiday hadn't been at the church a year yet, and Tina and Terry have only been here for about four or five days, and this is the first time they've visited here in a couple of years. They don't know that man! How could they? Like I said, I just don't get it."

Elder King cleared his throat. "I don't get it either. Do you think your grandfather knows more than he is telling?"

"Yes. Yesterday he said something about 'some things are better left unsaid.' Granddaddy said that they weren't going to press charges against Reverend Holiday. My grandmother told me something else interesting. According to her, it was Reverend Holiday's responsibility alone to pay the church mortgage, and she found out from her friend this morning that he hadn't been paying it. It's probably safe to say that he's cooked the books. My God, this is so sad. When I think about all of these people who worked hard all of their lives, giving when they probably couldn't afford to give . . ."

"It is sad. It's going to be even sadder for whoever is involved in stealing money from God."

"That culprit drained a lot of money from one member's bank account, and Grandma said that the church should have had around a hundred thousand dollars in the bank."

"Whew! That's a lot of money for a little old country church to have."

"True, but there are a few members at Greener Pastures who've done quite well for themselves. Some of them have children that send in large donations from time to time. Even my Uncle Charles once sent a five thousand dollar check to help renovate the church. I think Uncle Charles believes he can buy his way into heaven. How could the finance committee let something like this happen?"

"It happens. There are still a lot of churches out there where the pastor is in total control of everything, but I suspect there is at least one member on the board there who knew what was going on, but looked the other way for whatever reason," Elder King suggested.

Charlotte could hear one of Bishop Jonathan Lorne's sermons playing in the background. "Listen, I'm sorry," Elder King said. "I've got another call coming in. I will be praying for you and your family. Call me again if you need to talk."

Charlotte promised that she would do so and hung up the phone.

Mattie Mae, who had been listening, said, "I don't get how some folk can be so crazy about Reverend Holiday. I'm a little worried about Edmund. I don't know what Francine said to him, but it sho' did spook him. Edmund don't like to fly on nobody's airplane."

Charlotte tried comforting Mattie Mae by gently rubbing her broad shoulders. Shoulders that used to withstand anything. "Grandma, I need the keys to Granddaddy's car. Do you know where they are?" Charlotte sputtered out.

Mattie Mae pointed to the utility drawer. Charlotte retrieved the keys and headed outside toward Edmund's Lexus. The silver-colored luxury car, a Father's Day gift from Charles, was parked in its usual spot behind the house. Edmund rarely drove the car, and Mattie Mae never bothered to learn how to drive. Mattie Mae asked Charlotte to wait until she wrote out a shopping list for flour, cornmeal, grits, fatback, and onions.

Downtown Turtle Island was not what one would call a bustling area. In fact, it boasted only three intersections and two traffic lights. Main Street consisted of one grocery store, one post office, three gas stations, one drug store, two thrift stores, two banks, and a few small businesses. The black residents routinely hung out on Waller Street in front of Joe Green's Place. Joe Green's Place was virtually a hole in the wall, sandwiched between Busta Watkins's Barber and Beauty Shop and Waller Street Juke Joint, but it was the best soul food diner for miles around.

Joe's wife, Lilly, was unanimously and unofficially voted as the second best cook in town, next to Mattie Mae, of course. Mattie Mae occasionally baked desserts for Lilly to sell in the diner, allowing Lilly to keep all the profits. Lilly's crispy fried chicken dinners and Cajun seasoned fish sandwiches would usually sell out by the end of the day. Charlotte decided to make Joe and Lilly's diner her first stop, since Mary, John Edward's girlfriend, worked there and seemed to know so much.

Busta Watkins's Barber and Beauty Shop was another

major hub for social gathering, and knowing that it didn't take long for news to spread, especially in small towns, Charlotte figured that folks's lips were quite loose regarding Reverend Holiday. But her concern was for Tina and Terry.

Charlotte found a parking space in front of the Waller Street Juke Joint, which was a favorite watering hole for Turtle Island's black community. Although Charlotte was desperate for information, and given the fact that alcohol tends to loosen one's tongue, she still thought it not wise to be seen going inside a juke joint. Being a minister, one might misconstrue her innocent visit. Besides that, she didn't know anyone who worked there.

Dancing rhythmically challenged in the doorway of the juke joint was one of the regular barflies, sixty-five-year-old Cora Johnson, who was looking quite dehydrated as usual. Cora waved wildly at Charlotte as she curled her dried, cracked lips around a silver flask.

Waller Street housed most of the black-owned businesses, while the white business owners occupied the beautifully renovated buildings on Main Street and Flake Road. Even though the black and white community got along well, not that much had changed on the island since the days of slavery and Jim Crow laws.

The schools were still segregated. Black children attended poorly funded, run-down public schools while the white students received their education at a local private school named Turtle Island Academy. There were still a few black women who earned meager wages by cooking, cleaning, and babysitting the children of upper middle-class white women who didn't work. Like any other town, Turtle Island had its share of poverty-stricken families who did what they had to do in order to make ends meet.

Charlotte rolled up her window before getting out of the car. She overheard a silver-haired, middle-aged man talking to Cora.

"I told you, all these preachers want is your money! Didn't I tell you that? You see he done run off wit' them fools's money. Serve 'em right! I know one thing. I ain't fool enough to give no preacher my money. I know I'm goin' to hell in a gasoline suit, and I'll probably see that preacher there too!"

Charlotte winced at his comment. The impression Reverend Holiday left on people, who were already skeptical about spiritual leaders, would be hard to erase from their minds.

9

Charlotte walked past the laundromat to the next building, which had a BARBER WANTED sign posted in the window. The strong wave of Old Spice aftershave lotion and scorched hair was enough to keep her from entering the premises. Charlotte kept walking until she got to Joe Green's Place.

Before she even got to the door, Charlotte was greeted by the smell of old grease frying. The combination of all these odors on Waller Street made her nostrils burn. Upon entering the premises, she quickly got an earful of loud talking and laughter. Every chair in the diner was occupied with faithful patrons, who were either eating or waiting to be served.

There was nothing fancy about Joe Green's Place. Each square table was covered with plastic red-and-white checkered tablecloths. The floors were made of cold concrete, and the black paint on some of the wooden ladder-back chairs had begun to chip. The walls were a dull gray color, with crookedly hung photographs of Joe, Lilly, and various customers taken during opening day, some twenty-five years ago. Taped against the cash register was a faded dollar bill; presumably, the first dollar made on opening day.

"Is that Mattie Mae's grandbaby I see?" asked Lilly, who was still beautiful and shapely for a woman in her mid fifties, as she emerged from behind the counter. Her hair was cut short, slightly spiked and black as coal. She bore an uncanny resemblance to Lena Horne. Lilly wiped her hands on her ketchup and mustardstained apron and embraced Charlotte with a big bear hug.

"Hi, Ms. Lilly, how are you?" Charlotte responded warmly.

"It is so good to see you. I heard you were in town. I just got back myself about two days ago. I went down to Atlanta to spend some time with my grandbabies. How is Mattie Mae doing?"

"She's fine, considering everything that has happened," Charlotte said, well aware of the sudden hush in the once clamoring eating establishment.

"That's good. I'm glad to hear that. I've been meaning to call her, but we get so busy around here and by the time I get home . . . I don't even know how I manage to get to my bed sometimes. I heard about your cousins running off like that, and I wouldn't think anything of it if it weren't for these rumors flying around."

"Yes, ma'am, that's why I came here. Do you think I could talk to Mary and find out what she knows?"

"Honey, please! She won't tell you anything. You're a stranger to her. Mary is kind of shy when it comes to strangers. You'd have better luck making a mute talk than getting her to say something. As a matter of fact, she thinks that you might be in on it. Whatever 'in on it' means."

"In on what?" Charlotte asked, puzzled by the comment.

"Listen, honey, you don't need to ask her a thing. She told me everything, or at least all I believe she has, and since you're here, I'll tell you what she told me." Lilly turned around. "Y'all take over for me for a minute. I'll be right back," she shouted to the two women behind the counter. One of the women was Mary.

Lilly led Charlotte outside, away from the protruding eyes and perked ears, to an unoccupied picnic bench. Staggering from around the corner of Waller and Main was Otis Moss. Otis released a loud, gut-wrenching belch and flopped down on the bench opposite Lilly and Charlotte.

"If you don't get your rump up from here, Otis, smelling like a whiskey still so early in the morning. You should be ashamed of yourself!" Lilly scolded.

"You want me to buy you a fish sam'ich?" Otis offered, winking at Charlotte with his bloodshot eye. "I got plenty of money. I can buy you anything you want. You just name it. Go in there and tell Mary to fix you a sam'ich. Tell her Otis will pay for it. What's your name anyhow? You look familiar. Folks 'round here call me Coffee 'cause I grind so fine." Now winking almost erratically, Otis stood up and performed a painful-looking gyration of a dance.

"Close your mouth, Otis! How can you have plenty of money when you drink up every dime you get?" Lilly scolded. "Coffee my foot. You might need to drink a pot of coffee to sober up. Leave this girl alone. We're trying to talk."

"No thanks, Mr. Otis," Charlotte responded politely. "I don't care for anything. Don't you recognize me? I'm Edmund Morley's granddaughter, Charlotte." Charlotte couldn't tell if Otis was trying to remember her or if he was trying to adjust his focus on the dark green pickup truck as it pulled up to the curb behind her.

"Isn't that your nephew?" Charlotte asked him after turning around and seeing the truck.

Otis pretended not to see his nephew. Petey came to Waller Street on weekdays to pick up his uncle, to assist him in doing little odd jobs. He did it as a favor for Otis's wife, Nellie. She wanted to keep Otis busy and away from his drinking cronies. Unfortunately, having a job did not curtail Otis's drinking since he usually stopped by one of the neighborhood liquor houses to get pickled before going to work anyway. It was a good thing that Petey was wise enough to never allow his uncle to climb a ladder or handle sharp objects, heavy equipment, or machinery.

Petey waved to Lilly and Charlotte then beckoned for his uncle to get in the truck. Otis got off the bench reluctantly and sat in the passenger seat of his nephew's truck. Petey had barely driven a couple of feet when Charlotte and Lilly saw the passenger door of Petey's truck slowly open. They watched in horror as Otis spilled out onto the street. He was so drunk, he didn't even know he had fallen out of a moving vehicle.

Otis simply curled up in a fetal position as if he were in bed and started snoring. A humiliated Petey stopped the truck, got out, pulled Otis up from the ground like a sack of potatoes, and shoved him back inside the truck. Petey assured Charlotte and Lilly that his uncle wasn't injured and he would be taking him home instead of work.

Immediately after Petey Moss drove off, Charlotte and Lilly burst into laughter. "Nellie won't be happy to see Otis coming back home so soon," Lilly pointed out. "And I doubt if she'll let him get any rest. It's a shame how Otis and his brothers turned out. Their father used to be the pastor of Macedonia when we were growing up, and all of his children turned out to be drinkers—and I mean heavy drinkers at that!"

"That is a shame. Miss Lilly, I don't mean to cut you off, but I'm sort of pressed for time."

"Oh sure, I understand. Let me see . . . we were talking about Tina and Terry. Well, it seems no one knows where Terry is, but talk is that Tina and Reverend Holiday got married."

"Married?" Charlotte was totally shocked. "When? Wait a minute. That can't be true!"

"I'm afraid it is true," Lilly continued. "My friend, Vivian, works at the courthouse in Clark. Anyway, Vivian said that Tina and Reverend Holiday applied for a marriage license some time ago. Vivian knew Reverend Holiday because he pays property taxes in Clark, and she gave me a perfect description of Tina. She said the license was signed by John Cedric Holiday and Tina Annette Morley."

"Oh my God! What is Tina doing? And you say they applied for the license some time ago? I don't understand. When did they meet?"

"Honey, it's a small world out there. My daughter graduated from Spellman College the year before Tina and Terry graduated, and she remembers them. Shelley swears that she used to see Reverend Holiday around campus."

Charlotte's head was spinning like a top. "This can't be. This has to be some sort of joke. But I thought he was dating Lois Watkins," Charlotte said.

"Well, apparently he was using Lois Watkins. I heard that Tina knew all about it too."

"So, Tina came down here to get married to a thief? Why would she want somebody like that? On second thought, she's not known for her integrity either. I wonder what Terry has to do with all of this. Is Tina that sick of a person?"

"I don't know, and I can't pretend to understand it either."

Charlotte flinched as if someone had pinched her as she tried to process the news. She thanked Lilly for the information and excused herself to go shopping for Mattie Mae at the Piggly Wiggly grocery store.

10

Piggly Wiggly was crowded with shoppers pushing loaded carts and searching the aisles for so-called sales. Over by the fruit and vegetable section, a customer was arguing with a store clerk about the high cost of fruit as her child steadily stuffed himself with seedless grapes. Charlotte walked down aisle three and heard another intense argument coming from the meat department. Apparently, someone had stacked all of the chicken feet and pigtails in her cart, and this selfish act had aroused the ire of some unhappy customers who also came to purchase fowl feet and pig parts on sale.

Charlotte quickly found all of the items from Mattie Mae's list and patiently waited in the only open line to pay for them. After making her purchase, she drove home wondering how she was going to break the news to her grandparents. From a quarter mile away, she could see several cars parked in her grandparents' front yard.

Turning into the driveway, Charlotte parked beside a beat-up 1960 Cadillac convertible that had seen better days and appeared to be on its last leg. She was anxious to know what was going on after seeing cars snaked around the driveway.

As Charlotte got out of the car, she heard dozens of voices coming from the back of the house. She snatched her purse and grocery bags from the backseat and headed toward the backyard. Charlotte spotted her grandfather and three other men standing around a large black wash-pot that had a fire lit under it, frying fish. She couldn't believe they were having a fish fry at a time like this. And how in the world did they pull this off so fast? She hadn't even been gone that long.

"Come on 'round, baby girl," Edmund said when he saw Charlotte approaching.

"Hello." Charlotte smiled at Edmund's friends. "Grand-daddy, what is going on here?"

"Well, what does it look like?" Edmund said as he dropped fillets of fish into the hot oil. "We're havin' a fish fry."

"Now? And on a Monday?"

"You don't have to wait until Friday to eat fish."

"I really need to talk to you and Grandma," she whis-pered in his ear. Charlotte turned her head slightly and saw Mattie Mae carrying a large pitcher of lemonade in one hand and a pitcher filled with iced tea in the other. Sista was walking behind her carrying a silver tray filled with cornbread muffins. Seated at one of the picnic tables were Busta and Lois Watkins, along with a few other members she recognized from Greener Pastures.

Charlotte high-tailed it over to Mattie Mae and pulled her aside. "Grandma, I don't know what's going on here, but we need to talk now!"

"Girl, I know you were taught better manners than that. Ain't you gonna speak?"

"I'm sorry. How is everybody doing?" Charlotte asked, looking around at the guests.

Everyone, with the exception of Lois Watkins, greeted Charlotte. Lois looked as if she were heavily sedated. Her eyes were red and puffy from crying, lack of sleep, or both. Mattie Mae explained to Charlotte the reason for the impromptu shindig.

"We decided to have a meeting today to kind of celebrate. Some of the men got together and paid the chutch mortgage. The Lawd made a way. By the way, Charles called. So, we don't have to call and make arrangements for Edmund. Charles and Francine will be here tomorrow."

"They will?" Although surprised to learn that Charles and Francine would be coming to South Carolina, Charlotte found herself zeroing in on Lois. "I don't think Lois is celebrating. Look at her. She looks as if she has been crying all night. Well, one good thing about this, I'm glad the mortgage was paid. That *is* a blessing."

"It sho' is a blessin'. Don't worry 'bout Lois. She'll be just fine. God has a way of makin' up for our troubles. So, anyhow, we figured we might as well eat. No sense in starving. God's got it all under control." Mattie Mae patted Charlotte on her arm as an act of reassurance.

"True, but I found out something about Tina while I was in town."

Wrinkles framed Mattie Mae's face. "Charlotte, we already know 'bout Tina. We heard about her marryin' that man. Sista told me," Mattie Mae said sadly. "Go on. Put the groceries up and come on back and sit down wit' us."

Charlotte went inside as she was told and dutifully put away the groceries. She returned outdoors and sat across from Sista.

"I made a pot of sweet peas. I love me some sweet peas. I like how they pop in my mouth," Sista happily informed Charlotte. Sista continued to tell Charlotte about her strange love for sweet peas and how she had been eating them most of her life.

She should be sick of sweet peas by now, Charlotte thought.

Joe Green, who was average-looking but regal in stature, approached the table to say grace. Charlotte bowed her head and caught a glimpse of Edmund bringing the last few pieces of fried brims and catfish to the table. It seemed that no one cared that her crooked cousin ran off with the crooked preacher—no one except for maybe Lois. But Charlotte was mistaken.

The moment that everyone secretly dreaded had finally arrived. Sista opened her mouth and offered her condolences regarding the naughty nuptials. "I sho' am sorry that Tina saw fit to get herself married to that ole rogue. They out there somewhere spendin' the chutch money and Lois's money too, probably." Judging from the horrified looks on everyone's face, it was pretty clear to Charlotte that folks were ready to lynch and then dip Sista in hot oil.

With tears streaming down her cheeks, Lois shifted uncomfortably in her seat and sheepishly said, "I know about Reverend Holiday and Tina getting married. One day he'll get his. Besides, which of us have not been down that road before?"

"No, it ain't! Not all of us been down that road!" Sista declared as she continued to enjoy her precious sweet peas.

"Sista, hush up! You forgot how Johnny used to drive you, his own wife, to the store with his girlfriend sittin' right there between you two! Now, how foolish was that?" Edmund reminded.

"Yeah, but both of 'em dead now, ain't they?" Sista chuckled slyly. Sista looked apologetically at Lois. "You're right, Lois. The Lawd is the one who hands out justice. You just put yo' trust in Him. He'll work it out."

"Look," Mattie Mae said. "We're here to talk about the chutch and what we gonna do 'bout this Sunday's service. Come on, y'all, and eat up. Then we'll let Deacon Brown and whoever else wants to speak have a say."

"Oh, I can talk now," Deacon Brown said, his mouth dripping with corn kernels and butter. Deacon Alonza Brown looked so malnourished and was so bony in structure that he reminded Charlotte of someone from a third world country. She felt sorry for him. On the other hand, his wife, Julia, looked as if she had never missed a meal in her life. Deacon Brown wiped his hands and mouth with a soggy napkin, took a big gulp of water and then stood up from the table to speak.

"Most of you know by now that some of us men came outta our own pockets to help save the church, and there is no money to speak of left in the church bank account. Reverend Holiday almost wiped us out clean, and we're looking into why that happened. We had to use what was left in there, which wasn't much, to help pay the debt. If I remember correctly, there was less than a thousand in the account. We thought about having services at the old schoolhouse if we had lost the church, but God worked it out."

"What we gonna do come Sunday?" Sista asked, picking up the last two peas from her plate with her fingers.

"Well, Bishop Summers is aware of what is going on. One of the assistant ministers will preach this Sunday."

Charlotte sat quietly as she watched the fellowship between these lifelong friends who were at such peace. No one objected or bickered about their situation. Although it was obvious that Lois was heartbroken, Charlotte was glad to see her manage to smile every once in a while. Busta mentioned that he had struggled with leaving the fate of Reverend Holiday in God's hands, but eventually came to terms with how Reverend Holiday treated his daughter and agreed that God knew the end from the beginning.

Once the sun started to set, people began gathering their belongings and food to take home. Mattie Mae, who was inside the house, suddenly came out looking very upset. She looked around the yard until she found Lucille Johnson, who was standing by her car, waving goodbye to Deacon Brown and his wife as they started to drive off.

"Lucille, wait a minute," Mattie Mae said nervously. Mattie Mae rushed frantically over to Lucille and grabbed her firmly by the arm.

11

Due to Lucille's blood-curdling scream, everyone knew that Mattie Mae must have given her some very bad news. They quickly rushed over to see just what was going on. Mattie Mae struggled to keep the distraught woman from sliding down to the ground. Even Deacon Alonza and Julia Brown parked their car, got out, and rushed over and surrounded the two women.

Mattie Mae had received a phone call while inside the house. Lucille's daughter had died in New York from a drug overdose. The body had been found in the alley in a Dumpster. After several minutes of trying to console Lucille, Edmund offered to drive her home.

"Lucille, I know it's a hard pill to swallow, but she's in a much better place now," Julia Brown said.

Suddenly, Sista blurted out, "Not unless she accepted the Lawd she ain't, Julia. Furthermore, how is it that you always say that it's better to be alive than dead in a cold grave somewhere, but when someone dies you say it's better to go on home to glory than to stay here in this cruel world? Now, which is it? Oh, it ain't just you, Julia.

We need to make up our minds and we need to stop always sayin' everybody is goin' to a much better place. Not everybody accepts Jesus as their Savior."

Once again, everyone looked around in utter disbelief at Sista but remained quiet. Silently, Charlotte agreed with Sista. Sista may have lacked tact, but she was right. However, it was quite apparent that her opinion was not appreciated, at least not during this time fresh with bereavement.

"Not now, Sista!" Mattie Mae warned her friend in a threatening tone.

Nevertheless, Sista persisted. "I'm sorry, but I have to say this. People go 'round thinkin' they all goin' to heaven when they die. Just 'cause you ain't a mean person, or you don't smoke, drink, or cuss don't mean nothin'. And just because you go to chutch every once in a while don't mean you goin' to heaven when you die either."

Charlotte wanted to shout "bravo!" from the top of her lungs.

"Not now, Sista!" Mattie Mae warned a second time, gritting her teeth.

It was too late. An angry and hurt Lucille freed herself from Mattie Mae's mighty grip.

"Sista, I don't know if you're saying this to be mean, 'cause all these years I know you thought my daughter was yo' husband's child, but that ain't true. Sometimes you really don't know when to keep yo' mouth shut. Don't you think I know what you're sayin' is true? Where is your heart? How could you be so cold? I just found out that my only child is dead! Can I get past her being dead before you start talkin' about her going to hell?" Lucille screamed.

Joe Green and Edmund managed to put Lucille into the car before she hauled off and slapped Sista hard enough to leave a handprint. Edmund took Lucille's keys from her hand, inserted the key in the ignition, backed the car out of the lane, and drove Lucille home with Joe Green following so that he could bring Edmund home. Mattie Mae was totally embarrassed, but used to Sista's behavior. Sista, on the other hand, stood stoically. She couldn't care less.

It was now late in the evening, and the Morley household had settled down from the day's drama. Edmund had returned from Lucille's house and was now sleeping in his recliner. Noticing that her grandparents' bedroom door was ajar, Charlotte entered the room where Mattie Mae sat on the bed, reading her Bible.

"Grandma, excuse me, but it seems as if all heck is breaking loose around here," Charlotte noted, standing in the doorway.

"Sho' does, don't it? But this too shall pass, as they say." Mattie Mae sighed and shook her head.

"So, Uncle Charles and Aunt Francine will be here tomorrow? What brought that on?"

Mattie Mae closed her Bible, placed it on the doily-covered nightstand, and motioned for Charlotte to come sit next to her on the bed. Charlotte glanced around her grandparents' bedroom as she made her way to the bed. The plain white curtains were blowing from the breeze coming through the window screen. Family photos blanketed the walls, dresser, and nightstands, and a patchwork quilt that Mattie Mae had made was strewn across the rocking chair. Edmund's black leather strap that was used for chastening their children back in the day hung proudly on the wall like a retired NBA jersey. Charlotte nearly tripped over the curled edges of a pink-and-white chenille rug before sitting on the lumpy mattress.

Mattie Mae took off her wire-framed glasses and said,

"Charlotte, Edmund told me today that Charles and Francine are divorced."

"You're kidding! I live right there in the same city and I didn't even know they were separated. Then again, and I'm ashamed to say this, how could I know? It's not I like ever visited. Wow! I can't believe this. Do you know why?"

"Because my son is a liar," Mattie Mae answered harshly. "I talked to your father today while you were in town. He and the rest of my chi'ren knew that Charles and Francine weren't gettin' along. I asked him why nobody bothered to tell us. Esau said that it was up to Charles and Francine to tell us, which is true. That's how I brought my chi'ren up.

"You know, a mother knows her child, and I always knew that Charles was different. But not like this. When Charles told us that he was getting married, I was so proud of him and relieved." Mattie Mae paused briefly. "Back then, we used to call them sissies."

"Huh? Grandma, what are you talking about?" Charlotte was totally thrown off.

"Charles goes wit' men and women." Mattie Mae held her head down. "Charles and Francine got married for all the wrong reasons, and they had been tryin' to fool everybody only to end up foolin' themselves."

"Are you saying that Uncle Charles is bisexual? And you knew this during the time of your fish fry? You and Granddaddy were so calm."

"The peace of God is an amazing thing. Sometimes in life you have to take the good along with the bad. We was happy about savin' the chutch, but I was hurtin' real bad on the inside."

Charlotte wrapped her arms around her gray-haired grandmother. "And my parents knew Uncle Charles and Aunt Francine were divorced?"

"They didn't know at first. Esau said he knew they were separated, but later Charles lied and said that they had gotten back together. Esau said now he knows why Charles always made excuses for him not to come over to the house. Charles wasn't livin' there!"

"No wonder Tina and Terry are so jacked up," Charlotte guessed.

Mattie Mae shook her head and said, "There are reasons why they act the way they do. We did the best we could wit' raisin' Terry, but every time she came back here to go to school, it was like we got a wild animal to train all over again. That gal was so hardheaded and stiff that sometimes I wanted to send her right back to Charles and Francine to live. But I couldn't give up on her. She's still my gran'chile and I love all of my grandchi'ren."

"I know you do," Charlotte said as she got up from the bed and paced the floor. She thought about her grandparents having been hit, not once, but twice today, with disturbing news. Charlotte began to really feel sorry for her cousins. Surely they knew about their father's lifestyle.

Mattie Mae could no longer hold back her tears as she told Charlotte about the conversation she had earlier with Charles. She told Charlotte that Charles admitted to his bisexuality and that Francine had always known. However, Francine foolishly believed that she could change him, and at one point, she even resorted to witchcraft in an effort to turn Charles into a loving father and devoted husband. When that didn't work, Francine eventually began having affairs of her own.

Charlotte also learned the whole truth about the infamous "incident" that happened more than ten years ago. When Tina was a child, she caught her father in a compromising position with another man and was brainwashed into believing that she misunderstood what she had seen. This would turn out to be the same man who, one year later, molested Terry. The molestation, or "incident" as it was referred to by the family, was the ordeal that had brought Terry to Turtle Island to live with Edmund and Mattie Mae. No matter how hard Edmund and Mattie Mae tried, they just were not equipped to deal with the psychological damage Terry had suffered, and having a career in the medical field, Charles should have known this.

But Charles chose to gloss over the incident because he did not want his name to be synonymous with such a scandal. He thought that life on a farm and being around down-to-earth folk would be a good enough cure for Terry. Francine agreed. There were too many social ladders to climb. By the time Mattie Mae had finished telling the sordid story, Charlotte was truly sad.

"Grandma, God is *so* pulling the covers off. Uncle Charles and Aunt Francine sowed some bad seeds. What's sad is that Terry seems so influenced by Tina, and Tina keeps stabbing her in the back. Growing up, I'm sure Terry didn't trust adults. And the one person who did try to speak out against this pervert *and* their father was Tina, but they shut her down. Maybe that's why she lies so much. She was treated like a liar at an early age. I know this may sound twisted, but when you think about it, Tina was all Terry had."

"She had us!" Mattie Mae exclaimed. "I don't know. Maybe you're right. I don't understand all that psycho-mumbo-jumbo stuff y'all be talkin' 'bout. But I do know that God said that whatever is done in the dark will be shown in the light. Charles and Francine told us later that they had trusted the man and never thought he would do somethin' like that to a chile. And here it is . . . my own son!"

"No, Grandma, Uncle Charles is not like that. His

friend was the pedophile who was sexually attracted to children. Uncle Charles wasn't accused of molesting children. Plus, you have to understand. When most children are violated like that, they don't say anything. It's a combination of fear, shame, lack of trust, and God knows what else. To deal with it, many of these children act out in some way. Some grow up and do the same thing."

"That man could have started out likin' other men and got bored wit' that, so he moved on to chi'ren. Nothin' people do these days surprises me. I can remember years back, hearin' a story 'bout somebody catchin' one of Nellie Moss's relatives wit' a sheep. I didn't believe that was true then, but now I'm not so sure."

"My Lord, I hope that wasn't true. But you're right. Nothing is really shocking anymore. Well, it's getting late, and you need to get some rest. Do you want me to wake up Granddaddy before I go to bed?"

"No, let him sleep. He'll get up after while. I know he's tired. It's been a long day for all of us," Mattie Mae said as she started to unbutton her faded cotton dress.

Charlotte kissed her grandmother goodnight and quietly left the room. She could hear Edmund snoring downstairs as she entered her bedroom, closing the door behind her. She hoisted up the window to allow the cool night breeze to come in, which now contained a prominent scent of approaching rain. Charlotte knelt by the bed and prayed to the Lord. Knowing that there were seasons of good times and seasons of trying times, she prayed for the strength to handle yet another trying time.

Charlotte pulled off her dress and tossed it in the hamper. After brushing and flossing her teeth, she took a quick shower. After that, Charlotte slipped on her favorite nightgown, a Christian Dior number she had treated herself to on her last birthday. She turned on the ceiling fan, pulled back the white goose-feathered comforter and climbed into bed. Lying flat on her back, Charlotte thought about her family.

"You never really know what goes on behind closed doors," she said to herself. At least she knew why no one should envy Charles and Francine. Despite all of their material wealth, Charles and Francine lived miserable lives. That façade had to be tough to keep up, especially for Francine. Her prima donna ways were the reason most of the Morley family stayed away.

The rain arrived with great force. The sound pounding on a piece of flat tin played like a symphony to Charlotte's ears. When she closed her eyes, she saw a flash of bright light. At first, she thought it was lightning, but then came a vision of faces with no bodies attached. The faces moved around in a circular motion and had no features. The eyes, noses and mouths were missing. Next, Charlotte saw a clear blue sky above a large body of choppy turquoise water that was littered with debris. For some odd reason, the faceless people did not bother Charlotte, but the violent, crashing waves of water did. She kept her eyes closed until the vision faded. Soon, Charlotte drifted off to sleep.

12

After waking up to an early morning thunderstorm, Charlotte could hear movement coming from her grandparents' room as she reached for the clock to check the time. Yesterday, like most Mondays, had been a very exhausting day and had taken a tremendous toll on her.

Just as she was about to get up, Mattie Mae knocked on her door to see if she was up and wanted to participate in family prayer.

"Yes, ma'am, I'm up. Where do you want to have prayer?" Charlotte asked.

"We can say it in yo' room. Come on, Edmund. She's up."

Charlotte grabbed her robe from the foot of the bed and got up to open the door. She was surprised to see Edmund and Mattie Mae looking so haggard. In fact, Edmund shuffled into the room like a zombie. It was evident that the news of Tina's elopement and the revelation about Charles's double life had stressed them out.

Edmund led them in prayer, asking the Lord for forgiveness, guidance, and protection, not only for the members of his family, but for his church family as well. Edmund also asked the Lord to convict Reverend Holiday in his heart and to grant traveling mercies for Charles and Francine.

After conclusion of prayer, Charlotte offered to cook breakfast, and naturally, the offer was declined. No one cooked in Mattie Mae's kitchen but Mattie Mae. Charlotte laughed at her stubborn grandmother as she escorted her grandparents out of the room. Observing that the rainfall was now a torrential mess, Charlotte was ever so tempted to get back in bed.

Dressed in a brand new pair of blue denim overalls, Edmund sat on the front porch sipping his morning cup of black coffee. Mattie Mae sat next to him peeling peaches. Charlotte came out on the porch to join them and was about to sit down when suddenly the big, bright headlights of a black Mercedes sedan caught her eyes. It was Charles and Francine. Charles parked his car behind Edmund's truck and blew the horn.

Finally, the never-happily-married couple exited from the car. Francine, as usual, was a vision of elegance, dripping in Prada and Escada. To complete her look, she wore a pair of Christian Roth sunglasses that framed her oval-shaped face, and a pair of life-threatening pointed-toe stilettos that graced her pedicured feet.

Charles was casually but stylishly dressed in a pair of black leather sandals and black linen shorts that complemented his bowed legs. He wore a crisp white T-shirt that displayed the name of a well-known health spa resort. What really stood out about Charles, to Charlotte, was his flawless caramel-colored skin and naturally curly hair. Charles was a handsome and debonair man. He looked more like a catalogue model than a surgeon.

Charlotte admired the couple for taking great care of

their bodies and appearances. The two seemed like such a perfect couple. Charlotte was still grappling with the revelation of Charles's sexual preference and their divorce. She would have never guessed. He was not flaming. Then again, he liked both genders, so why would he be flamboyant? Charlotte concluded.

Mattie Mae was the first to get up to greet the pair. The three of them exchanged hugs and kisses. Charlotte was completely caught off guard by Francine's warmth. Normally, Francine was not a warm, touchy-feely type person. But Charlotte could tell that there was definitely something different about her aunt.

All eyes were now on Edmund, who so far had not moved a muscle or said a word. "Hi, Edmund," Francine said as she leaned down and planted a kiss on his cheek.

"You look good, Francine. How was the drive?"

Francine took a seat on the porch swing. "Not bad at all, considering we left so late and I hadn't slept much. Good thing there was no heavy traffic on the Interstate."

"How are you doing, Pop?" Charles asked timidly.

"I'm fine, and you?" Edmund replied in a cold tone. For someone who was so anxious to speak with his son, Edmund certainly didn't show it.

"Y'all want something to eat?" Mattie Mae asked.

"Nothing for me, thanks. I'm good," Francine replied. "We stopped by a Waffle House on the way here."

"Why are you wearin' them sunglasses, Francine? The sun ain't shinin'. In fact, the weatherman called for rain and clouds all day," Edmund noted.

"It's just a silly habit." Francine took off her expensive sunglasses and revealed a pair of the most enchanting green eyes. "I want to apologize for my daughters' behavior. Charles and I had a very long talk on the way down here, and we both agreed that we were rotten parents. And I want to thank you both for taking in Terry when you did. I don't think I've ever really thanked you." Suddenly, tears streamed down Francine's cheeks, prompting Charlotte and Mattie Mae to go over to comfort her.

"I'm sorry," Francine apologized. Her voice cracked. "I'm being emotional. I feel like someone who's been standing by the roadside just waiting for and watching a wreck."

"It's all right." Mattie Mae handed Francine some tissue from her dress pocket.

"Thank you. I know you mean well, Mattie Mae, but it's not all right." Francine dried her eyes with the tissue. "Anyway, one night last week, out of the blue, this colleague of mine called me. She said she didn't know why, but the Lord had placed me on her heart. Normally, I wouldn't want to hear any talk like that, but I found myself listening to her anyway. I don't know. This woman said that she could tell by my voice that something was wrong and she was convinced she did the right thing by calling me. She told me that she didn't know why she had to say this, but she felt led to tell me that I needed to take charge over my family, especially my daughters. How could she have known something was wrong? I don't even know what's going on with them. Although I work with this woman, we weren't friends. It's not like we even have lunch together or anything. Anyway, she invited me to her church last night. Greater Faith Center. They were having a special service."

"Did you say Greater Faith Center?" Charlotte asked.

"That's right. Bishop Jonathan Lorne is the pastor."

"That's my church, Aunt Francine! I'm an assistant minister on staff there," Charlotte exclaimed.

"Really, Charlotte?" Francine's face seemed to brighten with hope. "I didn't even know church service was like that. I thought the praise and worship was awesome enough, until your pastor came out and said some things that, if I didn't know better, I'd swear he had been spying on me. I can't explain it. It was like something wonderful came over me. I turned my life over to Jesus last night and joined the church, and I should be tired, but I'm not."

"Praise the Lord! I'm so happy for you!" Charlotte said, hugging Francine.

"The Lawd sho' is good! He sho' is good," Mattie Mae said, patting her hands.

Francine leaned forward and looked at Charles. "And I'm praying for healing and salvation for my Charles and the children as well."

Charles did not respond.

"Don't you have anything to say, Charles?" Edmund asked. "Don't you think that's a step in the right direction? I know this much: your daughters are somewhere out there doin' God knows what, and one of 'em ran off and married a man who is about to cause trouble in his household." As soon as Edmund said that, he wondered if Charles truly understood how his actions had affected his own family.

Charles grasped for words. "We, um, we did fail the girls, Pop. I know that. But we haven't heard from them yet, and it's true we don't know where they are. For all we know, Tina is on her honeymoon and Terry could be on a beach somewhere drinking cocktails."

Edmund rolled his eyes, took another sip of coffee, and said, "That's it? Tina is on her honeymoon! That's all you got to say? I just said that one of yo' daughters ran off with a preacher who stole the chutch money. And look at what you done to yo' marriage. Me and Mattie Mae didn't live in Washington wit' you two to see what was goin' on, but I know the girls weren't blind or stupid. No wonder that happened to Terry. And how could you let that happen?"

"Edmund, don't go and get yo'self upset," Mattie Mae interrupted, fearful of Edmund's blood pressure rising.

Charles looked Edmund squarely in the face and said, "Pop, I know you two are ashamed of me, and I'm sorry for that. I don't know if I can make a change like Fran did, and frankly, I'm not sure if I even want to. Please try to understand."

This time, Francine interrupted. "I only made a decision to repent just last night. There is no halo hanging over my head, and I'm sure there will continue to be struggles for me. Leaving an old life for a new one can't be easy. Being divorced is not easy for me. I've invested over twenty years of my life in our marriage. I tried everything else, Charles, and nothing worked. I've . . . we've been unhappy for years. Why do you think the girls act the way they do? I mean, look at us. I believe Christ is the only one who can turn this whole mess around. He loves us, but not some of the things that we do. I'm talking about our sins. If we don't admit our mistakes and turn to Him, things will only get worse for us. It's important to at least admit your faults."

"I know that, Fran," Charles said defensively. Judging by the tone of his voice, he felt threatened.

However, Francine refused to give up. "You say you know, but you never admit when you're wrong about anything. Listen, I don't want to argue with you. We are not here for that. I'm just grateful that God has allowed me to live long enough to come to the end of myself. I don't like the idea of Tina being married to someone who is shady, even though she's no angel either. Charles, God gave Tina and Terry to us to nurture, protect, and guide. We failed miserably as parents. I'm just hoping that it's not too late."

"Look at you, Francine," Mattie Mae said proudly. "Look at God."

"You all know that I didn't grow up in the church, and the few times that my sisters and I did go to church, we went with our next-door neighbor. I remember being bored out of my skull. I didn't get a thing out of it. But last night . . . last night was different. It was like God was speaking directly to me, and I could just feel His presence. Some people were laying at the altar praying, and some were giving awesome testimonies," Francine said.

"That's letting the Holy Spirit have His way in His church!" Charlotte exclaimed. "That's what I like about Greater Faith. Bishop Lorne is not a stickler for staying with programs and agendas. It's not a move of the Spirit when you have to stick with your agenda."

"Are you two gonna get back together?" Edmund suddenly blurted out.

"No," Francine stated. "Edmund, I cannot accept Charles back the way he is. He is not in love with me, and I have to accept that. We came here together as parents only, not as a reconciling couple. I've tried contacting the girls, but they are not answering their cells or returning my calls, so I know something is up. By the way, I want you all to know that we did hire a private investigator to find them, and we're prepared to file a missing persons report. I may not have been the best mother in the world, but I do have instincts, and my gut feeling is that something about this whole thing definitely stinks."

"I sho' hope this investigator can find 'em," Mattie Mae said.

"I hope so too," Edmund said as he got up from his chair and handed his coffee cup to Mattie Mae. He pulled a handkerchief from his pocket, blew his nose, and slowly started down the steps.

"Where you goin', Edmund, in all this rain?" Mattie Mae asked as the heavy downpour continued to beat against the roof.

"I'll be in town for a while."

"You want me to drive you, Pop?" Charles asked, really hoping that Edmund would say no.

"No! You stay right here," Edmund said before speeding off in his old pickup and splattering mud onto the Mercedes.

13

A s the rain showers increased, Charlotte wondered if it represented a cleansing away of sadness, or if it represented more tears to come. She heard a frog croaking nearby and noticed a small puddle of water inhabited by tadpoles by the front steps. "Now, this is good country living," she said to herself.

Just as Charlotte was about to excuse herself to call Elder King, she noticed that Mattie Mae, Charles, and Francine had already gone inside the house. She had been in such deep thought that she hadn't heard or seen them leave. Charlotte reached for the door handle and heard someone call out to her.

"Hey there, Charlotte!" Sista greeted from underneath a ratty old umbrella.

Charlotte could barely recognize the woman behind the familiar voice. Sista looked like a construction worker ready to go sit under the hair dryer. She wore an oversized plaid shirt, a pair of steel-toed work boots, and her thinning hair was rolled up in jumbo pink sponge rollers.

"Hi, Miss Sista. Come on in. I was just about to go in-

side. Grandma is probably in the kitchen as usual. Why
are you out in this weather?"

"Mattie Mae called me to borrow some sugar from
me," Sista explained, holding up the five-pound bag of
sugar as her proof. "I just come by to drop it off." Sista
closed her umbrella and glanced back at the sleek Mercedes as she landed on the top step. "Look to me like the
sugar is already here," she mumbled to herself, knowing
full well that Charles was due in today. Sista had always
been suspicious of Charles's sexuality and often told
Mattie Mae so. But Sista grew tired of Mattie Mae's denial of it over the years, and just stopped talking about it
all together.

Charles and Francine were seated at the kitchen table
drinking coffee and eating biscuits with jelly. Mattie Mae,
who was standing by the stove, turned around and saw
Sista entering the kitchen, "Oh, Sista, I didn't mean for
you to come out in this nasty rain! I was gonna send one
of these chi'ren over for the sugar. I'm gonna make some
sugar biscuits later on."

Sista laid her wet umbrella on the floor and handed
Mattie Mae the bag of sugar. "I don't mind. A little water
ain't never hurt no one. Hey there, Charles and Francine."
Sista grinned mischievously. "It's good to see you two.
How long has it been since y'all been home? Two or three
years, ain't it?"

Charles and Francine nodded their heads.

Francine knew that Sista had a knack for prying, so she
decided to speak up before Sista went in for the kill.
"This kitchen has always been the center of the house.
You know . . . good food, people having a good time."

"Yeah, and you two missed out on a lot of it," Sista
smarted off.

Since Mattie Mae knew that Francine was no match for

her acid-tongued friend, she also made an attempt to steer Sista off course. "Sista, any word yet 'bout the funeral arrangements for Lucille's daughter?" Mattie Mae asked.

"Oh yeah, I forgot to tell ya that it's gonna be at Caleb's Funeral Home this Saturday. The body should be here sometime tomorrow. I hope you know that I didn't mean to make such a fuss with Lucille yesterday. Sometimes I put my foot so deep in my mouth I could scratch my own palate. I don't mean no harm. You know that. I still say my husband was that chile's daddy. I don't care what Lucille says."

"I know you speak yo' mind, Sista, but you tend to do it at the wrong time. I'm just glad you didn't push the issue further about Johnny being that chile's daddy, or we'd have been scraping one of ya of the ground," Mattie Mae stated.

"Who? You wouldn't be scrapin' me off the ground!" Sista said adamantly. "That's for doggone sho'."

Charles slowly got up from his seat and said, "Mama, I don't mean to interrupt this intriguing conversation, but we need to know what rooms to sleep in. I can sleep in my old room, and I was thinking that Fran could take the first room up the stairs, but I didn't know which room Charlotte was using."

"Wait a minute! Y'all ain't sleeping together?" Sista asked anxiously. The inquiring mind of Nora "Sista" Jones wanted to know. Where Mattie Mae and Francine were successful in keepin' Sista out of their business, Charles failed.

"Sista, what did I *just* finish tellin' you 'bout yo' mouth?" Mattie Mae scolded. "Charlotte has the first room up the stairs, Charles. Take whatever room y'all want."

Sista stood in the middle of the floor waiting for one of them, any of them, to answer her question. Charles and

Francine simply smiled and excused themselves to go freshen up. Realizing that no one was going to answer her question, Sista took a seat at the table.

After Charles had finished unpacking his suitcase, he stopped by Francine's room to tell her he was going out to do a little sightseeing. It had been a while since he'd been home, and he wanted to see if anything had changed. Francine did not utter a word. She knew it was only a guise to leave the house and not face any issues. There were two things that Charles was good at: surgery and running from confrontation, and that was fine with her. She was anxious to read one of the books she'd purchased from Greater Faith bookstore.

Meanwhile, Charlotte was in her room on the phone talking to Elder King. "How are things going?" he asked. Charlotte brought him up to date on what was going on in her family and asked him to continue praying for them. Elder King promised that he would, and apologized for having to cut their conversation short again. He was running late for a meeting and would try to call back in a couple of days.

Charlotte said goodbye and was just about to hang up when Elder King said, "Oh, one more thing, Reverend Morley."

Charlotte placed the receiver back to her ear. "Yes."

"Mention to your aunt about our counseling services. I know that you will give her all the encouragement and support that you can, but let her know that we're here to help also."

"I will. I may be a minister, but this stuff has knocked the breath out of me, especially this business with my uncle. I just wish I knew all the answers."

"None of us have all the answers. We all are still learning, but you can do it. Feel free to call me again if you need some encouragement."

Charlotte hung up the phone and proceeded to the front porch. She could hear her grandmother and Sista in the kitchen trying to out-talk each other as she opened the screen door.

14

"Hi, sweetie," Francine said, looking up at Charlotte.

"Oh, I thought you were upstairs. Don't let me disturb you. I see you're reading."

After marking the page with a paper clip, Francine closed the book and laid it in her lap. "Don't be silly. You're not disturbing me. I want to talk to you anyway. I want to apologize to you for not being such a nice aunt."

"Okay, now you're being silly. That's not true," Charlotte said.

"It is true. It's bad enough that I haven't been a good mother, and I don't even know where to begin trying now."

"Well, God is the God of many chances. Forgive me for saying this, but I remember you and Uncle Charles always had this active social life, but look at what God is doing with you! I bet you never would have thought you'd be seeking after Him."

Francine folded her arms and crossed her legs. "I hear you, but you know what, Charlotte? Ever since I was a child, all I wanted to do was get away from South Carolina, marry a rich man, travel, and be able to afford the so-called finer things. I wanted to be respected and adored . . . just escape from the crap that I grew up in. I met your uncle when we were in college, and I was so determined to have him. And then I got him."

"Do you want him back? I mean, if he changed, would you want him back?"

Francine thought carefully before answering. "We should never have gotten married. I tried to make him love me, only to end up living with a man who tolerated me. Actually, we tolerated each other over the years. He tried in the beginning, but it wasn't long before he decided that the whole wife, kids, dog, and picket fence thing was not for him. In actuality, we both just wanted an image. I wanted the status image, and he wanted . . . well, he wanted a family to hide behind. I know Charles loves his daughters, but with his work schedule and battling his demons, it soon became obvious to me that the girls and I just weren't a priority to him. He knew it. I knew it, and my children suffered because they knew it. Don't get me wrong. I don't excuse myself. I caused some of the suffering by being in denial and not being a strict enough parent."

Charlotte appreciated her aunt's ability to pour her heart out, but she was not sure if she was ready to hear all of it. Elder King may have had confidence in her, but she didn't have enough confidence in herself to be objective. After all, she wasn't quite over her own divorce and the pain that her ex-husband, Anthony, had inflicted upon her.

"God knows I sure didn't have a role model to go by. My mother was crazy. She pretty much neglected us, and I turned around and did the same thing to my children," Francine said, fighting back tears.

"Aunt Francine, if this is too painful for you to talk about, I'll understand."

"It is painful, but it's also therapeutic to talk about. There has been no one I could really talk to about this. I didn't even know how. . . . I take that back. I didn't want to talk about it because I didn't want to expose the truth.

"My daughters have always been so jealous of other kids and their relationships with their families. They were even jealous of each other. My way of fixing things was to buy them everything they asked for. When my sisters and I were growing up, sometimes all we had to eat were potato scraps. I was determined that my daughters were not going to live like that. I gave them everything except the one thing they really wanted and needed . . . me!"

"Is it really true that Terry was molested by one of Uncle Charles's friends?" Charlotte found herself asking.

Francine sighed heavily. "That was an absolute nightmare. She was so young. I was so angry about it and all, but instead of dealing with it like we should have, I just helped Charles sweep it under the rug. We had to protect our precious image!"

"I vaguely remember something happening when they were young, but I was told that some boy at school messed with her and since neither the school nor the boy's parents did anything about it, you just sent Terry down here to go to school and help Grandma out around the house. I don't understand why it was such a secret," Charlotte said, shaking her head.

"It was such a despicable thing to happen to a child. Even ten years ago, you didn't hear or talk about child molestation like you do now, especially in the black community. And we still don't talk about it like we should. We like to sweep things under the rug and ignore them. We shouldn't say, 'only white folk do this, and black folk don't do that.' We all do it! I'm surprised that you didn't know the truth. That's not like Betty to not be open with you."

Charlotte shrugged her shoulders. "I know."

"Charlotte, to this day, I still blame myself. I remember that summer evening as if it were yesterday. It was during one of our fake and phony cookouts, and this colleague of Charles came over. I didn't know him very well, but I knew that he was a respected surgeon named Dr. Alvin Tifton. This man followed Terry into the house while the rest of us were outside. She just went inside to use the bathroom and that S.O.B was right behind her. I was too busy drinking whiskey sours and socializing to pay any attention," Francine recalled bitterly.

"Anyway, he came back outside as if nothing had happened. Hours later, it dawned on me that Terry had been inside for an awfully long time. When she came back out, I noticed she was withdrawn, but I didn't pay it too much attention. Who would have thought something like that would happen right under our noses? The next day, Tina told us what happened to Terry, but—"

Suddenly, Charlotte could hear the nearby chatting of Sista and Mattie Mae.

"Well, I reckon I'll mosey on back home before I have to swim back. Don't look like this rain is gonna let up. Francine and Charlotte, I'll see y'all later," Sista said as she made her way down the steps.

Charlotte offered to drive Sista home, but she declined the offer. The women said goodbye to Sista as she opened her umbrella and started on her way home. Once Sista was no longer within earshot, Mattie Mae asked, "What are you two up to?"

"I was just bringing Charlotte up to date on some things," Francine answered.

"Is that right? Francine, I'm sorry you and my son can't work things out. So many people can't seem to get

along these days. They treat marriage like it's dating,"
Mattie Mae said as she went back inside.

"You got that right," Francine replied softly. "You got
that right."

Charles parked his car in front of Busta's Barber and
Beauty Shop and took a trip down memory lane to his
childhood days. He happily remembered the times when
his father brought him to Busta's barbershop for his haircuts, even though he hated those bowl-styled haircuts.
He remembered seeing Waller Street crowded with people, especially on the weekends, but even as a small boy,
Charles knew that living on Turtle Island was not for
him.

If only his family knew how deep down inside he hated
his life. He was so sucked into a lifestyle that was made
to seem normal, and he couldn't help himself. If only
they knew how much he envied Francine's courage, but
was too prideful to tell her.

Charles had always been an overachiever and wanted
to experience life and all it had to offer. Aside from a lu-
crative career, life for him had meant social prominence
with his trophy wife by his side and creeping with
strangers for cheap sex.

Fearful of his reputation being ruined, Charles chose
not to press charges against his lover or to seek profes-
sional help for Terry. Terry would just have to be the sac-
rificial lamb, and her trauma would be medicated with
gifts and denial. Besides, she was young and resilient.
Children bounced back from things quickly . . . didn't
they?

Charles now had a deep respect for Francine. Here she
was, willing to make a change for herself and for their
children's sake, and he was nothing more than a coward.
"If my parents had made me take responsibility for my

actions as a child, maybe I would know how to step up to the plate," Charles muttered to himself, aware that he had issues, yet still casting blame. He learned early in life that being the youngest in the family carried certain perks, but being spared the rod too many times could be detrimental to one's character. It certainly was in his case. As a child, if he did something wrong, he'd lie on one of his older siblings. They were held responsible, and he got away, free and clear.

For whatever reason, no one ever admitted that Charles was the culprit who needed chastising. Charles's siblings didn't squeal on him when he broke the glass in the china closet, nor did they snitch on him when he took money from Mattie Mae's purse to buy candy from Ms. Lula, the candy lady.

Charles turned his focus back to Francine. She had a glow about her now, and he was envious of that. They had been through so much together—before, during, and after their marriage. Francine knew about his affairs, and he knew about hers. He couldn't blame her. After all, he drove her to that point. Now she was getting a handle on life without depending on him. If only things had been different. After having received what he thought he wanted, Charles realized that he was not so happy after all.

Charles found himself standing inside the Waller Street Juke Joint. The place reeked of thick cigarette smoke, stale beer, and dime store perfume. Cora Johnson sat in a corner booth swaying to the music and carrying on an intense conversation with herself. After she spotted Charles, she emerged from her dark haven and sashayed over to him, hoping Charles would buy her a drink. He refused, and after deciding that he had seen enough, Charles left, nearly bumping into Edmund and Busta, who were walking by.

"Will you look who is here! How you doin', Charles?" Busta said as he reached out for a handshake. "Edmund just told me that you and your wife was home. Glad to see you take time out for a visit."

Charles extended his hand and Busta gripped it like a lobster. Busta's hands, which had been strengthened by years of heavy farm work, were too much for Charles's pampered and protected-to-perform-surgery hands.

Charles asked about Lois while trying to ignore his throbbing hands.

"She's doing fine, just fine," Busta replied. "I'll tell her you asked about her."

Edmund suggested that he and Charles should get back to the house. Charles could tell that Edmund was hurt and disappointed in him.

He was hurt and disappointed in himself as well.

15

The past twenty-four hours of rain had finally ended by the wee hours of the morning. Charlotte threw the bed sheet back and stretched out her arms.

"Father, thank you for a good night's rest and waking me up this morning," she said. "I just want to say thank you. I'm not asking for anything. I know that you've heard my prayers and you've got it all under control."

Suddenly, she remembered that she had been recruited to drive Mattie Mae and Sista to Caleb's Funeral Home to view the body of Lucille's daughter. Guessing from the aroma coming from the kitchen, Mattie Mae would soon be ready to leave. Charlotte checked out the time and realized that she had better scurry.

Just when Charlotte was tempted to complain about the heat, she remembered a question she once asked Mattie Mae: "How could you guys stand it back in the day without air conditioning?"

Mattie Mae had replied, "Sometimes the summer heat made you feel like you was only a mile away from the sun, but you were used to it. We'd get up before sunrise to pick cotton, and we picked it 'til the sun went down. We came home, ate supper, took our baths, and we'd fan ourselves with hedge bushes to try and keep cool, but all that really did was stir up hot air. It did keep the flies and mosquitoes away, though. Chile, we didn't know any other way. We were just used to it."

Charlotte promised God that she would try not to complain about anything ever again. After she bathed and got dressed, Charlotte went downstairs.

"Oh, I'm glad you're up. Breakfast is on the stove," Mattie Mae said as she tore off a paper towel to dry her hands. "After you finish eating, I want you to put on a mess of greens for me. Use that pot in the drainer. I just washed it out."

Mattie Mae tightened the apron around her waist. "Mamie sent over a bag of greens she had in the freezer for us to cook for Lucille, but we don't have time to wait for it to finish cookin'. I'll ask Charles to watch the pot while we're gone. He can take it over to Lucille's later, or we can take it to her tomorrow to help feed."

"I'm not really hungry, so I'll do it now. Why can't Ms. Mamie cook the greens herself, Grandma?" Charlotte started washing her hands.

"Mamie is up there in age. She don't do much cookin' these days, but she wanted to do somethin' to help out."

Satisfied with the answer, Charlotte located a knife and started cutting and rinsing a few slices of bacon. She then started removing the frozen greens from the freezer bag. "Grandma, look!" she cried out.

Mattie Mae turned around to see what had Charlotte so excited.

"There is a dishcloth in these greens!" Charlotte said, holding up her discovery. To their amazement, nestled in the middle of the frozen collard greens was one of Mamie's dingy black-and-gray dishcloths.

"What? Oh, Lawd Jesus." Mattie Mae started laughing. "I'm sorry, baby. Mamie means well, but she is old and forgetful. I should have known to expect somethin' like this." The two women laughed so hard that they didn't hear Sista coughing as she came into the kitchen.

"What you two hens cacklin' about?" Sista asked as she got closer.

"We're laughin' at Mamie. She tries, bless her heart," Mattie Mae answered.

"What she done this time?" Sista went over to look in the sink.

Mattie Mae told Sista what happened.

"Yeah, she does mean well. Mattie Mae, you remember the time she called herself baking Petey Moss's family a cake when his daddy died? Cake turned out to be cornbread wit' icing on top! And then the cornbread was dry. It was drier than the—what's the name of that place again? The Betty Ford Clinic," Sista stated.

"Grandma, seriously, we shouldn't be laughing at Ms. Mamie," Charlotte said, even though she was still laughing to the point where her jaws started to ache. "How are you feeling today, Miss Sista?"

"Chile, that laugh done me good. I had arthritis pain so bad this morning 'til I felt like throwin' myself down some steps, but I feel much better now."

No one saw Francine standing in the doorway until they heard her giggling.

"Hi, Aunt Francine," Charlotte said. "It's been a long time since I've laughed like that. Even my stomach is hurting."

"Well, the day certainly seems to be off to a good start. Sista, you're a mess. You really crack me up," Francine said, pouring herself a cup of coffee.

"Y'all don't mind me. You goin' with us this morning, Francine?"

"No, I'm afraid I'll pass. I want to catch up on some reading."

Mattie Mae instructed Charlotte to throw the bag of greens and dishcloth in the trash. The three women said goodbye to Francine and loaded the car with food and drinks. Their first stop would be Caleb's Funeral Home.

Upon arrival at the funeral home, they saw a group of people gathered at the front entrance. The owner of the funeral home, Brother Caleb, Jr., stood at the door ushering in the visitors. Mattie Mae suggested that they should just poke their heads in for a minute to view the body and then go to Lucille's house while the food was still warm. Standing by the casket was Cora Johnson, Lucille's alcoholic sister.

"How she managed to tear herself away from the juke joint, I'll never know," Sista said, looking disgustedly at Cora, who was making an absolute spectacle of herself by falling out over the casket.

"Don't even look at her," Sista ordered Mattie Mae and Charlotte. "Cora just wants attention." But Mattie Mae and Charlotte did watch as Brother Caleb and his assistant pulled the drama queen away from the casket.

Sista led the way to the bluish-gray casket. "You know she just doin' that so somebody can feel sorry for her and give her a dollar to buy corn liquor. Lawd, have mercy. Look-a-here. The poor chile looks like a pig trussed up on a stick."

Charlotte and Mattie Mae noted how bloated the corpse appeared.

"And look at how drugs done messed this gal up. All that long, pretty hair she had on her head. Now look at her! Head clean as my hand," Sista said, holding out her palms.

Charlotte agreed that it was indeed a sad sight. A life cut short by drugs. As Mattie Mae, Sista, and Charlotte started to leave, a line of curiosity seekers began to file in. Everyone knew that Lucille's daughter was once a beautiful and successful model in New York who frequently rubbed elbows with the rich and famous, and Lucille had plenty of pictures to prove it. But now, look what the devil had stolen.

16

Lucille Johnson lived only two blocks away from the funeral home. Parking spaces were scarce on the narrow street, but fortunately, someone was backing out of her driveway as Charlotte drove up. Lucille's tiny three-bedroom, ranch-styled home looked as if it was about to fall apart, and her yard could have used some sprucing up as well.

Charlotte knew that Lucille and her sister, Cora, grew up dirt poor and that their single mother used to work as a seamstress at a factory over in Clark County. Although Lucille had always shied away from the bottle, Cora ran to it like a pig to a trough. Still, the two sisters were as close as two peas in a pod. Neither had ever married, but both of them had children. Lucille never said who fathered her only, now deceased child, but townsfolk speculated that it was Sista's late husband, and there was no telling who was the father of Cora's children.

"I know one thing; I better not see Otis here," Sista said emphatically as she canvassed the crowd gathered on Lucille's lawn.

"Why not? This is Lucille's house. You have no say over who comes here," Mattie Mae pointed out.

"I'm missing two chickens from my hen house, and ain't nobody but that darn Otis took 'em. If he's here and I see him with some fried chicken, I'll snatch it right outta his hand! I don't care whose house it is."

"Otis won't be here unless Nellie drags him here."

"Oh, they'll be here all right. There are three things Nellie Moss loves: food, funerals, and stirrin' up confusement," Sista affirmed.

No sooner than she said that, Charlotte saw Otis Moss, along with his wife, Nellie. Both were lifting large aluminum pans filled with fried chicken from the back of their Gremlin hatchback. Before Mattie Mae or Charlotte could stop Sista, she was halfway in the couple's face.

"Where did y'all get this chicken you totin'?" Sista asked.

"Don't start wit' me, Sista. It ain't none yo' business where this chicken come from," Nellie said in a hostile tone. "But since you must know, Otis bought this chicken on sale from Piggly Wiggly."

Nellie Rovenia Moss was a robust woman who looked like a prison warden, and it was a well-known fact that Nellie bossed Otis around. People figured Nellie was the reason why Otis drank so much, but that was doubtful since he and all of his brothers drank like fish long before he and Nellie married.

"I think you need to explain somethin' to me, 'cause you know good and darn well Otis ain't never bought nothin' from no store that he can't drink up. And since when did he start buyin' chicken from the store? He's been stealin' chickens from outta my yard like that *was* the store!" Sista shouted back.

The more a guilt-ridden Otis started slowly backing away, the closer his wife inched over to Sista. When he took one step back, Nellie took one step forward.

"Sista, I ain't the one, and we ain't the two, so you might want to leave me alone today!" Nellie yelled.

"That's right, ladies," Charlotte intervened as she came forward and squeezed her tiny frame between the two women. "Let us remember why we're here. This is not the time or place."

After a brief staredown match between Nellie and Sista, the two walked away from each other. Nellie hissed. Sista rolled her eyes, and Mattie Mae stood by the car with her arms folded and wearing a serious frown. When Sista got near Mattie Mae, she said, "You know good as me they done fried up my chicken. If today wasn't Sunday—"

"Well, today ain't Sunday," Mattie Mae interrupted. "And I ain't got no money to be gettin' you outta jail either. Both of y'all too old to be actin' like alley cats. So what if that was yo' chicken? She done fried it up now. You wasn't plannin' on puttin' fried chicken back in the chicken coop, was you?"

Sista shrugged it off and marched inside the house ahead of them.

Charlotte stopped Mattie Mae. "Grandma, what is it with Miss Sista, Mr. Otis, and Ms. Nellie?" With Sista out of the way, Mattie Mae told Charlotte how the rift between Sista and Nellie got started.

It was no secret that Otis and Nellie had a reputation for stealing. The couple had what Mattie Mae called "light hands." That was why no one ever invited them to events. People didn't want the hassle of nailing anything down because "Bonnie and Clyde" were coming over. That did not, however, deter Nellie from inviting herself. Well, at least not to weddings and funerals. No matter whose funeral it was, you were sure to find Nellie sitting in the second row with the family, grieving, just grieving her little heart out like she was kinfolk. Nellie would wait for any family of the deceased to line up outside the church, and when it was time for the family to go inside, she would boldly cut in line. No one ever dared to say anything to Nellie until one day several years ago, when Sista's husband, Johnny, died and Nellie saw fit to crash the funeral procession.

After having witnessed Nellie crash a couple of other funerals in the past, Sista knew that Nellie would try it at her Johnny's homegoing service. Not long after Sista had been seated in the front pew of the church, she turned around to find Nellie. Of course, she didn't have to look far. Nellie was sitting in the second pew next to Sista's children, black hat and all. Two of Sista's children were forced to sit in the third row because Nellie took up the last two spaces in the second.

Although livid, Sista got up calmly, threw back her black veil, went over to Nellie and whispered, "Nellie, I don't want to get loud in here, but make no mistake, I will if I have to. If you don't get yo' rump up, there will be two funerals in here. You ain't even kin to us! I mean it. Get up from here befo' I bust yo' head open 'til the white meat show. I'll stop this funeral, tell the ushers to take you out, and ask God to forgive me later. Why you always gotta be seen?"

Sista then just as calmly tiptoed back to her seat, and Nellie angrily did what she was told and found a seat in the balcony. The two women had been feuding ever since. However, the problem with Otis started one morning when Sista caught him climbing over her fence with one of her plump grain-fed chickens. By the time she got outside with one of Johnny's old hunting rifles, Otis was gone. Poor Otis was in such a hurry, he left behind crucial evidence—one of his elevated shoes.

The atmosphere at Lucille's house was almost carnival-like. Lucille, who was sitting down in the living room, gave a limp-handed wave to Mattie Mae and Charlotte when they came in. Charlotte briefly scanned the crowded living room and saw pictures and figurines scattered everywhere. One corner was set up as a shrine memorializing Lucille's daughter, Sasha. The wallpaper was faded and peeling and the sofa and chairs were in need of upholstering. Yet, the living room was very neat and orderly.

Charlotte followed Mattie Mae and Sista into the tiny kitchen where people were crammed in like sardines and were either bringing in food or helping themselves to it. Friends and relatives quickly gravitated to the chocolate layer cake that Mattie Mae brought, and no one objected to Charlotte's offer to wash the dishes that were piling up in the sink.

Soon afterwards, Lucille came in and asked Mattie Mae to help her search for a life insurance policy. Sista was in the living room giving her two cents to a group of people from Macedonia Baptist who were discussing the fate of Greener Pastures AME. Charlotte could hear Sista in the living room defending her beloved church.

"No, the chutch ain't closing down. Who told y'all that? Whoever said that told y'all a lie!" Sista declared adamantly.

Charlotte noticed a bowl of untouched rice on the table. She tossed the contents into the trash after seeing a dead fly sitting on top of it like a garnish. Just as she was about to squeeze a small amount of dishwashing liquid into the sink, she heard shouting coming from the front of the house.

One of Cora's daughters was laying claim to some personal items of Lucille's deceased daughter and was apparently upset about not being given charge to count the money in the sympathy cards. Out of concern for Mattie's Mae's safety, Charlotte stopped what she was doing to make sure that her grandmother was not caught in the crossfire.

"You *know* Sasha would want me to have this, Aunt Lucille!" the woman roared.

"My baby ain't even cold or in the ground yet and you yelling 'bout some stuff! Cora, you better come on in here and get this gal out of my face before I knock her head off. Get out of my room, Maggie!" Lucille shouted.

Charlotte pressed her way through the crowd to find Mattie Mae. People started stepping aside and Charlotte could see three men practically dragging a young woman, who was kicking and yelling obscenities, outside. Cora, who was cursing at her daughter for embarrassing the family like that, went staggering behind.

Charlotte peeked inside the front bedroom. After all of that ruckus, Mattie Mae and Lucille were in the room flipping through papers and going through shoeboxes as if nothing was going on. Charlotte felt led to go and speak to Maggie. As Charlotte got closer to the irascible young woman being restrained by the three men, Maggie stopped fidgeting and started glaring at Charlotte. "Who are *you*, and what do you want?"

17

"I'm Mattie Mae Morley's granddaughter, Charlotte."
A sudden spurt of courage came over Charlotte and
she asked the men to let Maggie go. They hesitantly
obliged.

"What do you want?" Maggie asked again, but this
time not so gruffly.

No longer nervous but keeping her distance, Charlotte
said, "Pardon me if I seem out of line. I don't mean to,
but if it's true that your cousin, Sasha, would have
wanted you to have her things, then do you think she
would still want you to have them after you've upset her
mother? Remember, you can catch more flies with honey
than vinegar. There is no telling what the Lord wants to
release into your hands if you would humble yourself,"
Charlotte said before praying silently that Maggie would
not embarrass her.

All of sudden, Maggie's countenance changed and she
thanked Charlotte for her kind words. She told Charlotte
that she was going inside the house to apologize to her
aunt.

Meanwhile, standing nearby was an attractive, well-dressed young man who had been watching the whole scenario. Charlotte noticed him only after Maggie left, but old eagle eye Sista, who had come outside, noticed him from the beginning.

"Whatcha lookin' at, Jeff?" Sista asked.

"I'm just admiring the view, Miss Sista. That's all. Do you know that young lady?" Jeff nodded in Charlotte's direction.

"Yeah, I know her. Admiring the view, huh?" Sista rolled her eyes. "Boy, that's your cousin. Your grandmama and her grandmama were sisters. That's Mattie Mae's granddaughter, Charlotte. So don't go gettin' no ideas 'bout courtin' her. I don't care if y'all was first cousins or tenth cousins. People these days don't mind goin' 'round messin' wit' their own kin. Actin' like a bunch of hillbillies!"

"Now, Miss Sista, you know me better than that. I was just admiring the way she handled Maggie Johnson, that's all. So, she's one of Aunt Mattie Mae's grandchildren?"

"Yeah, that's Esau and Betty's daughter. You need to come 'round more often so you can know yo' people." Sista gave Jeff a long, stern look and went back inside the house.

Folks satellited around Charlotte to praise her skills. She politely thanked them for their praises, but gave honor to the Lord for handling the situation. Charlotte began to feel the onset of a headache, or even worse, a migraine. She didn't want to cut Mattie Mae and Sista's visit short, but if they did not leave soon, she wouldn't be able to drive. Charlotte went inside the house and told her grandmother that she was not feeling well. She then went back out to sit in the car and waited for Mattie Mae and Sista as the pain continued to throb over her eyes.

"You sho' you feel up to drivin'? We can leave the car here and have somebody from the house come and pick us up," Mattie Mae suggested after she and Sista got in the car and before Charlotte pulled out of the driveway.

"I can drive. I just need to lie down for a while." Charlotte rubbed her head.

"You probably got a headache from all that commotion back there," Sista suggested.

"I'll make you a poultice outta some banana peels when we get home. I'll rub it on yo' forehead and neck. You'll feel better then," Mattie Mae said.

"Banana peels? Really! No, don't waste your bananas like that. I'll just take some aspirins or something," Charlotte told her grandmother.

"Who said I'd be wastin' bananas? We'll just have some banana puddin'. I haven't made one in a long time anyway," Mattie Mae said.

Charlotte admired her grandmother's resourcefulness. Mattie Mae went beyond making lemonade out of lemons. She knew how to make a dessert and a poultice from the same source.

When Charlotte pulled into Sista's driveway, she noticed John Edward chasing what she thought was a cat around the yard. "Boy, what are you doing?" Sista yelled as she got out of the car.

"I'm tryin' to kill this rat that came outta the woods," John Edward replied, violently swinging a shovel.

"Well, hurry up and kill it. I keep tellin' you we need some cats around this house. That thing look big enough to ride on." Sista ran into the house as if the rodent was chasing her.

Charlotte quickly backed out of the driveway and headed home before Mattie Mae got it in her head to offer up their assistance. She was not a rat chaser or catcher.

Edmund, Charles, and Francine were on the front porch

enjoying slices of fresh watermelon plucked from the patch. Feeling dizzy, Charlotte went straight to her room.

Mattie Mae went inside the house through the back door and immediately started whipping up the home-made remedy in no time. She then went upstairs and got Charlotte situated comfortably by making sure her bed-room was dark. Even though Charlotte had closed the blinds and the curtains, Mattie Mae draped dark fabric over the windows. Mattie Mae sat on the bed, applied the concoction on Charlotte's forehead and neck, and then wrapped a warm towel around her. Mattie Mae joined the rest of her family on the front porch once the banana pudding had finished baking.

"How Lucille doin'? I know that crazy family of hers was over there," Edmund said.

"I don't know what to say about Cora and her chi'ren, but Lucille doin' as well as can be expected. Anybody call while we were out?" Mattie Mae asked.

Francine spit a watermelon seed into a napkin and said, "The private investigator we hired called."

"What did he find out?" Mattie Mae asked eagerly.

"He believes Reverend Holiday and Tina are in the Ba-hamas and there is a strong possibility that Terry is in At-lanta somewhere. At least that's where she dropped off the rental car."

"What Reverend Holiday and Tina doin' in a foreign country?"

"I guess they're on their honeymoon." Francine said. "The detective did say it was possible that Reverend Hol-iday is preaching there. He has the name of some church, but he said something about the story not adding up. So he wants us to sit tight until he gets the facts straight. He didn't think it was anything to worry about, though."

"Nothin' to worry about!" Mattie Mae shrieked.

Charles decided it was time to speak up. "Hey, guys,

Fran and I are going over to her family's house this evening. We want to talk to her family together. We should be back in a few days."

"I think that's a good idea, Charles. At least you two seem to be gettin' along," Mattie Mae said with hope in her voice.

"I must admit that I'm proud of Fran," Charles said, holding his head down. "I'm not proud of the things I've done, and the best I can do for now is to be there for Fran with her family. As for my daughters, we just have to wait and see."

"I just have one question," Edmund said. "Where did we go wrong wit' you?"

Mattie Mae started humming to avoid hearing Charles's answer. After what seemed like an eternity, Charles finally responded after clearing the lump in his throat. "You did nothing wrong, Pop. Don't ever think that you did."

18

Charlotte woke to the sound of light tapping on her door. "Charlotte," Mattie Mae called out. "Are you feelin' any better?"

"Yes, ma'am." Charlotte lifted her head up from the pillow.

"Timmi is on the phone."

"I didn't hear the phone ring. I'll take the call." Before Charlotte picked up the receiver, she briefly closed her eyes. Immediately, she had another terrifying vision. Even though this vision had the same clear blue sky as the last one, this vision had a terrifying scene taking place that made her jolt. "Dear God, what was that?" she asked. Charlotte took a deep breath, lifted the receiver, and told Mattie Mae that it was okay for her to hang up. She wondered, what has Timmi gotten herself into now?

Charlotte and Timmi grew up in the same neighborhood and had been best friends since they were three years old. Timmi worked as an attorney for a very prestigious law firm that represented high profile cases. She owned a five-bedroom home in Bowie, Maryland, wheeled around town in a Jaguar convertible, was financially comfortable, and had the looks of a Hollywood starlet. But underneath all of that, Timmi was a deeply insecure person.

"Hi, Timmi, what's up?" Charlotte spoke into the receiver.

"Girl, I'm so fed up I don't know what to do! I need to get away for a while," Timmi began complaining.

"Uh-oh, what's wrong now?"

Charlotte knew that Timmi had been dating a guy she met two years ago named Bobby Cadwell, and figured the phone call had something to do with him. It was always the same old story with Timmi. Charlotte hoped that maybe, just maybe, this time would be different. Timmi had so much to offer and needed to stop showing her desperation to every man she met. She needed to see herself as God saw her. Charlotte never cared for Bobby and had been praying for the Lord to reveal Bobby's true nature to Timmi.

"I just found out that Bobby is getting married next month," Timmi said tearfully.

"What? To who?"

"Get this: the receptionist at my job! This chick and I used to go to lunch together, Charlotte! We've gone shopping together, and the little troll has even been to my house! I've mentioned her to you before. Connie."

"You're kidding me, right?"

"No joke. Both of them had been grinning in my face and seeing each other behind my back. You warned me about putting my business out there. Here I am bragging about what a good man Bobby is and come to find out that he was nothing but a counterfeit of a man. I guess I told her enough about him to make her go after him. You know yourself that Bobby and I had stopped talking to each other for about three weeks. I wanted him to get his act together. While I'm waiting for him to get his act together, she's pretending to be a friend to me and hanging out with him on the down low. Do you know Connie had the nerve to still want to be my friend after I found out about their engagement? In her mind, if I couldn't keep him, then he was fair game. In my mind, I'm questioning her loyalties. What does loyalty mean to this chick?"

"Wait a minute. You and Bobby had stopped talking to each other for what, three weeks, and then these two started dating and now they're getting married?"

"Oh no, sister girl! It wasn't even as correct as all that! He was seeing both of us at the same time."

"Well, now you know. Some people are not your true friends. You have to be careful of needy women who want to know your business. You know, the ones who have to have a man, any man, including your man, and on top of that, they will find a way to justify their actions. I don't care if Bobby was your ex-boyfriend. He's off limits to your friends, family, and even aliens. How could she think that the two of you could remain friends? Based on what? Most deceitful! How did you find out anyway?"

"In the wedding announcement section of the newspaper. Connie was walking around the office smiling in my face the whole time. No, I take that back. Last week, I did notice she started distancing herself from me. I wondered what was up, but I wasn't that interested to ask. We didn't hang out that much for me to be consumed with concern. And him, I can't stand his punk behind."

"Wait a minute, calm down. You've met his family. What did they have to say about this? Better yet, what did he have to say?"

"Oh, let me tell you. When I did talk to Bobby, his comment was, 'I never told you I loved you.' Charlotte, he was just *that* cold! He thinks he shouldn't have to say anything to me. He treated me like I was some one-night stand. As for his family, I only met his mother once. One day I got up the nerve to call her. She said Bobby told her that we were friends and that I was cool with it. Cool with it? He must be out of his mind. And get this: his mother also told me that Connie is pregnant."

"First of all," Charlotte said in a calm and soothing voice, "stop picking up these men in the clubs. I don't care if they are upscale clubs. The only thing Bobby has that your other boyfriends didn't have is a good job, and we'll assume a fat bank account and decent credit. Most, if not half of these men in the clubs are married, and if they aren't married, what are the chances of them looking for a serious relationship? So what if Connie is pregnant? One day he is going to look at her from across the breakfast table and resent her. He's going to feel like she trapped him, even though I'm sure she's not holding a gun to his head in order to make him marry her."

"You're probably right. And I understand what you're saying, Charlotte, about picking up men at the club, but I don't think just because a man goes to church it makes him a saint."

"No, and I don't think that either. The devil goes to church too. Remember my ex-husband? I thought I had a good man who loved going to church. It turns out he loved going to church to scope out the women. I want God to pick my husband for me. Otherwise, I might have to kill the next one. I'm sorry. I shouldn't have said that. I got in the flesh.

"Timmi, men don't realize how close to the edge they push us, and when you read about some woman killing some man, the first thing out of their mouth is that she's crazy. Sure, the woman would be wrong, but men had better learn about our emotional makeup and not take us for granted. We need to learn more about them as well. Women are so desperate to be covered that they do all of the hunting, and they're catching wild game in the process. Let what God has for you find you."

"I know. I'm just sick and tired of all the drama."

"Then don't be a part of it. Timmi, God gave you a sign for every man you met. You had more red flags than China. I tell you what: Why don't you come down here for a few days?"

"*Come down there!* Come down South? Come down there and do what? Pick cotton and eat chitlin' patties?"

"You need to quit. Seriously, come down and relax your nerves. Believe it or not, people here aren't backwoods-backwards like you think. You might have a little trouble understanding the language, but you won't need a translator for it. Come on, with your fly-girl self. The change will do you good."

"The *change* would do me in! You know the closest farm I've ever been to was a bottle of Boone's Farm wine."

"Girl, just come on. I know your schedule is flexible. My granny would love to have another mouth to feed. We can go into Charleston and shop. You know how much you love antique shopping. It's time to let yourself heal so that you can know what you really want."

Timmi agreed that she was tired of giving more than she got back in her relationships; giving before she got a chance to see what the man was willing to offer. That had always been one of her biggest downfalls.

"I might come down. Are the bugs real bad?" Timmi asked.

"Will you get off of it and just come down?"

"Okay, let's see. I've got some leave available. I suppose I could take a week off. I am preparing a brief, but there is no real rush on it. Let me check around with a few airlines and I'll get back with you. Of course, you know this means I'll be paying through the nose for a ticket on such short notice?"

"Whatever. It's a drop in the bucket for you."

Before ending their conversation, Timmi promised to call back as soon as possible with her flight information. Charlotte got up and took down the dark fabric from the windows to let in the few remaining hours of sunlight. She marveled at how nurturing and supportive Mattie Mae was. Not many women were like that anymore. She winced at the fact that women today were too concerned about catching a man, any man, your man, but not "The Man." So many women claimed to value themselves, but they really didn't. Too many people were running from one relationship to another, and to stab someone in the back meant absolutely nothing.

After retrieving her pen and journal from the night-stand drawer, Charlotte wrote about how people didn't really stab others in the back anymore; they were bold enough to let you see them coming with the dagger and plunge it in your chest. Lust had increased on all levels; enticing young girls to be sexy. Child molesters and sex offenders were multiplying faster than roaches. She remembered when most criminals were adults. Now, they were mostly juveniles.

Terrorism had straight sucker punched America in her face. People were running around having microchips inserted in their bodies for so-called identification purposes. It wouldn't be too long before people had their foreheads bar-coded and scanned.

She flipped through the pages of her journal until she found her notes on a sermon Bishop Lorne had preached entitled: "Things Are Lining up to Fulfill Prophecy."

Charlotte read her entry:

A visitor challenged Bishop Lorne today by saying that people have been declaring since the beginning of time that the end of the world was near. Bishop Lorne refuted the young man by saying, "I did not say that the world was ending now. The Bible clearly states that no man knows the hour of Christ's return. However, in the Book of Matthew 16:3, Jesus rebuked the Pharisees and the Sadducees for not interpreting the signs of the times. We are living in an age where we are quickly advancing in technology. Can't you see how it's possible for everyone to see Jesus through cable, satellite, and even on the Internet? Mind you, this is only one possible way. I'm not saying that it would be the way.

"Also, take the mark of the beast for example, and I'm not saying that chips and such are the mark of the beast either. I don't know that they are. But, just like microchips, the mark of the beast is a tracking device. Sir, the times that we are living in now are just a preview of things to come, and it takes spiritual eyes to see. As for people making comments about the end being near, you're right. They've always said that, and the Bible states that people will make this comment, but what I want to point out is that the conditions are much riper today than ever before. Jesus could come back tomorrow or a hundred years from tomorrow, but you could die today."

"Lord, I sure do hope that man received that message," Charlotte prayed as she closed her journal. She appreciated Bishop Lorne because he had no qualms about saying what needed to be said.

The sound of voices coming from the outside broke Charlotte's train of thought. Peering through the curtain, she could see Mattie Mae stooping down in the garden picking cucumbers. She chuckled at the sight of her grandmother. Mattie Mae was wearing a brightly colored scarf on her head underneath a large straw hat. She reminded Charlotte of Kizzie from the miniseries, *Roots*. Standing next to Mattie Mae was the young man Charlotte remembered seeing at Lucille Johnson's house during her little tête-a-tête with Maggie. Charlotte tossed the fabric onto the bed and went downstairs to investigate.

19

"Hello."

Mattie Mae and the young man were so busy talking that they were startled by Charlotte's voice.

"Oh, I'm sorry. I didn't mean to frighten you two."

Mattie Mae shook the dirt from the hem of her skirt and said, "I'm too old to be scared. Charlotte, this here is your cousin, Jeff, from Charleston. Jeff, this is Esau's daughter, Charlotte, from Washington, D.C. Jeff is my late sister, Beulah's, grandson."

Jeff hugged Charlotte and said, "Nice to meet you, Cousin Charlotte. I just stopped by to say goodbye to Aunt Mattie and Uncle Edmund before I leave."

"You stopped by for some sweet potato pie is what you stopped by for," Mattie Mae remarked.

"Now, Aunt Mattie, you know I always drop by to see you when I'm in town. I don't come as often as I should, but I make sure that I see you before I leave," Jeff said, winking at Charlotte. "I come up every so often to check on my grandmother's property. My family rents the house out, and since I live nearby, I come over whenever the tenants have a problem. This time one of the kids broke out a window while the other kid knocked a huge hole in the wall."

"I bet they was fightin' in there. People won't take care of yo' stuff like they would their own," Mattie Mae commented. "Shucks. Sometimes they don't take care of their own stuff."

Jeff agreed. "That is so true. I wouldn't have known about it if it weren't for one of the neighbors, Mrs. Jackson. She used to be a friend of my grandmother's, and one day she was over at the house visiting Alice. Alice is the young lady that's renting the house. Mrs. Jackson figured that I didn't know about the damage, and I didn't, so she called me."

Mattie Mae laughed. "Yeah, Minnie Jackson sho' will tell on ya as soon as she get a chance. She ever did been nosey. Wait a minute. You mean to tell me y'all got Alice Brown and her chi'ren stayin' in Beulah's house? I didn't know that's who was stayin' in the house. I could have told ya how triflin' she and her chi'ren was."

Although Charlotte was half listening to Jeff and Mattie Mae's conversation, her mind drifted back to Timmi and how it must be difficult for Timmi to be working with Connie. Then again, Timmi was a headstrong sister who never stayed down for long. One might be able to knock her down, but they'd better watch out when she got back up. God had always shown Timmi favor, even though she never recognized it.

"Boy, I'm just teasing you," Charlotte heard Mattie Mae say. "I got some stuff in the freezer for you to take back to Charleston. Let me go in the house and get some of these butter beans and collard greens. The collard greens made good this year. You can have a couple of chickens I bought on sale from Piggly Wiggly too." Mattie Mae picked up her basket of cucumbers and went inside the house to put together a care package for Jeff.

"So you live in Charleston? How do you like it?" Charlotte asked Jeff.

"It's all right. Actually, I divide my time between Charleston and New York."

"You do? Why is it that we've never met? I mean, I've been coming to South Carolina since I was a kid and I don't remember meeting you. I've heard my parents talk about Aunt Beulah and her children, but I've never met anyone from that side of the family."

"You and I have never met because I'm an Army brat. My dad is a retired lieutenant colonel," Jeff readily explained.

"There's a big difference between New York and Charleston. So when you're tired of the bright lights and snow, you fly south to unwind and thaw out?"

"Sometimes. I'm a real estate developer. My business is based in New York, but I appreciate quiet surroundings. I'm also an ordained minister, so times of peace and quiet are a must."

"So am I! I'm an ordained minister also. Wow! A real estate developer and minister; I bet your plate is full." Charlotte felt a check in her spirit. She immediately thought of the story of Mary's visit to Elizabeth and how Elizabeth's baby leaped.

"Yes, sometimes my plate runneth over," Jeff kidded. "I don't really spend a whole lot of time in New York these days, especially since I can conference in calls between Beechers and my home in Charleston. Of course, having a competent staff helps also. My life can get busy, but I like it."

Something in Charlotte's mind started to click. Beechers? She remembered that her Aunt Beulah's last name was Beecher. Charlotte had heard of Beecher Developers. *What was that CEO's first name again? Jack. No, it was Jeff. He can't be that Jeff,* Charlotte thought. "You know, it's a funny thing. You have the same last name as the president of one of the largest real estate development companies in America. I know you've heard of Beechers. They built the coliseum in Maryland a few years ago."

"I've heard of it." Jeff smiled. "I named it in honor of my mother's maiden name. My last name is Coates, and that coliseum was a monster of a project."

Charlotte was speechless. Here she had a cousin who was no doubt at least a millionaire, and an ordained minister, and she never knew it. "Are you serious? I mean, I can look at you and tell you've got a little change, but Beechers, the Fortune 500 Beechers?"

"You don't believe me?" Jeff seemed amused.

"Don't get me wrong, but . . ." Charlotte placed one hand on her forehead and the other on her hip.

"What's wrong?"

"I remember seeing your face now. You were featured on the cover of *Success, Inc.* magazine. I was impressed with your story. In just eight years, you exploded in the real estate business, but what I started to say is that I'm shocked to know that we're related. Then again, lately it's been one shock after another for me."

Jeff shook his head. "It can't be as bad as all that. Maybe we should plan a family reunion and stay in touch with each other."

Considering the last time the Morley side of the family got together for a reunion, Charlotte wanted to scream at the idea. Charlotte was excited about meeting most of Edmund's family, but unfortunately, they left a sour taste in her mouth. Edmund's sister, Ruth, who lived in Alabama, tried to rule over all the adults while her ten-year-old granddaughter, Tiffany, tried to reign over the children.

However, Ruth's son, Timmy, who was short, stocky, and mentally challenged, was a pure delight. Timmy just walked around all day in his muscle-hugging Spandex pants, a welterweight belt around his waist, and flexing his muscles. The family jokingly nicknamed him Built Timmy.

"Hello. Earth to Charlotte," Jeff called out while snapping his fingers.

"I'm sorry, Jeff," Charlotte said. "I guess I was off in Never Never Land. How are you able to manage a ministry and a large corporation?"

"It was a gradual process. I took a huge risk leaving my law practice in real estate, but only God knew that it would benefit me in the long run. Talk about ordered steps. Then, about two years ago, I was called into the ministry as a grief counselor. I also serve as a finance counselor in my church. I hope I get another chance to tell you a little more about it one day, and I want to hear your story as well," Jeff said, noticing Mattie Mae returning with his care package.

"Here, let me take that," Jeff said as he reached for the box.

"Grandma, is it me or I just don't remember hearing about Jeff?" Charlotte asked.

"You must be losin' yo' memory. I know you done heard talk about my sister, Beulah, and her chi'ren befo' now. And I know you done heard about Jeff somewhere down the line. He builds houses and things. Me and Edmund been to his house in Charleston once." Mattie Mae started laughing. "You remember that, Jeff? Me and Edmund got turned around in that big ole house. Thank God, Jeff, you have loud speakers in the wall."

"Loud speakers?" Charlotte asked, although she knew what Mattie Mae meant.

"Intercom," Jeff answered Charlotte. "My house is really not that big."

"Not that big? Charlotte, I want you to go see his house. Not that big! Beulah sho' would have been proud of you, Jeff," Mattie Mae said.

"Grandma, I couldn't impose on Jeff like that. Besides, I'll be going back to D.C. soon."

"What do you mean 'imposing'? You're family, so that means it wouldn't be an imposition. Besides, it would give us a chance to get acquainted and talk about our ministries. I live alone and look forward to good company."

Charlotte had forgotten that the article in the magazine stated that Jeff was, at that time, was a thirty-six-year-old widower.

Charlotte thought about the offer and asked, "Well, if you're not too busy tomorrow, would it be okay if my girlfriend and I stopped by? She should be arriving in Charleston at the airport sometime tomorrow. Her name is Timmi and she's never been down South before."

"Sounds good to me. Let me give you my numbers. Give me a call later and I will have something planned for us to do by tomorrow." Jeff pulled out a business card from his shirt pocket and handed it to Charlotte.

Charlotte was impressed. Not only was her cousin rich and handsome, but he was a Christian too! Hopefully, he would be able to help her talk some sense into Timmi.

"Charlotte, come on. Let's walk Jeff to his car," Mattie Mae said.

It looked like the antics of Tina and Terry wouldn't put such a damper on everyone's summer after all. Charlotte followed Mattie Mae and Jeff toward the front of the house, where Jeff's car, a taupe-colored Hummer, was parked.

"What kind of truck you call this?" Mattie Mae asked Jeff, rubbing her hand along the side of his vehicle as if she had been called to inspect for dust.

"It's called a Hummer," Jeff answered.

"It's a humdinger all right. Sista says it reminds her of those trucks that have money in it. You know, the ones you see at the bank and the stores," Mattie Mae said.

Jeff scratched his head and thought for a moment as he placed the box on the floor of the back seat. "You're talking about an armored truck, like a Brinks truck." He laughed. "I guess it does remind you of one. Leave it to Miss Sista." Jeff closed the door and kissed Mattie Mae on the cheek before getting inside. "Thanks for the groceries, Aunt Mattie, and Charlotte, I look forward to seeing you and your friend tomorrow." Jeff backed out of the muddy lane and blew the horn as he drove off.

As Mattie Mae and Charlotte slowly trekked back to the house, Mattie Mae said, "We hardly see Beulah's chi'ren these days, but both of her daughters call me every holiday."

"Where do Aunt Beulah's children live?"

"Jeff's mother, Lottie, lives in California, and her sister, Florine, lives in Buffalo, New York. Beulah's son, Ben, lives in Chicago. The family is just scattered all over the place. Florine used to visit y'all when she lived in Washington. Lottie and her husband traveled a lot when he was in the Army, so we didn't see much of 'em."

"Now that you mention it, I vaguely remember Florine now. I don't think I had started school yet," Charlotte recalled.

"I remember when Jeff first bought his house in Charleston. His father's sister, Frances, tried to make him feel bad about never callin' her when he was growin' up. Crazy woman. He was only a little boy then, and Jeff told her so too. He told her he couldn't pay for a phone bill as a little boy. Crazy woman had the nerve to say she didn't have money to call all over the world like his parents did. Frances is something else."

"I remember that time too," Sista said. "Frances's husband had just died." Neither Mattie Mae nor Charlotte had realized that Sista had been walking behind them. "Jeff sho' got her told. Frances was so upset she talked about that thing for a month. A hit dog sho' will holla, won't it? Look here, John Edward just told me he saw Charles at the drug store earlier today while we were at Lucille's house. Charles was talkin' to that little boy who works there. What's his name? Bruce, ain't it?"

Mattie Mae just looked at Sista, refusing to say a word. She knew what Sista was trying to imply.

"Well, you know that boy ain't nothin' but a sissy," Sista continued. "John Edward said they been talkin' for a long time too."

Mattie Mae could feel hurt rising from the pit of her stomach. "They could have been talkin' about the weather for all John Edward knows."

"They was probably talkin' sissy talk," Sista mumbled as she marched toward the vegetable garden.

Mattie Mae turned to face Charlotte. "I almost forgot. Jeff did a nice thing today. Lucille never did find that insurance policy, and she was short on money for burial. We didn't know Jeff was standin' out in the hall. He came in the room and gave Lucille a check for twenty thousand dollars. Seen it wit' my own two eyes. Said he hoped that was enough for expenses. I wanted to cry."

"That was beyond nice. That was even beyond generous," Charlotte commented as she opened the door for

Mattie Mae. Charlotte found herself in the mood for some of that banana pudding Mattie Mae made.

Just as Charlotte was about to place a generous amount of banana pudding in her mouth, Mattie Mae informed her that while she was sleeping off her headache, Charles and Francine had gone to visit Francine's family in the southeast part of South Carolina.

20

"Anyone see my box of bullets in there on the kitchen counter?" Edmund called out.

"Yes, sir," Charlotte answered after spotting the black and gold box on top of the counter.

"Whatcha fixin' to do?" Mattie Mae asked.

"I saw a possum out by the barn. I ain't had possum and sweet potatoes since hatchet was hammer."

Edmund stood in the doorway. "Just chunk it here," he said to Charlotte.

"Edmund, it's gonna be even longer befo' you eat any possum and sweet potatoes. You ain't cookin' that mess in my pots," Mattie Mae said.

"Woman, what is wrong wit' you? You used to eat it."

"I used to eat it. You don't see me fixin' it anymore, do you?"

Charlotte started laughing at her grandparents. It seemed that every once in a while, Edmund would acquire a nostalgic taste for "road kill." During the early years of their marriage, Edmund always wanted deer, possum, rabbit, squirrel, or coon for supper, and Mattie

Mae would remind him that he shouldn't eat critters from the woods.

"You don't know what kind of disease these animals have. It's a blessin' the Lawd let us live. That stuff we been eatin' back then could have had rabies," Mattie Mae told her husband.

"You still eat chitlins and pigs' feet. You still eat pork," Edmund pointed out defensively.

"Well, some habits take longer to break than others." Mattie Mae winked at Charlotte.

Forsaking the bullets, Edmund left the room muttering something about the Bible speaking against eating pork, forgetting that he still ate pork also.

Charlotte got on the phone to call her mother. By now, she had so much to tell her. After Charlotte told her mother about the latest happenings, Betty had a little news of her own. She had recently run into Charlotte's ex-husband.

"How is he doing?" Charlotte asked, not really wanting to discuss anything about Anthony. She wished him well, but as far as she was concerned, Anthony was a part of her past that was dead, buried, and never to be resurrected.

"He said he was doing fine. He asked about you. I told him that you were doing well and that you were in South Carolina visiting your grandparents."

"Good answer, Ma. Where's Daddy?"

"He's at work. You know that man feels that every prescription needs to be filled by him and him only. Let me speak to your grandmother for a second."

Charlotte said goodbye to Betty and handed the receiver to Mattie Mae. She then peered through the screen door to check on Edmund, who was talking to Sista as she filled her apron pockets with cucumbers from the garden.

After briefly chatting with Betty, Mattie Mae resumed her conversation with Charlotte. "Jeff has always been a good person, and I never heard a bad thing about him or his brother."

"He does seem to be a man of integrity. How did his wife die?" Charlotte asked after polishing off the banana pudding.

"I think she had breast cancer." Mattie Mae removed the last piece of chicken from the frying pan.

Charlotte heard her cell phone ringing in the living room, but got there too late to answer. She checked the message. It was Timmi calling with her flight schedule. When Charlotte returned to the kitchen, she looked through the screen door and found Edmund removing the laundry off the clothesline.

"I'll get these for you, Granddaddy," Charlotte said as she walked toward an exhausted looking Edmund. She stopped to sniff the sun drenched laundry hanging on the clothesline.

"Thank you. If you'll just get the ones on the back line, I'll take down these on the front."

"What happened to your possum?" Charlotte asked, looking around cautiously.

"Oh, it ran off in the woods a little while ago. If you see any around here, let me know. Those things will fight ya if you ain't careful."

Charlotte promised that she would before freeing the laundry from the clothespins' grip. She neatly folded and laid the sheets and towels inside the plastic laundry basket. Afterwards, Charlotte and Edmund went inside the house where Mattie Mae, Sista, and Busta were already seated in the dining room watching television and feasting on hefty portions of red beans and rice and southern fried chicken.

Being accustomed to entertaining guests, Mattie Mae

had the good sense to have a dining room set that could comfortably seat eight or more people. A large hurricane lamp served as the centerpiece on the dining room table. The wallpaper was light green in color with dark green hurricane lamps as the design. Dark green crushed velvet valances hung over the windows. Placed in each corner of the room were artificial plants that needed light dusting.

Edmund joined his wife and friends at the table while Charlotte fixed their plates, walking carefully so as not to slip across the damp floor. Since Mattie Mae was always baking, it was not unusual to see flour wasted all over the floor and table. Upon entering the dining room, Charlotte noticed Sista frowning toward the television.

"I don't like some of that ole music these people singin' these days," Sista complained. "Some of that stuff sounds like that ole hippity-hop music. I hope whoever we get for a pastor don't come here wit' some crazy notions. Y'all know I heard that some of our members are talkin' about joinin' Macedonia."

Mattie Mae looked disappointed. "Well, Sista, we do need a change. If we keep doin' things the same way, we won't be able to reach our young folk. Shoot, some of the folk *our* age can't be reached. We really need somebody who can reach the people, especially the young people. Most of 'em ain't even interested in the chutch. We need somebody to explain things plain to 'em. They see some of our members every weekend drinkin' at the juke joint and shoutin' in chutch Sunday. They call us hypocrites, and I don't blame 'em! Reverend Holiday and my own granddaughter just made things even worse."

"You right, Mattie Mae. We do need some life in the chutch. Folks been sittin' up in there 'sleep since the chutch been built. Half of 'em come just to see what other folks are gonna have on," Sista said.

"Greener Pastures is stuck in tradition," Charlotte chimed in. Everyone looked surprised by Charlotte's comment. However, she did not let that keep her from speaking further. "It's like you both said. You need a change. You need some life. People need to hear an anointed word, a prophetic word, not a feel-good word. A feel-good word doesn't change a person. People need to get the congregation to participate. I've heard Reverend Holiday talk about we need to praise the Lord, but you really don't praise there, and Miss Sista is right. People sit there and go to sleep. I'm ashamed to say this, but I fell asleep in there last Sunday."

Charlotte took another bite of chicken and waved her fork in the air like a magic wand. "The average person is going through something, and most of the members at Greener Pastures sit there like they aren't going through a thing. There is no real move there. It's just tradition and formality. They just come there because that's how it's always been. You get up on Sunday, and you go to church. If I were God, I don't think I would want to go anywhere that I didn't feel welcome. Would you?"

Everyone at the table kept silent for a moment, and Charlotte could tell that she struck a nerve. She didn't want to offend anyone or sound superior, but since the subject had been brought up, she had to respond. Charlotte realized that it would be hard, but Greener Pastures needed to get unstuck. More than half of the black population on Turtle Island went to church, but did so out of religion, not relationship.

"You mean we should do stuff like all this dancin' I see them do on TV?" Sista asked, picking her teeth.

"Yes, as a matter of fact, I think dancing should be added. It is a form of praise. You know the Bible says that David danced out of his clothes," Charlotte replied. After noticing the disapproving looks on Edmund's and Busta's

faces, she continued to explain. "Granddaddy, I'm not talking about shake-booty pole dancing, but God does want
our praises. I can show it to you in the Bible."

"No, you don't have to do that. I know it's in there. It's
just that we never did that kind of stuff befo'. Some of the
mothers of the chutch would pass out if we did somethin' like that. I can see 'em now," Edmund explained.

Charlotte would not give up. "That's just what I mean.
Stuck and nobody is growing or changing. Church the
way you guys know it was good for you when you
started out, but we have a new breed of people out here
now. Maybe, and this includes the mothers of the church,
maybe some people need to pass out; in the Spirit, that
is."

"I don't understand what ya meant by a new breed of
people. People still doin' the same things they've always
done," Mattie Mae replied.

"That's true, but now things are done on another level,
and the church needs to keep up and step up another level
as well. People are hungry to be taught, not preached at.
Plus, we are the church. We represent the church. Does
your church, and by this I mean Greener Pastures as a
whole, do anything to help educate, feed, and clothe the
community? Is there any type of program to help people
find jobs? In other words, are members reaching out instead of just meeting amongst themselves on Sundays? Is
there anything appealing going on to draw people in?"
Charlotte asked.

"I don't think we should be tryin' to bait folk in. That
ain't what the chutch is for," Sista said, sounding as if she
had been personally insulted.

"I'm sorry, but that *is* what the church is for—in part
anyway," Charlotte explained. "The church shouldn't be
just a place to go sit and sleep for two hours."

"Well, do you have any ideas on how to do these

things? We ain't a big city chutch with big city money. Besides that, we don't know who we gettin' for a minister. He might be the type that won't go for any of this," Busta pointed out.

"Maybe so, but if he's a true man of God, he will at least agree that the church should be doing something outside of its four walls. Are you willing to try some ideas? Who knows? Whenever the new pastor comes, you might find that he will be thinking along the same lines," Charlotte said, trying to encourage them. "You don't have to be a big city church to make changes. No church started out big. Just start with asking the Lord to send you the right leader. Ask Him to impart the wisdom and guidance needed for the building of His church." Charlotte decided to leave them with a little food for thought.

"May I make a suggestion?" Charlotte offered. "Why don't you go ahead and have your choir lead the congregation in songs as usual, but let's also put together a praise and worship team."

"Go on," Sista said.

"I can help with that. Also, I'll get Timmi to create some flyers on her laptop when she comes and we'll distribute them throughout the community. This would be a way of inviting the people who don't normally attend church. You all can ask for volunteers to pick up the people who don't have transportation, and instead of feeding the pastor every Sunday, why not serve dinner to people who are less fortunate? Maybe you can do it on a once-a-month basis. A hungry person does not want to hear a sermon when his stomach is growling for a sandwich. And why not have a clothes drive also? Sometimes people don't attend church because they feel that they don't have anything decent to wear. Anyway, these are just a few suggestions."

"You know, that does sound good," Busta admitted. "But who we gonna get to do all these things?

"Busta, hush up," Sista commanded. "You know there's a whole heap o' folk that would love to show off their singin' for this praise and worship choir. You know Bessie Moss, Otis's cousin? She swears she can sing like Mahalia Jackson, and some of the men will be glad to pick up people for chutch, especially Abraham. He likes to feel important wit' his big-doin' self. And the only time the chutch feed folk is after a funeral. Folk show up in the fellowship hall like we was givin' away free lunch. Of course, some of 'em is really hungry, but a lot of 'em is just plain greedy!"

"Miss Sista, you are something else." Charlotte shook her head.

"You do have a point, though, Sista. I think most members would be glad to help out, even though some of 'em would do it just to be seen. I think you got some good ideas, Charlotte," Busta said.

"I think so too," Mattie Mae agreed proudly. "But who can we ask to do this Bible study? I guess Reverend Glass should be the first choice since he is an associate at the chutch. Oh no, I forgot he's outta town."

"Might as well be outta town! That man can't preach as good as me," Sista blurted out. "Why you think Bishop didn't mention Reverend Glass? Bishop knows that man can't preach. The only thing Reverend Glass knows how to preach on is how Eve tricked Adam into eatin' that apple."

"Come to think of it, that sho' is the truth," Mattie Mae said. "But we have no choice but to let him preach this coming Sunday. But after that, he'll be out of town. I don't know what we're gonna do then."

"I have a suggestion," Charlotte offered. "What do you all think about Jeff being the guest speaker? He's a

Christian and he is a minister. I don't mean to come off as if I'm trying to take over your church, but you need some help. Now, I don't know how the AME affiliation does things and I can't honestly say that I know how good of a speaker he is, but I sense that he's called to do this."

Looking quite suspicious, Sista asked, "Why him? You're ordained too. Why don't you do it?"

"I think I would be more useful in helping you put together a praise and worship team. I'm one of the leaders on my team at my church," Charlotte explained.

Sista then turned to Mattie Mae. "Mattie Mae, you did tell Charlotte that Jeff is her cousin, didn't you? I know he's a nice catch and all."

"Sista, they know they're cousins. Charlotte's just tryin' to help us out, and here you go talkin' crack!" Mattie Mae assured her friend.

"I seen how Jeff been lookin' at Charlotte, and you know just because you're kin don't always stop folk from courtin' each other. Look at the Moss family, and they breed like rabbits. So many of them runnin' 'round Turtle Island 'til it ain't funny. Cousins marrying cousins and they have no shame 'bout it either. Otis's daddy might have been a minister, but I heard that he had chi'ren by one of his own daughters. I believe it too. Look how crack they all act. Everybody knows Emma and Sammy Moss are two first cousins . . . married to each other. If you ask me, I think Nellie and Otis is some kin, but gettin' back to these ideas of Charlotte's, if we gonna serve dinner on Sundays, we can't have just anybody cookin' it. Like Mamie, for example. Ain't no tellin' what you'll be eatin' on. I know she means well, but I don't know what she be thinkin' sometimes. And you know Gert Mitchell will want to read the scriptures, knowing good and well she can't read a lick!"

Mattie Mae decided that she had better stop Sista before she got too carried away. "Okay, Sista, we got it. We are gonna have to meet with the board members. We don't want nobody thinkin' we sittin' here tryin' to take over."

"I'll go right now and call up the members of the board and see what they think," Edmund said as he left from the table.

Busta thanked Mattie Mae for supper and said that it was time for him to go. Lois was away in Detroit visiting her sister, and he wanted to call to see how she was doing. Sista decided it was time for her to leave also. She wanted to call her sister in New York just to be nosey. Charlotte went to clean and mop the kitchen before Mattie Mae's splashes and spills hardened and they would have to call it artwork. Mattie Mae, Busta, and Sista walked to the front door discussing how proud they were of Charlotte. Greener Pastures needed a shot in the arm and needed it fast.

Charlotte decided that after Edmund had finished his calls, she would call Jeff to see if he was willing to come back with her to speak at the church on Sunday; that is, if it was okay with the board members. As she started putting away the food, she could hear Edmund telling Mattie Mae that, so far, half of the board members were fine with the idea and there would be a meeting tomorrow at the home of Deacon Brown.

After Charlotte finished mopping the kitchen floor, she went upstairs to her room to dial Jeff's number. She was thrilled about Timmi's upcoming visit and wanted to show her friend how to have a good time other than in a nightclub.

Jeff picked up the receiver after the third ring. Charlotte apologetically informed him of how she offered up his services for Sunday without checking with him first, and he told her that he would be honored to teach on Sunday if the church agreed. He would ride back to Turtle Island with her on the condition that she and Timmi stay overnight at his home. Charlotte was delighted about the offer, and after hanging up the phone, she pulled out her journal to write another passage:

There is a slight glimmer of light, a ray of hope at the end of this dark tunnel. I pray for the safety of my cousins and for the health of our churches. It is my desire that Timmi is reached somehow during her visit on the island. No one is really talking about, or to, my Uncle Charles. In the short time that I've seen him, he has spent most of it avoiding everyone. I can't help but feel that something sinister is going on concerning Tina and Terry. Dear Lord, I hope that I am wrong.

21

A side from a nagging cramp in her left leg, Charlotte slept well and woke up excited about helping out her family's church. The scandal that Reverend Holiday and Tina had caused seemed to be a blessing in disguise. In fact, she was becoming sure of it.

It was already 9:00 AM and it would soon be time to pick up Timmi from the airport. After making up her bed, Charlotte knelt down to pray. Once she finished praying, she stayed on her knees to listen to the Lord, but all she heard was the humming noise coming from the ceiling fan. Charlotte got up from the floor and walked over to the closet to get her overnight bag. She checked out the time again before going into the bathroom.

She peeked out the window. Edmund was on his tractor plowing in the soybean field, and Mattie Mae was walking on a path that led to Sista's house. Charlotte took a hot shower using her favorite orange-ginger sugar scrub, which had the ability to leave a scent in the bathroom like potpourri.

Charlotte didn't consider herself to be a clothes horse,

but she did like to look nice. She picked out a white DKNY tank top and a pair of light blue capri pants to wear. The blue and white espadrilles she purchased at an upscale Maryland boutique would go perfectly with the outfit. After removing the hard plastic rollers from her hair and fingering out the curls, Charlotte decided that she was not satisfied with the look. Pulling out a hairbrush from her purse, Charlotte brushed her hair back into a long, curly ponytail.

Charlotte double checked her directions to Jeff's house and closed the door behind her. She then made a pitstop in the kitchen to fix a bacon and egg sandwich and grab a bottle of cold water from the refrigerator. After leaving a note for her grandparents that she was on her way to Charleston, Charlotte drove Edmund's car to the nearest gas station, filled the tank with gas, then proceeded toward Old Bay Bridge, the only road to and from Charleston.

The route to the airport was rather scenic. Wildflowers grew rampant along the side of the highway, and terra cotta–colored outlet malls and shopping centers were just beyond the exits. Charlotte was amused by the artificial pink flamingos perched on the front lawns of modest homes built along the access road, and the air hinted of freshly cut grass.

It didn't take long for Charlotte to reach the airport terminal's crowded parking lot. She pressed the button on the metal box for a ticket and sought out a parking space. After finding a space on the second deck, she headed toward the baggage claim area, where Timmi would be waiting. As Charlotte crossed the walkway, she immediately spotted her childhood friend, who looked radiant in her white linen pantsuit and diamond pendant with matching diamond teardrop earrings. Timmi flashed Charlotte her much talked about one hundred–watt smile as she saw her best friend approaching her. The two friends embraced as if they hadn't seen one another in years.

"You look great, Timmi. You really do!" Charlotte said, standing back to take a second look.

"Girl, I don't know what it is, but I feel great too. Wait a minute. You act as if you hadn't seen me since forever. Did I sound that bad on the phone the other day? Don't answer that. I know I sounded like somebody calling the suicide hot line," Timmi said as she followed Charlotte to the car with her luggage.

"You are as silly as ever. How was your flight, silly? I'm so glad you're here. I still can't believe you're here."

"I'm just so glad to get away," Timmi said.

Charlotte lifted the trunk of the car to put in Timmi's bags.

While Charlotte was driving toward their destination, she informed Timmi of their sojourn at her cousin's house.

"Jeff Coates is your cousin?" Timmi asked in disbelief. "How could you not know that Jeff Coates was your cousin? Girl, if you weren't a minister, I'd slap you."

"I'm glad you're afraid of slapping me, because then I'd have to repent from slapping you back." Charlotte laughed. "Jeff is not my first cousin, but he is a cousin. He says that he has the whole day planned for us."

"I'm all for that. Plan my day! I read about him. Widower with no children."

"I read the same article. Now, Timmi, he *is* saved, so don't expect to go clubbing with him."

"You wound me. Seriously, Charlotte, you don't know how much I've been thinking about what you said to me. You know . . . about the whole club thing? I go out to have some fun only to come home feeling empty. I want somebody decent in my life. I *deserve* someone decent in my life. I don't even want to share the same airspace with trifling-behind men."

"Okay, let's not even talk about trifling men. They're not worth talking about. Read these directions for me." Charlotte handed Timmi a single sheet of paper that had the directions to Jeff's house written on it. "I pretty much memorized it, but tell me about how far we've got to go."

"Let me see," Timmi said, looking out the window before looking at the directions. "Judging from this, we've got about a half a mile to go. You know, it's really pretty here. I was expecting to see dirt roads, out-houses and farm animals crossing the street."

"Yeah. They've made a lot of progress over the past century. They still have the dirt roads, but only certain farm animals can now be licensed drivers."

Confused, Timmi stared at Charlotte for a moment and then started laughing after she realized Charlotte was pulling her leg.

Charlotte smiled and said, "Seriously, I think Charleston will surprise you. It's quaint and really very nice. Now Turtle Island, that's a different story. That may take some adjusting for you."

"Right now, I don't even care. Okay, let me see these directions. It looks like once we go through this light, we should be close to his house. Does he live by a lake or something?" Timmi asked, noticing a family of ducks huddled near a grassy knoll.

"Yeah, he did say something about a lake. That must be it over there," Charlotte said, pointing to an area where there were two mansions sitting on a hill and partially obscured by large oak trees. Charlotte slowly drove up to the closed iron gate displaying the words "Palmetto Lake Estates" and waited for the security guard to come out of a small brick booth. With pad and pen in hand, the badly sunburned man asked Charlotte, "How are you ladies doing today? Who did you come to see?"

"Jeff Coates," Charlotte replied as she showed the guard her driver's license.

The guard dialed Jeff's home, and after getting an approval, opened the electronic gate. The huge iron gate slowly opened up and revealed a winding, tree-lined street. Charlotte and Timmi were both speechless as they drove past the homes. Each home was different in architectural structure, and each had award-winning landscaping. The tony enclave proudly boasted enormous wealth.

The first house they passed on Sycamore Street was enormous in size, almost bordering on monstrous. This particular homesite came with a horse stable and two mother-in-law suites. Tucked away at the end of the street was Jeff's majestic gray-and-white Victorian mansion. The column-lined wraparound porch was loaded with dozens of healthy Boston ferns.

"Girl, I'm sick. This place makes my subdivision look like a concentration camp," Timmi said. "Forget skyscrapers. This is breathtaking, absolutely breathtaking. I could definitely live here. Oh . . . my . . . God!"

22

Charlotte turned in to Jeff's circular driveway, where he was anxiously waiting. "Hi, Charlotte. I take it this is your friend. Timmi, right?" Jeff said, smiling at Timmi. "I'm glad you ladies made it safely. I'll get your bags for you."

Charlotte released the lock to the trunk and got out to hug Jeff. Timmi stood by watching.

As Jeff retrieved their luggage from the trunk of the car, Charlotte said, "This is unbelievably beautiful. I've always dreamed of having a home like this."

"Thank you. I know it is a lot for just one person, but I like it. My wife and I had hoped to raise a family here, but that was not to be." Jeff turned his head slightly, just in time to see the look of admiration on the faces of Charlotte and Timmi. "You two are welcome to stay as long as you like," Jeff offered.

Timmi said, "I want to thank you for allowing me to stay here, and forgive me for being blunt, but an attractive, successful brother such as yourself . . . well, I guess what I'm trying to say is . . ."

"Why do I live alone? Why haven't I remarried?" Jeff guessed. "I'm not like most men who rush into a relationship to get past my pain. It's been a couple of years since my wife's death, and sometimes grief can linger a little longer than we'd like it to. Thank God it doesn't hurt as bad as it used to, but it still hurts. When you rush to fill a void, you usually fill it with something you'll later regret. I've learned that you must take the time to heal. I loved my wife. She was a good woman. And I do hope to remarry some day.

"I've attended some really good Christian conferences for men lately. It was basic stuff, but you know us. Most of us aren't willing to learn even the basics, and that's really what we need. If we don't learn the importance of healing first, we run the risk of making painful mistakes because we don't like to be alone. I have dated some very nice women since my wife's death, but not anyone steadily. There are women out there who tried to convince themselves, and me, that they were really into this relationship, but they were really looking at the material things. So, I'm careful. The heart can be deceitful."

Timmi was impressed. Charlotte was curious. "You haven't met any Christian women who sparked an interest?" Charlotte asked.

"Not for a wife. Just because a person is a Christian does not necessarily mean that person is the one for you. Come on. Let me show you two to your rooms."

Jeff led Charlotte and Timmi up the steps onto the spacious wraparound porch. The front door of the house opened to a classic black-and-white checkered marble floor with a crystal chandelier imported from Italy that hung from the ceiling. Near the base of the stairway was a large round cherry wood table with the largest floral arrangement Charlotte or Timmi had ever seen. As Charlotte and Timmi followed Jeff upstairs to their guest rooms, he informed them that he had seven bedrooms, and thought that they might like to have the two rooms that were across from each other.

Once they got to the top of the stairs, Jeff steered them to the left and down the end of the hall where the guest bedroom suites were. Jeff's room, the master bedroom suite, was to the right of the stairs. He leaned the luggage against the wall and opened the French doors to Charlotte's room. The first thing she noticed in the room was the mini-bar and a dorm size refrigerator. Then Charlotte saw the glass-enclosed fireplace and a huge sitting area in the corner.

The bedroom was tastefully decorated in royal purple and meadow green. The California king-sized Scandinavian bed was plump and inviting. It was covered with purple and green pillows. The sitting area had two green chaise lounges with beaded purple throw pillows. Mounted on the wall was a twenty-seven-inch flat panel television, and the only other furniture in the room was a Scandinavian-style dresser. On top was an 8x10 silver frame with a scripture from thirty-seventh chapter of the Book of Psalms printed on parchment paper on it.

Installed in the private bathroom was an extra wide garden tub with whirlpool jets, with a gigantic porthole window trimmed in mahogany above the bathtub, which complemented the mahogany double vanities. The double-door walk-in shower was large enough for four people and featured a marble sauna bench and two wide showerheads.

Charlotte went back into the bedroom, opened the closet, and marveled at its size. She estimated the closet to be about the same size as her bedroom in Washington. In fact, Charlotte figured that her whole house could fit in a few rooms of Jeff's home.

Jeff could tell that Charlotte was pleased with her room. He placed her overnight bag on top of the bed and suggested that they follow him to Timmi's room next.

"If your room looks like this, then I'm afraid to see what the master suite looks like," Timmi whispered in Charlotte's ear.

Timmi's room was a kaleidoscope of crimson red, white, and navy blue. The carpet was a deep rich navy blue color, and on each side of the wrought iron king-sized bed were wrought iron and glass pedestal tables. Each table held a small bouquet of crimson red roses in crystal vases and small Tiffany lamps, similar to the Tiffany floor lamp in Charlotte's room.

The comforter was fluffy and white with two oblong pillows; one navy and the other one red. The room had no fireplace or sitting area, but it did have a beautiful carved antique armoire with a television and stereo system inside. The bedroom's eight windows had shutters that were distressed and painted in antique white. The window seats were covered with fabric that had hand-painted roses on it.

In one corner of the bedroom stood a 1950's floor model television that had been converted into an aquarium, complete with miniature African frogs, seahorses, and rare tropical fish.

"How cute. Fish TV. I'm impressed," Timmi told Jeff.

The bathroom featured a claw foot bathtub, a pedestal sink, separate shower, and a floor-to-ceiling mirror. Sprinkled on the bathroom dressing table were red, white, and pink rose petals centered around a jasmine-scented candle. Both bed and bathrooms had a nautical-meets-French country theme, and the closet, which was just opposite the wall where the dressing table was, had built-in storage space.

Jeff informed Charlotte and Timmi that he would be outside waiting for them after they got settled and had a chance to freshen up.

"Do you remember that show *Lifestyles of the Rich and Famous*?" Timmi asked. But before Charlotte could answer, Timmi said, "I hate to sound so materialistic, it's not like I've never seen anything nice before, but this is awesome! You know what I'm saying? This is nicer than the senior partner's home and *he* thinks he lives in a palace, with his arrogant self. I can understand why Jeff wants to be extra careful about who he marries and brings into his home."

"I know, but before you get too excited and get too used to this, I have to warn you, once we leave here, Turtle Island may send you into remission, and I want you to be prepared." Charlotte laughed. Charlotte's laughter was cut short by a sweet hickory-laced aroma that went straight to her head. "Do you smell that?" she asked Timmi, racing over to one of the windows. Jeff's sprawling backyard resembled a Hawaiian luau.

Charlotte could see a large, grassy hut-like structure next to an open barbecue pit. Underneath the hut was a half-moon–shaped granite counter complete with rattan barstools. Closer to the house, Charlotte could see a couple of willow wood chairs and a Chimnea outdoor fireplace. Standing over the pit with tongs in one hand and a cell phone in the other, was Jeff, grinning as he caught his guests surveying the backyard.

"Hope you two are in the mood for some barbecue chicken and grilled corn," Jeff said.

"Smells and sounds good to me. I'll be down in minute, but I think Timmi wants to change clothes first," Charlotte replied.

"Take your time." Jeff gave a thumbs-up sign before continuing his telephone conversation.

With tears welling up in her eyes, Timmi faced Charlotte and said, "Thank you for inviting me. I feel better already."

"Okay, you're welcome, but why are you crying?"

"I don't know. Yes I do. I've been so stressed out lately, and now I finally feel a sense of peace, like everything is going to be all right."

Charlotte hugged Timmi and silently thanked God for His reassuring presence, knowing that one day, everything would be all right.

"You go ahead and change. I think I'll unpack later. Right now, I'm going to take a look around, case the joint, as they say. I'll be outside," Charlotte said as she left Timmi's room to venture downstairs.

Once Charlotte reached the bottom of the stairs, she noticed a room to her left with only one item in it: a baby grand piano in the center of the floor. The room to her right was a Shaker-styled dining room, which was also decorated in purple and green with a touch of eggshell white. It included a large abstract painting on the wall done in purples, greens, and cream. As Charlotte entered into the living area, she was beginning to think that purple and green was either a favorite color combination of Jeff's or his late wife's. The suede sectional sofa was a deep plum color with lime green suede pillows.

Sitting on the fireplace mantle was a wedding photo of Jeff and his late wife and a small collection of Faberge eggs. Healthy green plants filled out the room. Charlotte had to admit, whoever was responsible for the décor of the house definitely had a creative eye. Although interior decorating had once been her profession, she didn't think she would have changed a thing.

The kitchen had cherry wood cabinets and built-in stainless steel appliances. She loved the low-leveled, stainless steel stove and the kitchen island, with its base made out of red brick, which complemented the exposed brick wall in the kitchen. As Charlotte was about to join Jeff outside, he entered the kitchen.

"Charlotte, help yourself to anything you see. I was just coming in to get the salad. If you don't mind, would you bring some salad dressing from the refrigerator? We'll put them in the one outside," he said.

"Outside? You have a summer kitchen?" Charlotte asked Jeff.

Jeff smiled. "Yes."

Charlotte selected four types of salad dressings and followed Jeff outside. "Jeff, I don't know about anything else in your life, but it's apparent that the Lord has blessed you financially. I imagine it wasn't always easy for you. You know, to whom much is given, much is required," Charlotte stated as she sat down in one of the cushioned willow wood chairs.

"God has been good to me, and you're right, it has not been easy. Everything has its price. I had to endure a lot of pain, jealousy, betrayal, rejection, you name it."

"True. But you relied on God."

"I didn't know God until I went through those things." Jeff laid the tongs on the counter and sat next to Charlotte.

"Really?" Charlotte was surprised. Given her family's religious history, she had assumed that Jeff had been saved all of his life. She then remembered that not even all of her immediate family had followed Christ, so how could she be so presumptuous?

"Really," Jeff answered. "It took all of those things to bring me to a point where I felt that I needed somebody bigger than me to help me get through those challenges. Life had to be better than what I was going through. Soon enough, I came to realize that the Lord blessed me with good health and a career that afforded me nice things. I am blessed to the degree that I can give generously, and I no longer feel guilty about being blessed financially."

"You've got a testimony many need to hear. I sure do hope the vote is a yes for you to preach at my grandparents' church. I have a feeling that you will be a powerful influence next Sunday."

They both turned around to see Timmi joining them. She was dressed casually in a pair of shorts with a light cotton peasant blouse. She was about to sit in the chair in front of Charlotte when Jeff got up and offered his seat instead.

On his way back to the barbecue pit, Jeff looked at Timmi and said, "Timmi, you look like that light brunch type, and that's too bad. When Aunt Mattie gets through fattening you up . . . oh well."

Charlotte winked at Jeff.

Jeff announced that chow was ready as he removed the chicken, which was pulling away from the bones, from the grill. After he said grace, the three new friends settled down at the counter to enjoy good food, good conversation, and a spectacular view of the lake, occupied by boaters and swimmers.

"Since it's still early in the day, what's the plan, Jeff?" Timmi asked eagerly.

Charlotte was glad to see Timmi so at ease and enjoying herself. Even though Charlotte had just met Jeff, she did not believe in coincidences. She truly believed that God had ordained their meeting for such a time as this, not only for the members of Greener Pastures, but for Timmi as well.

"I thought we might go to the market and then go to an antique shop in this village called Antique Row. Timmi, Charlotte has informed me that you like antiques. If we have time later, I thought a boat ride might be nice, especially while the sun is setting," Jeff suggested.

"A boat ride sounds relaxing. I take it you own a boat?" Timmi asked, picking out the cherry tomatoes from her salad.

"I do. That's it over there." Jeff pointed to a small yacht docked several feet away at the pier. Charlotte could see that the vessel was christened "Angela" and assumed it was named after his late wife. The vessel was docked at the pier, which was just a short distance away from the house.

Timmi glanced in the direction where he was pointing and said, "Well, that certainly isn't a paddle boat."

Timmi studied Jeff as she helped herself to a soda. He seemed to be too good to be true, and while she found him attractive and intelligent, she really wasn't interested in getting close to any man right now. Besides, it felt good to be in a relaxing atmosphere where no one was flirting or putting on airs.

"You're a good cook, Jeff," Charlotte complimented as she chewed her chicken.

"Thank you, ma'am," Jeff replied. "Don't ask me for the secret seasonings. If I tell you, well, you know the rest."

Charlotte and Timmi threw their paper plates into the rubber trashcan. With keys already in hand, Jeff said that he would get the Hummer out of the garage. That gave Charlotte a chance to be alone with Timmi for a moment. She reached over and pinched Timmi on her arm.

"Ouch! What was that for?" Timmi screamed.

"I saw the wheels turning in your head, Timmi. Remember, you're trying to get over a bad breakup. This time let the man show you that he's interested or I'll hurt you myself," Charlotte scolded.

"What are you talking about? You didn't see any

wheels turning in my head. Look, you have nothing to worry about. I've had enough heartache and have no intentions of chasing after your cousin. I was just sitting there thinking about how respectful he is. I know we haven't been here long enough to tell, but I get a really good vibe about him. I mean, look at all of this. I would be as conceited as all get out. If this house were mine, you'd be walking around in socks and wearing gloves, baby!" Timmi snapped her fingers. "And then I'd do a strip search before you left, 'cause you know I can't let the silverware and the bling walk out with you."

"I sure hope you're not this crazy in the courtroom." Charlotte shook her head.

"I sure am," Timmi declared with pride.

23

"Just before you came outside, Jeff started to open up about being betrayed and dealing with petty jealousies," Charlotte whispered after looking over her shoulder to make sure that Jeff was not close by.

"In other words, life!" Timmi said as she gently pushed Charlotte inside the kitchen. She was more than ready to go antique shopping.

"Yeah, life, but whatever *life* was for him, it brought him to the Lord," Charlotte said.

Jeff peeked in the kitchen and asked if they were ready to go. Timmi made a mad dash for the stairs and quickly returned with her leather backpack and Charlotte's saddlebag.

Charlotte complimented Jeff on the décor of his home as she followed him to the foyer.

"Angela did it. She was a licensed interior decorator," Jeff said.

"She had good taste. Everything is so beautiful. I used to dabble in interior decorating myself. I also did some freelance work as an illustrator for children's books," Charlotte said as Jeff locked the front door. Timmi had already made it back downstairs and was outdoors, ahead of them.

"Sounds like you're every woman. I'll have to get you to sketch something for me when we get back," Jeff challenged.

"Jeff, I haven't sketched anything in so long, I couldn't draw a stick-man right now if I wanted to."

"Right! I'll let you off the hook this time. How did you like interior decorating?" Jeff asked as he opened the passenger doors of his vehicle for Charlotte and Timmi.

"I enjoyed it very much," Charlotte answered.

Displaying the manners of a perfect gentleman, Jeff helped Charlotte into the front seat and then assisted Timmi. As Jeff drove slowly up Sycamore Street, he pressed his remote to open the gate and waved at the security guard as they rode past. He didn't tell Charlotte or Timmi that their first stop would be a tour of an old historic market. Jeff discerned Timmi to be a city girl with some radical opinions, and felt that the tour would either enlighten or incite her. Hopefully, it wouldn't be the latter.

Visiting an old slave plantation was a risky move, especially since he secretly planned to win her to Christ. Timmi might use slavery as an indictment against God. If she did, then his next plan would be to point out to her that God had even warned Abraham that his seed, "God's chosen children" at that, would be slaves for four hundred years and suffer greatly. While it may seem unjust to us, it was God's way.

Jeff was so busy concentrating on how to handle Timmi that he didn't realize Charlotte was talking to him until she nudged his shoulder. He looked at Charlotte and apologized for not paying attention. "I'm sorry. I was thinking about something. What did you say?" Jeff swerved around a car that was hardly moving. In fact, the driver was moving so slowly that Timmi was under the impression that the car had stalled on the highway.

"Does this market we're going to have a wide variety of seafood? After all, this is Charleston and Timmi can hook us up with some mad seafood dishes. Will you listen to me? We just ate and I'm talking about food again. I've been around Grandma too long," Charlotte said.

"We'll stop by the seafood market on the way back, but the market that we're going to now is an old slave trade market in a small town near here." Jeff didn't have to wait long to hear their reactions.

"What? A slave market? You mean to tell me we're going to an old auction block?" Charlotte asked in a high-pitched voice.

"You have got to be kidding me!" Timmi exclaimed. Then both Charlotte and Timmi asked, "They still have those around?"

"I'm not kidding, and some of these places are still standing," Jeff answered. "I think you two will find it quite interesting. And get this, some of the original slave cabins are still on site. You'll see the rice fields they worked in, a slave cemetery, so on and so forth. It's one thing to read about it, but it's something else to actually see history. Our people have come a long way. It amazes me how we as a people have so many doors opened to us now and our ancestors went through so much just trying to survive. Come to think of it, it wasn't that long ago that our people, and some of our white brothers and sisters, lost their lives for us. The civil rights era was not that long ago."

"You're right, Jeff," Charlotte agreed. "And we still

blame the white man for everything, but we act out our hate on each other. How messed up is that? We never left the plantation. Well, the plantation mentality never left us, I should say."

Although Timmi was a little apprehensive about trusting Jeff's decision in going to the slave market, she had to admit that she was enjoying her visit so far. While totally out of her element, she could not deny the fact that this visit was indeed refreshing.

Hold up, Timmi said to herself. *Before I get too excited about being here, I can't forget that I haven't seen Turtle Island yet. For all I know, people there are still using mules for transportation.*

Timmi came from a long line of Washingtonians, and there was always someone in her family stirring up strife. That someone was usually her maternal grandmother, Mary Jane Parsons. Mary Jane normally left you alone if you gave her some money.

As a young child, Timmi always looked forward to Charlotte's return from South Carolina so that she could hear Charlotte's latest family stories and adventures. They were so much better than her own. The only stories that circulated within her pitiful family centered around who stole what from whom, who did what to whom, and most importantly, who had the audacity to spend money on themselves and not on Mary Jane.

She yearned for the type of family gatherings that Charlotte had. She and her brother, Craig, did celebrate traditional Thanksgiving and Christmas holidays at her parents' home; however, holidays at Grandma's house were another story. Mary Jane's idea of a holiday celebration meant an all-night game of cards at her house with plenty of beer and crab legs to go around. Thank God for a friend like Charlotte, who had instilled so much in her, and Timmi wanted to tell Charlotte just how much she valued their friendship.

Watching the view from her window, Timmi noticed a beautiful sea of green and presumed it to be a golf course, but then Jeff made a sharp right turn onto a driveway that sloped downward. At the bottom of the hill was a massive antebellum plantation surrounded by magnolia trees and plum trees bearing a striking resemblance to *Gone with the Wind*'s Tara Plantation. The hedges on the front lawn had been artistically carved into letters that spelled "Capehart Plantation."

The Capehart Plantation was owned and operated by a woman named Ivey Wells, who was a descendant of the original owner, Samuel Capehart. Allegedly, Samuel Capehart was said to have been a ridiculously wealthy man who was unusually kind to his slaves, and his mercy toward his slaves had earned him ridicule from his peers. However, because of his wealth, power, and influence, no one dared to mock Samuel Capehart to his face. There had also been rumors that Samuel Capehart saw to the education of his slaves, which would explain why so many of his slaves were able to read.

Jeff circled the parking lot twice, looking for a parking space. Finally, an elderly couple backed out from a space near the front and he swiftly replaced their vehicle with his. Judging from the number of cars present, Charlotte and Timmi could tell that the plantation was a hot tourist attraction. Jeff locked the doors of the vehicle once Charlotte and Timmi got out.

Charlotte looked back at Timmi and said somberly, "Look at us, dead men walking."

"I know, right. We act as if we're going to be auctioned off," Timmi responded. Jeff chuckled at the comment. "Don't laugh, Jeff. You'd make a good, strapping buck of a field hand," Timmi said, playfully poking him in his back.

Waiting at the door to greet them was their host, who wore a nametag with his name printed on it. Leo was a frail-looking, freckle-faced twenty-something white male.

"Hi, my name is Leo, and I will be your host," Leo said cheerfully. "I tend to speak a mile a minute, so please feel free to stop and ask me any questions," he politely said. Charlotte figured that Leo was either extremely eager to do his job or very eager to get it over with.

Leo escorted Charlotte, Jeff, and Timmi through a corridor plastered with documents on the walls. Jeff chatted with Leo while Charlotte and Timmi read the actual documentations of slave purchases, census records, and newspaper articles that kept track of how many times a slave tried to run away. Timmi shook her head in disgust.

They walked over to a corner at the end of the hall where there was a glass cabinet that displayed iron shackles, a whip, and a slave code which read: *No slave is permitted to hit a white man or woman; gather together in groups of more than six; testify in court; learn to read or write or have church without a white man present.* Timmi was justifiably angry and wanted to lash out at the nearest white person she saw, which was Leo.

After they turned the corner, Charlotte and Timmi found themselves in a room that was the exact replica of Sam Capehart's parlor. Proudly displayed on the walls and tables were pictures of Samuel Capehart, his family, and his family of slaves. There were just as many photos of sad and sweaty slaves posing in the fields as there were portraits of Samuel Capehart and his family dressed in their Sunday best.

Even though Samuel Capehart may have been one of

the more compassionate slave owners, it was obvious from the pictures that his slaves did endure some hardship, and Charlotte was disturbed by one picture in particular. The photo was that of a slave girl who looked to be no more than thirteen years of age and no less than nine months pregnant. The shot was taken in a huge cotton field, capturing clearly how the child was struggling with a heavy burlap sack on her back. Legend had it that whatever Samuel Capehart lacked in cruelty, his wife, Eunice, was filled with in abundance.

Charlotte overheard Leo telling Jeff a horrible story about how Eunice would spit into the pots after dinner had been served to the Capehart family in order to keep the house servants from eating any of the healthy meals prepared by their own hands. Evil Eunice, as the slaves secretly referred to her, felt that the scraps the slaves were given to eat was nutritious enough for them. Eunice even enjoyed pitting the house servants against the field hands. The hateful look etched on her face in the photographs was proof of an evil and unhappy woman.

After touring the inside of the mansion, Jeff, Charlotte, and Timmi were led outside to the slave quarters. Standing a few yards away from the house were four well-preserved wooden shacks.

"These were the slaves' living quarters," Leo proudly announced, as if they couldn't guess.

Charlotte chose not to be offended by Leo's enthusiasm, telling herself that he was young and he was only doing his job. However, the look on Timmi's face said that she wanted to shut Leo up, permanently.

Leo opened the creaking door of one of the shacks. It was a sight to behold with its dirt floor, one wood stove, and a mattress made from straw and old rags. Rags were commonly used to stuff the cracks in the walls in an attempt to prevent cold air and critters from coming in. Although the tour was highly educational, it was equally depressing, and Charlotte and Timmi felt that they had had enough.

24

Jeff remained quiet as he drove away from the parking lot. "Well, that was an experience," Charlotte said, fastening her seat belt. "I'm still trying to wrap my mind around those images."

"For real," Timmi agreed. "It was enlightening, but I don't feel all warm and fuzzy inside. And that Eunice Capehart . . . if she were alive today, I'd like to put my Jimmy Choos in her you-know-what."

"I know what you mean," Charlotte chimed in. "If I wasn't saved, I'd aim north with my Nine Wests my doggone self!"

The comment made Timmi laugh right in the midst of yawning. "I've always known that they auctioned off slaves like they were furniture, but my God! And reward notices for runaways. Please!"

"And through it all, they kept praying for God to rescue them." Jeff interrupted in an effort to lighten the mood and reveal God to Timmi.

"That may be true, but look at how long it took God to do it," Timmi said bitterly. "Animals were treated better than they were. Given scraps to eat . . . they didn't have time to do *anything* for themselves after working in the fields all day, and those shacks they were living in were disgraceful. Slumlords provide better housing than that! They were better off dead. I can't understand why our people had to suffer so much."

Jeff suddenly slammed on the brakes, jerking Charlotte and Timmi forward. Apparently, the driver of a Porsche Carrera decided to jump in front of him without turning on his signal, nearly causing Jeff to ram into the car. Jeff, whose feathers were not easily ruffled by someone's lack of driver's etiquette, looked in the mirror at Timmi and said, "Do you think our people suffered as much as the Jews?"

"What?" Timmi asked, leaning forward.

Knowing that the trip to the plantation would probably affect Timmi as it no doubt had, Jeff was ready to explain. "Don't get me wrong. I'm not making light of our ancestors' suffering. Remember the movie *The Ten Commandments*, where Charlton Heston played the part of Moses? So you know that long before there were African slaves, there were Hebrew slaves. Jewish slaves. Well, they cried out to God long before our ancestors started singing 'Swing Low, Sweet Chariot' in the cotton fields."

Timmi was still angry. "I still think liberation took too long, even for the Jews."

Jeff could tell by Timmi's demeanor that faith and understanding for her had been a battle. Charlotte listened closely to the interaction between Jeff and Timmi and was arrested in her spirit to stay out of the conversation.

"Generation after generation suffered for hundreds of eons. For all of the beatings, lynching, and poverty, where is the justice and love in that?" Timmi asked angrily as she huffed and leaned back in her seat.

"Timmi," Jeff said calmly. "I can't tell you why any of

them had to suffer for such a long period of time. I know such things make you question why to serve a God like that. But, I can tell you this: a seed cannot bear fruit unless it falls to the ground and dies. If you notice, eventually a generation comes along that reaps the benefits of the previous generation's suffering. For instance, if our ancestors had not lost their lives fighting for our civil rights, you and I would not be enjoying the freedoms that we have today. You're an attorney. Consider the fact that slaves were forbidden to even learn how to read or write. I'm a widower, and I rest in knowing where my wife is. If we were alive four hundred years ago, she probably would have been taken away from me, sold to another plantation owner, constantly getting raped by her master, and I wouldn't have been able to do a thing about it. Sometimes it takes an act of injustice to enact justice."

"That's true, I'll give you that," Timmi said with slight reluctance. "But why is there still so much poverty?"

"I'll give you my opinion on that later, but first, back to the suffering. God said in His Word that we would have trials and tribulations. He warned us that we would. Yet, we, the children of God, act so surprised and indignant when we go through hardships. Jesus suffered more than any human being has ever suffered. As for poverty, God also said that the poor, we would have with us always. I do have a couple of theories on poverty. One is that God knew we would have enough resources on this earth that no one should be poor and starving, but God also knew that the help would not be forthcoming.

"We have so many people with so much money and so many people who waste it on trinkets when it could be used to provide shelter or feed and clothe others. I'm not saying that the rich don't help, because so many do, but there are so many people who give money where it really does not benefit anyone. Do some research on some of these so-called charities and see what I'm talking about. If little Johnny needs a decent place to live, the money that is funneled into Save the Snails Charity Dinner won't help him. I mean, come on. Let us get our priorities straight. You know what I'm saying?"

Timmi, who had calmed down, responded, "I hear you. I never thought about it like that. I don't really read the Bible, but I have heard that scripture you're talking about, the one about the poor, you will have with you always. I can remember wondering why God would allow people to starve and be homeless, and what you just said makes sense. There sure is enough money floating around the universe to help people, and even if it wasn't, there are enough trees to cut down to make some. You're right. We do have enough people to lend a helping hand. We just don't have enough hands lending help."

"So, we really can't beat God up about our sins. See, you're getting it. I just bet you graduated summa cum laude," Jeff said as he turned to wink at Charlotte.

Timmi giggled and said, "No, actually it was more like "come by here, please, Lawdy!'"

"When you get a chance, I want you to read the Book of Habakkuk in the Bible. Habakkuk was a prophet who was troubled by all the injustices he saw. Read what the Lord told him. That should encourage you," Jeff said with certainty.

However, Timmi still felt a twinge of anger for what her ancestors, and even the Hebrew slaves, had to go through. Although she understood Jeff's explanations for some of the problems in the world, she still was not completely satisfied.

I should take the time and read the Bible, Timmi thought. Timmi's anger dissipated the moment Jeff turned off an exit marked ANTIQUE ROW.

Antique Row's cobblestone street was filled with antique shops, thrift stores, and bistros. Timmi was so excited that she literally leaped out of the vehicle before Jeff made a complete stop to park.

"Jeff, I really liked the way you handled Timmi's questions," Charlotte whispered to Jeff before getting out.

He patted Charlotte's hand and simply said, "It wasn't me."

"We'll go in the shop across the street." Jeff pointed at the largest store on the block.

Etched on the burgundy-colored marquee of the two-story building was the name of the store: House of Solomon. The ringing of bells hanging from the door alerted the owner that he had customers entering his treasure trove. The storeowner greeted Jeff as soon as he opened the door. "May I help you?" the man asked.

"We just came to browse around," Timmi answered instead. Knowing that she had a passion for antiques, Timmi doubted that she would leave the shop empty-handed.

House of Solomon was cluttered with all sorts of interesting antiques, art deco, and other relics. Jeff collected outdated *Life* and *Look* magazines and stumbled upon many editions that were in mint condition and dirt cheap.

Charlotte had made a conscious decision to start wearing hats to church. She thought that while change was good, some traditions were becoming a lost art. Charlotte had always admired the Easter Day Parade photographs shown in old magazine articles and books and in her opinion, the crème de la crème of the fashion statements were the hats. During the 1950's, African-American women were known to stroll along the streets of Harlem dressed to the hilt, and hats and gloves were a major part of their ensemble. Charlotte searched the store for vintage hatpins and struck California gold in the costume jewelry section. She found a pink pearl hatpin and an adorable chocolate brown, felt pillbox hat.

Timmi, on the other hand, chose to seek out black memorabilia. The visit to the plantation, unbeknownst to Charlotte and Jeff, ignited a desire to study more about African-American history and gain spiritual knowledge.

As Jeff and Charlotte stood at the cash register waiting to purchase their items, they both saw Timmi getting in line with her arms full. Timmi had great success in finding some noteworthy rare collectibles. Timmi arranged her items neatly on the counter and happily told Charlotte what she found.

"Look at this!" Timmi held up a piece of paper that had yellowed from age. "This is an actual tobacco stock certificate and they had the nerve to depict a slave family on it. I also found these Aunt Jemima and Uncle Mose salt and pepper shakers, an unopened box of Gold Dust Twins washing powder, and a set of art deco canisters that comes with a biscuit barrel."

Jeff stepped aside so that Charlotte could pay for her items next. Charlotte handed the clerk a crisp fifty dollar bill and said to Timmi, "I'm surprised no one has bought this certificate before now. Then again, I guess the local residents don't want to be reminded of the past."

Timmi looked at the clerk and then said to Charlotte in a low voice, "True, but I'm sure *some* of the people around here must collect this stuff, and we can't be the first set of visitors from out of town to visit this shop. I'm not complaining, because the way I see it, since this certificate was still here, that means it was meant for me to have it."

The owner handed Charlotte her change and looked sheepishly at Timmi as she moved her items closer within his reach. "Ma'am, we just got that stock certificate the other day. Some workers were tearing down this old house over on Sheff Road and found it stuck underneath the floor boards."

"Get out of here!" Timmi screamed, raising her eyebrows. She then showed the owner the certificate, pointed at upper right-hand corner and said, "Look at this date. You mean to tell me this piece of paper had been buried inside a house for over two hundred years?" Timmi was still in shock about her authentic find.

"Yes, ma'am. Believe it or not, it's not uncommon to make a discovery like that. Y'all have a nice day and come back," the clerk said as he handed Timmi her receipt.

Once outside, Jeff asked if they wanted to browse around in some other stores. Timmi and Charlotte opted not to, noting that they were anxious to check out the seafood market.

"That's right, I completely forgot," Jeff said as they crossed the street. Jeff turned on the engine and proceeded to Water Street Fish Market, which was only about three blocks away.

Sitting outside the seafood market were several women weaving straw baskets and placemats at lightning speed. After considering the fact that a purse, an accessory tote, and a pullman were more than enough for two hands to struggle with through an airport terminal, Timmi decided not to buy any of the handsomely crafted baskets.

Once inside the market, Charlotte and Timmi were amazed. Water Street Fish Market sold practically everything derived from the sea, including fresh seaweed. One merchant sold strictly ocean-themed souvenirs and seafood gift baskets from his booth. Jeff spotted one of his neighbors near the lobster tank and excused himself to go over to speak with the man.

"Timmi, get whatever you want and I'll pay for it," he told her.

"Oh, no you're not. I'm a stranger staying in your home. The least I can do is pay for this," Timmi argued as she grabbed his arm.

Jeff freed himself from her clasp and started walking away. "I'm insisting on this, Timmi."

"Insist all you want, but I got this." Timmi walked away, feeling confident that she had won her case.

Jeff slowly walked over to his neighbor and looked back at Charlotte, as if to say, "Don't let her pay for anything."

Charlotte shrugged her shoulders and mouthed the words: "You don't know her. I couldn't stop her with a gun."

Charlotte followed Timmi to one of the glass encasements and slipped a twenty-dollar bill in her hand. Immediately after taking a numbered ticket, Timmi was the next customer called to be served. By the time Jeff had finished talking with his neighbor, Timmi and Charlotte were walking away from the checkout counter.

25

Jeff was in his office conducting business while Charlotte assisted Timmi, who was a culinary genius and knew her way around anyone's kitchen, by preparing a carrot soufflé. Timmi gathered the Worcestershire sauce, mayonnaise, mustard, eggs, saltine crackers, hot pepper sauce, and salt and pepper for her tasty Maryland crab cakes. A skillet filled with corn oil was heating on the stove, ready to receive the catfish fillets. Timmi wanted everything to be perfect for her gracious host.

She kicked off her shoes, washed her hands at the sink, and said, "Charlotte, I've been meaning to ask you if you've heard anything about your cousins."

Charlotte, who completely forgot about Tina and Terry, got down from her stool. "Oh, Lord! Thanks for reminding me. I totally forgot to call my grandparents. Hopefully, they've heard something by now." Suddenly, there was a loud clamor of thunder accompanied by sharp streaks of lightning that seemed to split the sky.

"Well, so much for sailing on the Angela," Charlotte said, sounding disappointed. "It doesn't really matter anyway. Timmi, I'm going to call my Grandma and find out what's going on. Put the soufflé in the oven for me; it's already preheated. I'll be right back."

"All righty then. Tell your folks I look forward to seeing them tomorrow."

"I will." Charlotte went into the family room to retrieve her cell phone from her purse. She sank down into the plush sectional sofa and dialed her grandparents' phone number. "Hi, Granddaddy. How is everything going?"

"Hey there. Is that you, Charlotte?" Edmund asked.

"Yes, sir. I called to find out if you guys heard anything regarding Tina and Terry and if you've made a decision about Jeff. By the way, where's Grandma?" It suddenly dawned on Charlotte that Edmund usually didn't answer the telephone unless Mattie Mae wasn't home.

"She over at Sista's house. You can tell Jeff to be ready on Sunday. Francine hadn't called yet, so I don't know what's going on. I just pray the good Lawd keep them girls safe."

"So do I, Granddaddy. So do I. Well, anything else going on? Oh, before I forget, Timmi says that she is looking forward to seeing you guys tomorrow."

"Tell Timmi we'll be glad to have her. Betty called right after you left. She said it wasn't nothin' important and she might try and reach you on yo' cell phone later. The only thing goin' on that I know 'bout is Maggie *and* Cora is actin' funny wit' Lucille. They heard 'bout Jeff writin' out a big check for Lucille, so now they mad wit' her. That's one set of crazy people."

"That's a shame."

"Cora is too far gone to change, and poor Maggie just can't help it. She got ways just like her mamma *and* daddy."

"Who is her daddy?"

"Otis Moss. Nellie and Cora used to be best friends ever since they were chi'ren. That friendship ended when Nellie found out Cora was goin' wit' Otis behind her back and got herself pregnant. I remember Nellie was walkin' around here lookin' like a cut dog when she had found out, but Otis ended up marryin' Nellie anyhow. That just goes to show you."

Charlotte wasn't sure that Nellie ended up with the prize after all. After seeing a long bolt of lightning, Charlotte said, "Listen, Granddaddy, I'd better go. It's starting to storm here. We should see you guys sometime tomorrow. I love you."

"I love you too, and y'all drive carefully."

"We will." Charlotte rejoined Timmi in the kitchen.

Jeff was now in the kitchen talking to Timmi. Lightning constantly flashed across the Carolina night sky, and moments later, the clouds unleashed a heavy downpour, dashing Timmi's hope of going for a boat ride. So, the three of them settled down in the den like old friends and discussed nearly every topic under the sun.

It became obvious to Charlotte that Timmi had been filled with questions about God for years, and there were moments when Jeff and Timmi got very close to arguing . . . for real. During those heated moments, Charlotte prayed quietly for the confusion to stop. She clearly recognized it as a trick brought on by the enemy, especially when Timmi expressed her opinion on what she considered to be unfair practices by the Jews. Jeff quickly pointed out to her the fact that the Jews are God's chosen people. It was his final answer, and it was not up for debate.

"What God gave to them He meant for them to have, and they have every right to fight for what is theirs," Jeff stated.

Timmi had to admit that she had started to believe in

the Bible after seeing fighting in the Middle East via the news media. She questioned why war was still going on thousands of years later, and was astounded at what Jeff showed her in the Book of Judges 2:20-23 and 3:1-5. Apparently, the Lord left other nations in the land to teach the Israelites and their future generations about warfare and how to obey His commands. It was a test.

For every question that Timmi posed, Jeff was ready with an answer. Perhaps it was that inquisitive legal mind of Timmi's that was to blame. Nevertheless, Charlotte recognized it as a sign from the Lord that He was wooing Timmi into the fold. It also gave Charlotte a chance to observe Jeff's teaching skills. She knew she took a big risk in suggesting that he be a guest speaker at Greener Pastures. Now, Charlotte was totally confident in his ability.

All of a sudden, Charlotte was feeling a need to be protective of Jeff, and a wave of compassion swept over her. She could only imagine how women may have tried to manipulate him. Although she was positive that Jeff could take care of himself, she also knew that prolonged loneliness could lead to temptation for any person, even a Christian.

Charlotte was in the bedroom studying her Bible and felt an urge to pray. "Lord, I know that you are our protector, and right now, I strongly sense the need to ask that you protect my cousin, Jeff. Lord, I know that you know all things, and I ask that no weapon formed against him prosper—" Before Charlotte could finish her praying, she heard the doorbell ring and felt the need to listen.

"Who could be at the door at this hour?" she said to herself. Charlotte could hear a woman laughing as she got up from the chair. She cracked open her door and said to herself, "I need to mind my own business." But when she heard a female voice asking Jeff to show her around, Charlotte felt an urgency to go downstairs to investigate.

Charlotte ventured down the stairs and saw two women standing in the foyer. One of them, who appeared to be in her late teens or early twenties, had on a psychedelic print dress that was so tight it could pass for sausage casing. The other woman, who looked to be in her early forties, spotted Charlotte coming down the stairs. Jeff turned around to see what they were looking at and introduced Charlotte to them.

"This is my cousin, Charlotte. She's visiting from D.C." Jeff looked at Charlotte and pointed to the two women. "Charlotte, this is my neighbor, Brenda, and her niece, Yolanda. Yolanda is visiting from southeast D.C."

"Nice to meet you," Charlotte greeted.

Yolanda looked Charlotte up and down and then turned her back. *Oh, no she didn't!* Charlotte thought to herself. No wonder Charlotte was feeling so protective of Jeff. The devil was sending over an imp.

"As I was saying," Yolanda said. "We're sorry for the intrusion. I know it's late, but we did see a light on upstairs and thought you might still be up."

Charlotte thought Brenda looked fairly decent, but Yolanda had on more makeup than a clown.

"What can I do for you ladies?" Jeff asked.

"My aunt and I were wondering if you had plans tomorrow." Yolanda rolled her eyes at Charlotte.

"I plan to take Charlotte and her friend around some more before spending the week on Turtle Island," Jeff answered.

"I've heard of that place, haven't I, Aunt Brenda?" Yolanda asked her aunt and shrugged her shoulders.

Charlotte doubted that Yolanda had ever heard of Turtle Island. In fact, she doubted if Turtle Island was even on a map.

Yolanda moved closer toward Jeff and asked, "If it's not any trouble, I would like to ride with you guys. I've never been to an island before."

Now Charlotte was really disgusted. *This girl is either crazy or rude. How can she include herself like that? Oh, she's a bold one!* Charlotte fumed to herself.

Brenda rescued her niece by grabbing her hand. She reached for the doorknob. "Let's not keep Jeff and his cousin any longer, Yolanda."

Brenda nearly shoved Yolanda out the door.

Charlotte waved goodbye and told them that it was nice to meet them also. Once the door was closed and a few seconds had passed, Charlotte and Jeff looked at each other, dumbfounded.

"Did that seem weird to you?" Charlotte asked.

"Yeah, it did. You want some coffee? I just put on a fresh pot."

Charlotte nodded as she followed Jeff into the kitchen. She sat down on one of the barstools by the kitchen island while Jeff retrieved two coffee mugs from the dishwasher and placed them on the island. "Jeff, be careful," Charlotte warned. "I have a gut feeling Brenda is not all she seems. Yolanda, on the other hand, is pretty obvious. Who knows? Maybe Brenda is trying to snag a rich husband for her young niece."

"It can't be that. Why would you think that?" Jeff poured coffee into the cups and then handed Charlotte the sugar and cream.

"What? The way Yolanda was acting. She was flirting pretty hard and she was definitely annoyed at the sight of me. It's only natural to be annoyed when someone interrupts your flow," Charlotte said.

"You are funny. Anyway, I'm not interested in Brenda or her niece, but good looking out. Work that discernment, girl."

"Thanks for appreciating my discernment. A lot of men hate that about a woman. But we all know that's nothing but an ego issue."

"A lot of men have a problem with it because they don't want to recognize insight. Most men don't like to be told anything. It's a pride issue. But I do appreciate anyone who has a strong gift in discerning, so I'm not taking what you say lightly. Aunt Mattie told me about the summer camp incident when you were young. I'd say you have a strong prophetic calling."

Charlotte was stunned. No one in the family had talked about those serial child murders in years, and she had just remembered that tragic summer the other day. But what really shocked her was Jeff's comment about her having a prophetic calling. "You're the second person to tell me that I had a prophetic calling. It took me a while to admit it to myself," Charlotte said solemnly.

"I'm sure it did. Gifts may be given without repentance, but they do come with a price. I bet you realize by now you've had this gift since you were a child." Jeff took a sip of coffee and waited for her response.

"Looking back, I would have to say yes. But where was this gift when I got married? If I knew then what I know now . . ."

Jeff took another sip of coffee. "Don't punish yourself. We don't always see things coming. You're prophetic, not all-knowing. Love is not blind; lust is. My wife was very discerning also. I was a knucklehead when we first got married, and I took her for granted. I had to receive some hard knocks in order to appreciate what I had, but by that time, it was too late. When Angela first got sick, we went to one doctor after another who couldn't find anything wrong at first, and then she started feeling better. A month later, she fell ill again, and this time, after we had gone back to the doctor, she was diagnosed with cancer that had already metastasized."

"I'm so sorry. How could they have missed breast cancer?"

"She didn't have breast cancer, although it did eventually spread there. The cancer initiated in her stomach. Listen, do you mind if we changed the subject?" Jeff asked. "You just met Brenda and Yolanda for all of two seconds and you could tell that something was not right with those two just that quickly?"

"I can't explain it, but yes, I could. All I know is, I was upstairs feeling like you needed protection. I started praying and then I heard the doorbell ring. Normally, I'm not *that* nosey, I promise you. The minute I laid eyes on Yolanda, I knew. I can't put my finger on it, but there's something about that aunt too. Did you notice how quickly Yolanda forgot about their plans?"

"She did, didn't she?" Jeff frowned. "Last year I hosted a cookout and I invited Brenda over. Greta Morgan, who is the pianist at my church, was here also. Every time Greta and I got to talking, Brenda took every opportunity she could to interrupt us. Now, it was okay for me to socialize with anyone else, but not with Greta. I didn't realize what she was doing until Greta pointed it out to me. I still didn't pay it too much attention, but now that you are seeing something too . . ."

"Well, I didn't see Brenda flirting with you or anything, but Yolanda was blatant. Is Brenda married?" Charlotte got up to place her cup in the sink.

"Divorced. Brenda got the house in her divorce settlement. Rumor has it that she used to be her ex-husband's secretary and she's thirty years his junior. Brenda was married to Judge Steven Baxter, who happens to be Caucasian, retired and living somewhere in upstate New

York with the rest of his wealthy family. You know the type; old money that just grows into more money."

After being convinced that Brenda and Yolanda were up to no good, Charlotte asked, "Brenda sounds interesting. Would it be okay if we stayed one more day and leave Monday morning instead?"

"That is perfectly fine with me. Now, if you will excuse me, I'm going upstairs to get ready for bed. Help yourself to whatever you want." Jeff picked up the newspaper from the chair and left.

Charlotte figured that if Brenda and Yolanda saw that they hadn't gone anywhere, they wouldn't be leaving either. Charlotte didn't like schemes or schemers, and if she was right about these two, she needed to come up with a plan to stop Brenda and Yolanda in their tracks. Charlotte went back and knocked on Timmi's door to solicit her help.

"Come in," Timmi answered.

Charlotte eased the door shut behind her.

Timmi was sitting on the floor polishing her toenails. "Charlotte, I'm glad you're here. I was feeling a little guilty. I felt like I had put Jesus on trial during our conversation earlier."

"You did." Charlotte chuckled as she sat down on the bed. "But we'll just call it a mock trial. At least you showed that you've got a hunger for Him. He wants us to seek after Him, you know."

"I hope so, because I didn't know if I was being blasphemous or not. I'm just grateful that I'm not burning in hell right now."

"You're so silly. Listen, I am getting this funny feeling," Charlotte said as she rubbed her chin.

"Uh-oh, what now?" Timmi rolled her eyes.

"I really feel like, and I know you may not understand this, but I feel like Jeff is being set up."

Timmi pulled the straps of her pink-laced camisole over her shoulders. "Set up how? By who?" she asked, sounding like an attorney working a case.

"My gut feeling . . . a gold digger. Maybe I shouldn't say that, but that's how I feel."

Timmi listened intently as Charlotte told her about what had just happened. "You're probably right," Timmi agreed. "I might not understand this from a spiritual aspect, but I definitely know it from a street aspect. Let's not forget, we're from the hood and we know vermin crawling out of the sewer when we see it. Jeff has some pretty deep pockets, and what woman wouldn't want a man who made some *real* paper? Why don't we try a little experiment?"

"You are reading my mind, but you can't be street about this, Timmi."

"Street! I am a lawyer, an attorney at law . . . esquire. I don't get street anymore. Well, not in places where people know me," Timmi said, grinning slyly.

26

Charlotte and Timmi had devised a plan the night before to see if their suspicions about Brenda and
Yolanda were correct. Timmi took a quick shower, got
dressed and went downstairs to the kitchen for a glass of
milk. Jeff was in the kitchen removing blueberry pancakes from the skillet. She briefly informed Jeff about the
discussion she had with Charlotte. Jeff agreed to go
along with the idea, since the plot was simple and harmless. Timmi passed on his offer of pancakes and told Jeff
that she would meet him outside.

Timmi met Jeff outside, where he was preparing to
give the Hummer a good washing, while Charlotte was
upstairs peering through the bedroom window, which
happened to face Brenda Baxter's Tudor-style home.
Outside her window, she could hear Jeff and Timmi talking and playfully throwing suds at one another. They did
appear to genuinely be having fun. It didn't take long for
Yolanda to come out of her aunt's house and make a bee-
line straight toward Jeff and Timmi. Charlotte noticed

that Yolanda had on a pair of skimpy shorts that provided about as much coverage as a piece of dental floss.

"Look at her!" Charlotte fussed as she raced out of the bedroom, nearly colliding into the wall in her haste to get outside.

Charlotte got outside and leaned against Edmund's car just in time to hear Yolanda ask, "So, is this another cousin?"

"No, I'm a friend," Timmi answered smugly.

Yolanda smirked at Timmi and turned to face Jeff. "My aunt said that you were a nice man and she feels that you could really help me."

"He *is* a nice man, and right now, he's a very busy man," Timmi said rather possessively.

Yolanda gave Timmi a look that clearly said, "I was not talking to you." Timmi could tell that Yolanda was the type of woman who figured she could get whatever she wanted by swaying her statewide hips. However, Yolanda was still no match for Timmi. Yolanda looked at Charlotte and Timmi as if she was on to them. Charlotte went over and stood beside Timmi.

Jeff turned around and saw a limping Brenda approaching them. Timmi, who caught Yolanda placing her hand on Jeff's arm, took the water hose to rinse the suds off the tires, and *accidentally* doused Yolanda's hands in the process. "Oops, I'm sorry," Timmi lied. "I need to pay attention to what I'm doing."

Just as Yolanda was about to respond, Brenda walked up to Yolanda and whispered something in her ear.

"Jeff, I did the dumbest thing right after I left your house last night. I sprained my ankle. At least, I hope it's just a sprain. I twisted it going down the steps to my basement." Brenda pointed at her bandaged left ankle.

"Here it comes," Charlotte whispered in Timmi's ear.

Timmi shook her head.

"Jeff, if you're not too busy, would you mind taking my niece? As you can see, I'm in no shape to drive around." Brenda tried to look pitiful.

"Normally, I wouldn't mind, Brenda, but remember I have plans with Charlotte and Timmi," Jeff pointed out.

Now you're showing your true colors. Apparently, you don't care what our plans are as long as yours are carried out, Charlotte said silently to herself as she observed Brenda closely.

Brenda gasped as if she suddenly remembered. "Oh, that's right. Jeff, I completely forgot." Both Brenda and Yolanda looked disappointed.

Jeff politely apologized for not being able to drive Yolanda around today. Brenda claimed to have understood, and Charlotte watched as Yolanda escorted her limping aunt back to their house.

Timmi tossed her rag into the bucket and shook her head in disgust. "Ms. Brenda, or should I say fake Hopalong Cassidy, is coaching her niece on how to snag a rich man. You can see through that like glass."

"Something is definitely not right with those two," Charlotte agreed.

Jeff shrugged his shoulders and said, "I really don't want to be bothered with Brenda or her niece. Charlotte, I got a check in my own spirit when Yolanda pranced over here in her Underoos. I gave her the benefit of the doubt earlier. I know she's young and all, but . . ."

"I hope you did get a check in your spirit because girlfriend was purposely showing all of Victoria's secrets," Timmi said as she poured the dirty water out of the bucket.

Jeff nodded his head as he leaned forward to spray the inside of his vehicle with a woodsy pine scent. "I'm old enough and savvy enough to see through some people.

It's a beautiful day. Why don't we just go out and enjoy the day like we planned? Oh, and Charlotte, since I'll be staying for the remainder of the week on the island, why don't you just leave Uncle Edmund's car here and we can pick it up after we drop Timmi off at the airport?"

"Sounds good to me," Charlotte replied. "I can't wait to show Timmi the *real* dirty South; strip her of her big city ways and bring her down a peg or two. By the time those folks on Turtle Island get through with her, she'll be wearing bonnets and gingham dresses and taking homemade biscuits to work."

"Whatever!" Timmi remarked, pushing Charlotte as they followed Jeff inside the house.

Jeff led the duo upstairs. Soon afterwards, Charlotte and Timmi trailed behind Jeff to do a little shopping and sightseeing. When Jeff pulled out of his driveway, he checked his rearview mirror and saw a "miraculously healed" Brenda sprinting from her house, trying to flag him down. He lifted his sunglasses from his shirt pocket to protect his eyes from the sun's rays and kept driving.

PART TWO

Who is wise and understanding among you? Let him show it by his good life, by deed done in the humility that comes from wisdom.

James 3:13

27

Charlotte started to doze off the minute Jeff exited from his gated community. Timmi offered to drive, but he declined the offer, pointing out that he usually heard from the Lord while driving. As they got closer to Turtle Island, Timmi noticed the scenery change from majestic homes and new shopping centers to farm equipment, growing crops, barns, and a few dilapidated outhouses. Even the four-lane highways had transformed into two-lane roads with faded yellow lines.

"Why are you so quiet?" Jeff asked Timmi as he slowed down to let a squirrel cross the road.

Timmi rolled down her window and said, "I was just thinking. Listen, I hope I didn't aggravate you with my questioning. I guess it's the attorney in me."

"Not at all. Everyone has questions about something, but many are too afraid to ask them. Most people don't want to appear ignorant."

"People in the South believe in going to church and knowing their Bible. I'm the one who grew up clueless," Timmi said softly.

"Oh, you'd be surprised at how many people carry a Bible and don't understand it," Jeff assured her.

"I probably would be surprised." Timmi smiled and reached in her purse for a mint. "I want to thank you for being so nice to me. You and Charlotte come from good stock. She and I have been friends since we were in diapers practically, and we've seen each other through some real difficult times. I'm at a point in my life where . . . I don't know, I guess I am searching, but I see so many people going to church, and some of them are the biggest hypocrites I've ever met. I don't get it."

"Keep in mind that you can't let people stop you because they're doing wrong. You don't want to go to hell with them. So, if the deacon is cheating on his wife or the pastor is the most arrogant person on the earth and they all call themselves Christians, don't let that hinder you, because guess who they have to answer to? The same God you will have to answer to. Besides, the Bible tells us that we shall know them by their fruit."

"How do we really know there is a God or that He's still alive?"

"How do we know?" Jeff was astounded by the question. "Do you see that sun up there?" he asked, pointing to the sky. "Now, I know there is this Big Bang Theory, but ask yourself these questions: If there was an explosion billions of years ago, what happened in this explosion that still causes the sun, the moon and the stars to rise? I mean, is an explosion that happened so long ago still telling the sun when to rise for daylight and when to set for nightfall? Do all races of people, who speak different languages, come from monkeys, who, by the way, *cannot* talk? Don't get me started."

Looking as if she had received a startling revelation, Timmi said, "That does make sense that there has to be a God, but I still can't get past all the suffering and evil in the world. I know we touched on that a little, but I just can't understand it, especially when there is no justice."

"You have to remember that Jesus suffered also. Now, the Lord has so many followers. Remember our talk about a grain of wheat falling to the ground?"

"I know, and I believe what you're saying, but doesn't that make it seem like we're somehow pawns in a game of chess of good and evil? Besides that, I can't understand why even Jesus had to suffer."

"As for being pawns in a chess game, I suppose one can view it that way, but consider which side you would rather be on if that was the case. The thing is, Satan wants us, and God wants us back."

Timmi looked out the window and recognized Edmund and Mattie Mae's wood frame house from pictures Charlotte had shown. Mattie Mae was standing in the yard talking to Miss Sista.

Charlotte leaned over to tell Timmi, "You are going to absolutely love Miss Sista."

"I thought you were asleep. Why would I love Miss Sista? What's her story?" Timmi asked.

Charlotte loosened her seatbelt and said, "Miss Sista is a very funny and very blunt woman. She's an older version of you."

Jeff chuckled as he parked underneath the oak tree. As soon as Timmi stepped out from the vehicle, Mattie Mae went over to greet her.

"Timmi, I'm so glad you're here, and I want you to make yourself feel right at home. My goodness! You went from a pretty little girl to a beautiful young woman," Mattie Mae said. Timmi blushed as Mattie Mae dragged her over to introduce her to Sista. "Sista, this here is Charlotte's friend from Washington."

Sista hugged Timmi. "That sho' is good. Real friends are hard to come by these days."

"Yes, ma'am, they sure are." Timmi looked back and grinned at Charlotte and Jeff.

"Jeff, I hope my girls weren't no trouble," Mattie Mae said, tugging on her hair scarf.

"No, ma'am, not at all. I was glad to have them over," Jeff said.

Mattie Mae grabbed Jeff by the arm. "I hope you plan on stayin' with us too. Just leave the bags in the car. You can get 'em out later."

"Aunt Mattie, you already have a house full. Are you sure?" he asked. "I can always stay with my Aunt—"

"We got plenty of room," Mattie Mae interrupted.

"Grandma, have you heard from Uncle Charles or Aunt Francine?" Charlotte asked.

"No more than a message on the phone from Francine saying that they'll be back as soon as they can. Sista, why you lookin' at Jeff like that?" Mattie Mae asked after noticing Sista eyeing Jeff suspiciously.

"Ain't nobody studyin' Jeff," Sista said, leading the group to the front porch.

"Miss Sista, why do you always give me such a hard time?" Jeff asked.

"To keep ya on yo' toes," she replied. Jeff planted a kiss on Sista's cheek before he sat down. "Go on now," Sista said, playfully pushing him away. "You can't handle this."

"How y'all doin'? Turn out to be a nice day today, ain't it?" Otis Moss yelled from the road. Walking alongside Otis was one of his teenage nephews. Both men were carrying gallon-sized jugs.

"It sho' is a nice day, Otis. Where y'all headed to in this hot sun?" Mattie Mae asked.

"Down here to the well. My pipes at the house burst, so we goin' over yonder for some water."

"Burst? That's too bad. It's always something, ain't it? Is Petey coming over to take a look at yo' pipes?"

"He said he'd be over soon as he finished haulin' a freezer from Sallie Gibson's house."

"I wonder what caused yo' pipes to burst. It ain't even winter yet," Mattie Mae pondered out loud, scratching her head.

"That's what I said too. Whatever it is, I hope Petey can fix it."

"I hope so too, Otis."

"Well, we'll see y'all later," Otis said as he and his nephew walked onward.

"All right then. We'll talk to ya later." Mattie Mae waved goodbye and took a seat next to Sista.

"That boy looks familiar. Sista, who is that walking with Otis?" Mattie Mae asked.

"You know that's one of Floyd's sons," Sista answered. "Don't you remember Otis's brother, Floyd? Floyd's chi'ren got those "wee little" heads like their mama, Mary Frances, wit' her funny-shaped self. Mary Frances' head ain't no bigger than a doorknob, but the rest of her body is bigger than a doublewide trailer."

Jeff, Charlotte, and Timmi started laughing hysterically. Timmi was now beginning to understand what Charlotte meant about Sista.

"Grandma, where is Granddaddy?" Charlotte asked.

"Somewhere with Busta Watkins and Joe Green. You couldn't beat those three men apart wit' a stick." Mattie Mae then looked at Timmi. "Timmi, how did you like Charleston?"

"It was pretty nice. I hope to visit the place again," Timmi answered, smiling at Jeff.

"Jeff, you got a sermon ready for Sunday?" Sista asked, all the while watching Timmi.

"I'm not really doing a sermon, Miss Sista. It will be more like a Bible study," Jeff said. "Is there anything in particular I should know about, Aunt Mattie?"

"Everything has been taken care of. Janie Frost will read the chutch announcements, and the deacons will be leadin' devotion," Mattie Mae answered.

Jeff winced at the comment. "May I make a suggestion?" Jeff asked. "Sunday service will be new and different for all of you, and I'm sure there are some people who are apprehensive about my speaking, but why don't we eliminate the announcements if there is nothing new to announce? As for devotion, I thought the plan was for Charlotte to organize a praise and worship team."

"What do you mean eliminate the announcements?" Mattie Mae asked, sounding appalled. "And why can't we have Charlotte singin' *and* have devotion?"

"Well, Aunt Mattie, I've only attended Greener Pastures a few times, but I noticed that during devotion, most people tend to just sit there or fall asleep."

You got that right, Charlotte said to herself.

"When ya think about it, we very seldom have anythin' new to say in the announcements, but we've always had devotion," Sista added.

Jeff squirmed around in his seat, trying to figure out how to make Mattie Mae and Sista understand without offending them. "Praise and worship is different. The congregation is encouraged to participate in songs of adoration."

"Folk sing durin' devotion!" Sista pointed out.

"Yes, ma'am, but only a few people do. It's not done corporately." What Jeff really wanted to point out was how dry their singing was. "Can we give praise and worship a try?"

Mattie Mae seemed to be a bit skeptical. "I'll get Edmund to tell the deacons we won't need 'em," Mattie Mae said reluctantly.

Sista cautioned Charlotte. "Be careful 'bout what ya

sing. I still say some of that music don't belong in the chutch."

"Yes, ma'am, I know. We'll be careful about the selections. They will be songs that will help people express their thanks and acknowledge God for who He is," Charlotte explained.

"I understand what y'all sayin', but people 'round here is used to certain songs," Sista stated.

"In my heart, I know you're right, Charlotte," Mattie Mae stated. "Too many people around here are stuck! Stuck in their minds and stuck in the way they do things. Of course, some of 'em are gonna buck about this 'cause they don't want change. Shucks, let's do it! Maybe some of these leaders in the chutch will straighten up and set an example if we step up and change things. We got one deacon who will lead devotion every Sunday and everybody knows that every Saturday he's over at Carrie Jones's house."

Timmi was very impressed. Jeff and Charlotte made some very valid points that even she understood, and being around them made Timmi want to re-evaluate her life; to be rid of toxic relationships and seek after this peace that God gave them. Although Timmi had always been able to land on her feet, she thought about how devastated she would have been if she had lost her true love to death like Jeff had, or to endure a troubled marriage as Charlotte did. While the others continued to chat, Timmi watched as a butterfly landed on the armrest of the swing. Although she would never want to live in the country, Timmi was beginning to see why Charlotte appreciated the simplicity of Turtle Island.

28

After Jeff placed his luggage in the spare bedroom, he drove into town to visit his cantankerous Aunt Frances. Charlotte was on the front porch putting together plans to hold an audition with people interested in forming a praise and worship team.

Timmi, who went upstairs to get her laptop so that she could get started on her assignment to create eye-catching flyers, was actually looking forward to the upcoming events. Mattie Mae showed Charlotte a list of the names of all those she had contacted and who expressed an interest in joining the praise and worship team. Charlotte suggested that she and Timmi post flyers around town since flyers would be a feasible way of reaching local residents on such short notice.

Mattie Mae informed Charlotte that she and Sista had already organized the clothes drive, which was specifically targeted for needy children and would greatly benefit several single mothers living in an impoverished section of Turtle Island called Cabbage Patch. Mattie Mae was also happy to report that many of the elderly living in that same area were ecstatic about the meals-on-wheels delivery.

"It sho' is a blessin' that Lilly is cookin' the food for these families," Sista remarked as she removed wax from her ear with a hairpin.

"Yes, it is. Joe and Lilly Green are blessed to be a blessing," Charlotte stated as she jotted down the information Timmi would need for the flyers.

"Joe and Lilly don't mind helpin' nobody out," Mattie Mae said as she went inside the house to answer the ringing telephone.

Sista sat on the edge of her seat, anxiously waiting for Timmi's return. Sista had memorized a round of questions to ask Timmi, but when Timmi did return with her laptop, a flustered Mattie Mae was right behind her.

"What's wrong, Grandma?" Charlotte asked.

"Yeah, what ail you, Mattie Mae? Who was that on the phone?" Sista asked, eager for information.

"Is it something about Tina and Terry?" Charlotte asked nervously.

Mattie Mae sat down and drew a deep breath. "No. Y'all not gonna believe this, but that was Lilly on the phone. Some ole roguish somethin' broke in her shop last night and stole everythin' outta her deep freezer! Can y'all believe that?"

"What?" Charlotte, Timmi, and Sista shrieked together.

"Sho' did," Mattie Mae said. "Anyway, they know who done it."

"Who was it?" Sista asked with her eyes nearly popping out of their sockets.

"Sue Martin's boy, Troy. You know he's on that stuff too," Mattie Mae said sadly.

"You can look at that boy and tell," Sista commented. "How they know he the one done it?"

"Because he was still in the diner . . . 'sleep! He broke

in the liquor store too. Larry opened up the liquor store this mornin' and found the back door wide open. Troy was passed out on Lilly's floor wit' liquor bottles all around his stupid tail."

Charlotte and Timmi laughed at the irony. Sista also found the botched robbery to be comical. "You mean to tell me that fool ain't had no better sense than to steal from one place, get drunk, and pass out across the street?"

"Well, Grandma, at least they recovered the food," Charlotte noted.

"Well, they only found 'bout two or three packages of chicken and ribs by his feet, and Troy was layin' down wit' his head on a bag of French fries like it was a pillow." Mattie Mae chuckled.

Sista crossed her legs and huffed. "I hope he got frostbite from layin' on those French fries!"

"Frostbite! Hot as it is, Troy probably done that to stay cool. But you're right, I bet he sold the rest of that meat," Mattie Mae said, shaking her head.

As if she had just received a hot news flash, Sista snapped her fingers and said, "On the other hand, I wouldn't be surprised if he didn't give Otis and Nellie that meat and he broke into the liquor store too! Food and liquor is right up Otis and Nellie's alley."

"So, does this mean that Joe and Lilly won't be able to do the meals-on-wheels drive?" Timmi asked while logging on to her laptop.

"No, not at all. Thank the Lawd for that," Mattie Mae answered. "I'm just mad at the devil for tryin' to stop us."

"No weapon formed against us shall prosper," Charlotte said. "I guess we shouldn't be surprised by distractions since we're trying to bring about a change for the better."

"Well, I need to run on to the house," Sista announced as she got up. "I left a pot of chicken backs and tails on the stove cookin', and John Edward liable to let 'em burn. Sometimes I can't trust that boy 'round no fire."

Both Charlotte and Timmi frowned at the thought of cooked chicken backs and tails.

"I'll see you girls later on," Sista said as she and Mattie Mae walked down the steps then toward the edge of the lane.

"Chicken backs and tails? Will I have the honor of being served that delicacy while I'm down here?" Timmi asked as she clicked on the clip art tab on the toolbar.

"I doubt seriously that you will." Charlotte laughed. "I've never had it. Although, I have heard Granddaddy go on and on about how chicken feet made such good gravy."

"Yuck! Who taught black folk how to eat from the rooter to the tooter?"

"Come on now. You just left the plantation. You read what Mrs. Capehart fed her slaves. We're creative and we know how to make a meal out of anything. Speaking of creative, what have you got so far for the flyers?"

Charlotte got up to look at the laptop screen and was pleased with what Timmi had done so far. In the top left-hand corner was a picture of clothing and tables, giving the perfect depiction of a yard sale. In the top right-hand corner was a picture of food with steam rising from a turkey. In the bottom left-hand corner was a picture of a three-member chorus group dressed in black robes and holding hymnals, and in the bottom right-hand corner was a picture of a small white church with a steeple.

In the middle of the document, Timmi had typed in large bold letters:

ATTENTION! ATTENTION! ATTENTION!
COME ONE, COME ALL

Everyone is invited to come out to Greener Pastures AME Church

Friday, August 21, 2007 at 12 noon.

There will be a clothes drive bonanza (FREE clothes for your children).

Nothing over $5.00 for adult clothing.

Chicken, ribs, and fish dinners to be sold on premises for $3.00 a plate.

Free dinners to be delivered around noon to the elderly living in the Cabbage Patch area.

There will be a table set up for job applications for the new automotive plant in Clark. Also, we will be auditioning for saved, gifted singers for the choir and/or praise team.

DON'T MISS OUT ON A GREAT OPPORTUNITY!

"I love it. We'll save it on a CD so we can print it out on Granddaddy's printer," Charlotte suggested.

"Your grandparents have a printer? I thought we'd have to go to the library or somewhere to print these," Timmi said. As she followed Charlotte inside the house and upstairs, Timmi studied her surroundings. Edmund and Mattie Mae did not live lavishly, but they weren't paupers either. All of their furnishings, though not trendy, were modern. Timmi just could not picture senior country folk having an interest in technology.

Charlotte led Timmi to a bedroom that also served as Edmund's office. The tiny bedroom reminded Timmi of a quaint little bed and breakfast she had once visited in New England. The room was tastefully decorated in powder blue and white with faded floral wallpaper and a blue-and-white crochet bedspread.

"Believe it or not, Granddaddy likes his gizmos and gadgets," Charlotte said, pointing to a computer and printer located in the alcove of the room. "He even treated him-self to this flat panel monitor for his birthday. Grandma says he hardly uses it because he spends most of his time with his buddies, which is true. I know I haven't seen him use his computer since I've been here. Grandma swears he got it for us kids to use when we come down to visit, and she's probably right."

"Charlotte, where y'all at?" they heard Mattie Mae call out.

"Upstairs, Grandma. We'll be down in a minute," Charlotte answered as she pressed the power button.

"What do you want for dinner?" Mattie Mae shouted back.

"It doesn't matter. Why don't you rest from the kitchen for a minute?" Charlotte suggested as she retrieved a CD from the desk drawer and inserted it into the disk drive.

"Rest!"

Charlotte knew that the word *rest* was practically a curse word when it came to Mattie Mae and her kitchen. She also knew that whatever it was her grandmother de-cided to cook, Timmi was in for a treat. Timmi's mother was no chef, so it was a mystery where Timmi learned how to cook so well. Charlotte and Timmi could hear a gospel quartet singing on the radio downstairs, with Mattie Mae singing along as they waited for the flyers to finish printing.

"Charlotte, can I ask you something?" Timmi asked with a puzzled look on her face. "What made you believe in God? I took to heart the things Jeff explained to me, and it all makes sense, but what really did it for you? I've known you all my life, and I've seen the change in you, yet we've never talked about your faith. I know that you're sincere, and I know that you don't go to church just to be going. You're constantly reading all these inspirational books, you go to all of these conferences, you have a gifted voice, and I believe you would give a person your last drop of blood if they needed it."

Charlotte thought carefully about the question as she gathered up the flyers from the printer tray. "For me, it was a process that really began when I was a child. God chose me, and all I wanted to do was be a kid and play outdoors."

Timmi leaned against the dresser and folded her arms. "You remember last year when you dragged me to that women's convention and the ushers tossed out pamphlets? I didn't get to see what they were passing out because some old crazy woman snatched it right out of my hands. You know me. I wanted to smack her silly. I look at people like that and I get turned off."

Charlotte laughed. "I remember that. You've got to keep in mind that some people go places to see a man and not 'The Man!' Who knows? Maybe the woman was having a bad day and the Lord convicted her later about her behavior."

"I don't know what her problem was, but I still wanted to smack her." Timmi jerked her head.

"All I can tell you, as you already know, is that I grew up in church, and you know all about my heartaches and disappointments. When I got sick and tired of being sick and tired, I cried out to God. I prayed, studied the Bible, and read everything about God that I could get my hands on, then one day I realized that I was developing a relationship with God. It was like my eyes had opened up for the first time in my life, and I could see how he had been with me all the time. The Lord had been speaking to me since I was a kid," Charlotte explained.

"I vaguely remember hearing you say that God actually talks to people, but people say that all the time, and I never heard God speak to me. You really can hear his voice?"

"Yes, but He speaks in different ways. Let me give you an example. One Saturday night, about two years ago, I was lying in bed and this poem popped into my mind. I'd never heard it before, but I did write it down. Don't you know the next day the guest speaker at church pointed me out and said that God will be giving me more poems to write for His glory."

"Whoa!"

Charlotte got up and searched for an envelope to place the flyers in. "You never told me about God telling you beforehand, though," Timmi said.

"I know. I don't tell you everything. Anyway, when we're so caught up in day-to-day things, we are not always able to see how God has done or is doing something in our lives. He could be speaking to you by saving your life, and using something like allowing you to forget to set the alarm clock and you oversleep. If you had left the house on time, you might drive off and get involved in an accident. Who knows? We don't, but God does. And Timmi, God does speak to you too."

Timmi hung her head down. "It's sad. Here I am with a law degree and never even thought about such simple things. It sounds like what we claim is our conscience is really God speaking."

"Exactly! You know how sometimes you'll do or say something and then you'll think, 'something told me not to say anything' or 'something told me not to go there'? Well, most of the time that's the Holy Spirit trying to tell you something. However, that can be tricky. Sometimes we talk ourselves out of things that He wants us to do." Charlotte checked her watch. "We'd better go and pass these flyers out. It's a good thing Granddaddy is riding with his friends and left his truck. I don't know what I was thinking leaving the car back in Charleston."

After the two left the room, Charlotte stopped by the kitchen to get a hammer and some nails. "Grandma, we're going into town and post these flyers. Where are the spare keys to the truck?" Charlotte asked.

Mattie Mae was at the sink vigorously washing out a muffin pan. "Look in that top drawer behind you," Mattie Mae replied.

Charlotte pulled out the drawer and found the keys underneath some old receipts.

"Miss Mattie, it sure smells good in here. What are you making?" Timmi asked, taking in a deep breath as she poked her head in the kitchen.

"I've got a roast with potatoes and pearl onions in the oven and some green beans on the stove," Mattie Mae said proudly.

"I hope you didn't go to all that trouble for me."

"Timmi, this is how my Grandma relaxes," Charlotte said. "Grandma, we shouldn't be gone long. What road is it again that I turn on to go to Cabbage Patch?"

"You make a right on Miller Cross Road. It's the first street after you cross over the railroad tracks. Cabbage Patch ain't nothin' but a long dead-end street. If you see Edmund out there, tell him to come on home so he can eat."

"I will. We'll be back in a minute," Charlotte said as she and Timmi went out the back door.

"I wonder why they call it Cabbage Patch," Timmi asked.

"Because years ago our people didn't talk about sex. So, when kids asked where babies came from, they were told the cabbage patch. This part of town is known for its amount of single mothers with kids," Charlotte answered.

"So, hence the name Cabbage Patch."

Charlotte nodded as she pressed the gas pedal and

proceeded on her journey, making frequent stops to post flyers on trees and light poles.

Timmi got a kick out of downtown Turtle Island. "Now, *this* is country," Timmi said jokingly as she checked out the view.

"Don't go making fun of my heritage. You're just jealous," Charlotte joked. "Do me a favor and look inside the envelope. Count how many flyers we have left. I want to be sure we have enough in case some people will have to share one." Timmi opened the envelope and counted out forty remaining flyers.

As soon as Charlotte spotted the street sign marked Miller Cross Road, she turned on the signal and made a right turn. The residents stared suspiciously at them as they drove down the street. Miller Cross Road was filled with shotgun shacks that needed to be boarded up and condemned. Many of the front porches had clothes hanging out to dry over broken banisters, and the children were either slightly dirty or just downright filthy. Some of the front yards were littered with broken wine bottles and empty beer cans.

"No, I take back what I said earlier. *This* is country," Timmi declared, shaking her head. "I don't care where you go, there is always a ghetto."

"You can say that again! We'll go all the way down to the end of the street and work our way up," Charlotte said as she parked between a blue-and-white Cutlass Supreme and an old rusted Corvette resting on concrete blocks.

"This street reminds me of the movie *Mississippi Burning*. You remember the part where the FBI dropped one of the Klan members off in this black neighborhood?" Timmi stated.

"Sad, isn't it? This is disgraceful. People should not have to live like this."

The house that Charlotte parked in front of was in much better shape than most homes on Miller Cross Road. Whoever lived there had a healthy-looking garden on the side of the house and nice patio furniture on the porch. Sitting on the porch in a wheelchair was an elderly, gray-haired woman who asked them who they were looking for. Charlotte got out of the truck and introduced herself as she gave the woman a flyer. The friendly old lady simply introduced herself as Rosa.

"Miss Rosa, my grandmother's church is having a clothes drive tomorrow and will be delivering meals to the elderly as well. If you're interested in having a meal delivered to you, I'll take down your name, address, and order so that you can receive one."

"Praise God! That sho' is nice. Who is your grandmother, baby?" Rosa said.

"Mattie Mae Morley." Charlotte turned around to see where a slapping noise was coming from. It was Timmi, who had just violently squashed a mosquito that had been trying to suck her arm dry.

"Is she all right?" Miss Rosa asked.

"She'll be fine." Charlotte chuckled. "Miss Rosa, you have a choice of a chicken, barbecue ribs, or fried fish dinner, and they all come with potato salad or macaroni and cheese, green beans or turnip greens, and a slice of red velvet cake or pecan pie."

"That sounds good, and sho' I know Mattie Mae. I know Edmund too. He used to be a rascal, that Edmund. I'm older than they is, but we all grew up together on the same road. It's about time the chutch did somethin' for all us ole folk. I used to go to chutch, but I ain't able no more on account I ain't got but one leg. I had sugar so bad the doctors had to take my leg off."

Miss Rosa held up the beach towel that was on her lap to reveal one leg dangling from her skirt. "Put my name down for one chicken dinner wit' macaroni and cheese and green beans and I'll have some of that red velvet cake for dessert. I don't mess wit' pork no more on account of my high blood pressure. Who doin' the cookin' anyway. 'Cause I don't eat just anybody's food."

Charlotte's heart was filled with compassion for Miss Rosa. "Lilly Green is preparing the food. Miss Rosa, if you don't mind my asking, do you have someone to shop for you or take you to the doctor? Do you have anybody to help cook and clean?"

"Oh, that's all right then. Lilly is a darn good cook. My neighbor across the street takes me wherever I need to go. That's so kind of ya to ask. My husband and my only chile died years ago. My husband had a stroke, and Junior, my son, was killed in a huntin' accident. So, it's just me now. Y'all send me over a plate. Edmund knows where I stay."

Charlotte hugged Miss Rosa and reached in her purse for a ten-dollar bill, slipping the bill into the woman's hand. Miss Rosa thanked Charlotte as she and Timmi left, but before they got to the next house, two men in their early twenties approached them.

"Girl, look at this. Everywhere I go I attract throwbacks," Timmi whispered to Charlotte.

"Y'all must be lookin' for me," the toothless guy with processed hair said.

"No, but since this is your hood, you can help pass out these flyers, Denzel," Timmi smarted off.

"She's just kidding. We've got it covered," Charlotte said while handing the men a flyer and rolling her eyes at Timmi.

"I ain't never seen y'all around here befo'. I'm lookin' for a friend, a nice young lady to take to the club sometimes," the other guy said, looking Charlotte and Timmi up and down. Although this one did seem to have teeth in his mouth (gold teeth, at that), he didn't look quite as bad as his friend, who was tore up from the floor up.

Good Lord. I've seen better teeth in a dog, Timmi thought to herself. "These flyers are about a function that will be taking place at *church*. We're not passing out flyers for the grand opening to Bubba's Disco, nor do we want to go to Bubba's Place, or whatever the name of your local night-club is. So, you can safely guess that these aren't entry forms for the Drop It Like It's Hot contest either. By the way, do you have a job?"

Charlotte, who was looking quite flushed, pinched Timmi on the arm. Just like Sista, Timmi was well sea-soned in giving out tongue-lashings, but Charlotte felt Timmi's attitude was rude and uncalled for.

"I work right up the street at the gas station. Why? You wanna bring me lunch or take me out to lunch?" the guy with the gold teeth said, apparently unmoved by Timmi's crudeness.

"Unbelievable!" Timmi said, apparently unmoved by Charlotte's attempt to shut her up. "I tell you what; go buy yourself some lunch and charge it to the game!" Timmi huffed and walked away, visibly irritated. Charlotte apol-ogized to the men for Timmi's behavior and rushed to catch up with her. Just as she was about to correct Timmi for being so rude, someone yelled out of a nearby window.

"Sherman and Eric! Y'all leave those girls alone! Don't nobody want y'all. Y'all all the time up in somebody's face!"

Charlotte decided to leave Timmi alone for now, since she was already across the street talking to a young woman. A half-hour later, they each had interesting sto-ries to tell one another when they got back to the truck. Timmi told of meeting a surly, but fresh old man who wanted her to sit on his arthritic knee and tell him about herself. She also met a young woman in her early twenties who was a mother of five. "Those kids made Bebe's kids look like sweet little angels," Timmi told Charlotte.

Charlotte told Timmi that she met one of Otis Moss's aunts. However, a neighbor of this particular aunt eagerly told Charlotte that the aunt didn't need any meals delivered to her because she had some of the meat that was stolen from Joe and Lilly Green's shop in her deep freezer. Troy Martin was a close relative of the woman's. Charlotte also visited the home of a family of ten who lived in a three-bedroom house. Cabbage Patch was no more than a tract of land filled with tenant dwellers, and as one tenant told Timmi, they all paid their rent to ole man Johnson. Charlotte and Timmi left Cabbage Patch feeling sorry for the residents, but hoped that most of them would be able and willing to come out for tomorrow's events.

Charlotte turned into her grandparents' lane just as Jeff and Edmund were driving out. "Where are you guys going?" she asked. Jeff told her that they were going to meet with members of the board. Charlotte smiled and drove on to the back of the house and parked the truck. Upon entering the kitchen, Timmi waved at Mattie Mae who was on a three-way call with her daughters.

After Charlotte and Timmi washed their hands and helped themselves to a plate of dinner, Charlotte placed her food on the dining room table and went to turn on the television. On the screen, live and in living color, was Yolanda in handcuffs. Screaming behind her, while trying to cover her face as if she were on *COPS*, was her Aunt Brenda—Jeff's neighbor.

"Oh my God! Turn it up, turn it up!" Timmi shouted at Charlotte. Charlotte turned up the volume and joined Timmi at the dinner table. The two of them watched and listened in disbelief to the news report detailing Yolanda's arrest.

29

According to an unidentified caller, Yolanda Yvette Yates was wanted in Washington, D.C. on suspicion of murder. A few months ago, a wealthy socialite from a Washington, D.C. suburb had been found murdered in her home, and the woman's husband had recently been arrested. Since his capture, the husband had been singing like a canary. He confessed his involvement in his wife's murder to the police, but also implicated a young lady named Yolanda Yates, whom he met at a sleazy nightclub on the outskirts of Washington, D.C. about a year ago. According to the husband, he claimed that Yolanda came on to him and reeled him like a fly to a spider web. Charlotte and Timmi were stunned.

According to the husband, he and Yolanda had a one-night stand, which he now regretted. The man said he made it clear to Yolanda that he was happily married and that the affair was a mistake, but Yolanda became obsessive and demanded that he leave his wife. He told of constant hang-up calls to his home and he was sure that it had been Yolanda calling. The man also claimed that Yolanda stalked him constantly and he was in fear for his life. However, there were no police reports filed to support those accusations. The police, though, did have reason to believe that the man was still seeing Yolanda after his wife's death and that he seduced her into a murder-for-hire scheme. Supposedly, there was a witness who could prove that Yolanda was used and dumped once payday came.

Meanwhile, Yolanda had been singing a different tune. The cable network then played a video recording of Brenda defending her niece. According to Brenda, Yolanda told a tale of a married man chasing after her, begging for her affection, and complaining of being trapped in a loveless marriage. Yolanda claimed that the man rambled on and on about how much he hated his wife and that he'd do anything to be rid of her, but when she learned of the woman's death on the news, she became suspicious. Yolanda told her aunt that she started avoiding him and was afraid for *her* life. However, he was so persistent in trying to contact her, she decided to come to Charleston. She didn't run away because she was involved in a murder; she was running away from a man she suspected to be a cold-blooded killer.

"Can you believe this?" Timmi said, shaking her head. "This sounds like a made-for-TV movie."

"Right! I knew something wasn't right about Yolanda, but I never would have guessed this. So, she's down here on the run," Charlotte said as she scooped up a spoonful of vegetables. For some quirky reason, Charlotte usually ate her food with a spoon instead of a fork.

Timmi slowly chewed her beef before swallowing and said, "You might not have known Yolanda was involved in murder, but you knew she was bad news. It's one thing to be about the dollar bill, but murder is a little extreme. And I'm not saying that she's guilty. I am an attorney, so I know better than to act so presumptuous."

"Yeah, but from a legal standpoint and from your experience, what's your gut feeling on this?"

"First, after having met the girl, I think it's safe to say that she probably did the chasing. She's a huntress. It's hard to tell whether Yolanda and this man were in cahoots. I *do* believe she's in over her head. If memory serves me correctly, the victim's first name was Melinda, Melinda Albright, and I think her husband's name is Harold. I know she was born into money. He wasn't. Melinda came from a very affluent family, and they didn't approve of Harold. I'm sure they didn't want him near the family jewels. Rumor has it that Harold was known for cutting out on Melinda. And I'm talking about with girls *and* boys."

"I remember that murder. She was an heiress. Not that it's a good thing one way or the other, but please say you mean he's bisexual and not a pedophile. I've had enough of—"

"Rumor has it that Harold is bisexual. As a matter of fact, the same was said about Melinda. Some people get bored easily, I guess. That's why when the news first broke, there was speculation about the killer being one of her lovers. Let's see. Melinda's body was found on the floor in her foyer, but what really stands out in my mind about it is that Melinda was found dressed in all black leather: leather boots, leather dress, and leather dog collar. You know, the whole dominatrix thing. Whoever killed her strangled her with her own doggie collar. She was a beautiful girl, too. I'm almost sure Melinda was somewhere around our age."

"Lord, decadence."

"Hey, like I said, some people get bored easily. No telling what they were into."

"Look at where it got her. No, I'm wrong for that. There is *no* reason to commit murder."

After the news anchorman announced a break for commercials, Timmi laid her fork on the plate and said, "Charlotte, I don't know how to tell you this other than to just say it, but I think I've seen your Uncle Charles with Harold Albright once."

"Huh?" Charlotte was stunned. She wondered about how sordid her uncle was. Charlotte began to wonder how long and how much did Timmi know about her uncle's life.

Timmi could tell that Charlotte was struggling with something, but felt that Charlotte needed to know about her Uncle Charles, or least all of what she knew about him.

"There is this place that is sort of an underground club and attracts mixed company, if you know what I mean," Timmi said.

"No, I don't know, Timmi. What *do* you mean? Are you implying that you are adventurous?" Charlotte was fearful that her heart just could not take any more shocking news, not right now.

"No! Now, you know me better than that," Timmi exclaimed. "Calm down. I didn't know what kind of place it was at that time. I went there with that same little back-stabbing Connie and one of her sisters, who I found out later calls herself bi-curious. Anyway, tucked away in a cozy little corner in the back of the club were these two men: Harold and another man who strongly resembled your Uncle Charles. I noticed the man kept trying to hide his face from me anytime I came near them or looked in their direction. At first I thought I was being silly, but then it became obvious to me that he did not want to be recognized. He didn't know I would have ignored his butt if he weren't so obvious. As fate would have it, I got a good look at his face when one of the waiters came out of the kitchen. You know how when they swing open those doors and light from the kitchen filters in?"

Charlotte felt that Timmi was stalling in an effort to protect her, but it was too late. She already knew what Timmi was going to say. "Timmi, you don't have to hold anything back. I already know about my uncle being bisexual."

Timmi was relieved. "Whew! Charlotte, I didn't think you knew since we talk about everything and you never mentioned that."

"I didn't know. I just found out a few days ago, along with my grandparents."

"Wow! That must be hard on them. There are some other things that I'm sure you don't know about. Your uncle's name has indirectly come up in some of our court cases. As far as I can tell, it's nothing serious, but my concern is that he seems to hang around with some very unsavory characters. I just find it odd for a man in his profession to be associated with these people. Then again, what is odd these days?" Timmi stressed.

"You mean Uncle Charles has business dealings with shady folk?"

"Yes and no. A couple of years ago, we represented a client who was charged with child molestation."

Charlotte's heart sank and she wasn't sure if she wanted to hear anymore about her uncle, but Timmi continued. "Our client wasn't convicted, but he did drop your uncle's name as a good friend, sort of a reference, who would be an excellent character witness. I personally felt that the man was guilty, but we have some attorneys at the firm who could convince a jury that there really is a tooth fairy and an Easter bunny. Anyway, it turned out that we didn't need to call on your uncle. I'm sure he was relieved.

"There was another case we had that involved a male escort service and your uncle's name—well, not his name, but one of the plaintiffs gave a description that fits your uncle right down to his stethoscope. This plaintiff was a male escort who was suing his employer, and he didn't know your uncle's real name, but he said your uncle was a regular. This particular escort said that his 'regular' was a prominent surgeon. He named the hospital where this 'regular' was employed at. He knew that he had adult twin daughters. What are the odds on that? Next thing I know, our client's legal fees are taken care of quick, fast, and in a hurry, and the suit was settled out of court. Of course, any surgeon's salary could afford this, but—"

"You think Uncle Charles paid for the man's legal fees?" Charlotte asked in a disappointed tone. Since she no longer heard Mattie Mae's voice in the background talking on the telephone, Charlotte assumed that her grandmother must have ended her telephone conversation. Charlotte did not want Mattie Mae to hear her conversation with Timmi.

After noticing Charlotte's lowered tone, Timmi spoke softly also. "What I'm saying is that your uncle seems to be a bit careless. He tends to frequent places that are questionable. Look, I never said anything to you before because who am I to judge? It's none of my business unless it comes across my desk, and Charles's name has come across my desk. I didn't think anything of it until that night at the club. That sealed it for me." Timmi threw down her napkin and crossed her arms. Charlotte was so disappointed in her uncle that she had now lost her appetite.

Suddenly, Mattie Mae entered into the dining room and said, "Willa Belle and Mattie Lee said to tell you girls hello. Both of 'em talk like they might come home for Christmas. It would be nice if all of my chi'ren could come home. It's been a long time since the whole family got together." Immediately after she said that, they heard Edmund and Jeff talking as they came in through the front door.

"Miss Mattie, I must tell you this is the best meal I've had in a long time," Timmi complimented.

"I'm glad you enjoyed it. Now you know this is your home too. Y'all back already?" Mattie Mae said, joining Edmund and Jeff, who were seated in the living room.

"I'm going to tell Jeff about Yolanda," Charlotte said as she got up from the table.

30

Timmi went into the kitchen to get a second helping while Charlotte sat in the living room with Edmund and Jeff. Jeff listened as Charlotte informed him about his neighbor's niece. Mattie Mae, who was in no mood to hear more distressing news, announced that she was going across the street to visit Ms. Mamie, who was feeling a little under the weather. Edmund only grunted as he got up to go back outside and feed the hogs. After Charlotte finished telling the story to Jeff, he stood up and shook his head.

"That's some story, but how did the police catch her?"

Charlotte shrugged her shoulders and said, "I don't know, but I do that know Brenda and Yolanda need prayer. Well, on a hopefully lighter note, how did the meeting with the board go?"

"Everything went well. All I can say is you've got to love plain honest folk. Now, I hate to seem antisocial, but if you will excuse me, I need to go to my room to type out some notes."

About midway up the stairs, Jeff looked back at Charlotte and said, "I don't know how they caught Yolanda, but just think; I could have been driving her around Charleston when the cops tracked her down, and they would have thought I was harboring a fugitive."

As Timmi washed the last dish, she heard her cell phone ring, and Charlotte quickly tossed her a dishtowel to dry her hands. Timmi pulled out the small silver phone, placed it to her ear, and cheerfully answered without looking at the caller ID display panel.

"Wassup, boo?" Bobby said in his soulful baritone voice.

"Who is this? Bobby?" Timmi wanted to kick herself for not looking at the caller ID before answering.

Charlotte pretended that she hadn't heard Bobby's name being called out and mumbled to herself, "Just like a dog trying to dig up an old bone." Charlotte continued drying the dishes, dismissing the notion to leave the kitchen to allow Timmi some privacy.

"You got some nerve calling me," Timmi shouted with one hand on her hip. Timmi laid the phone down on the counter next to the dish drainer and pressed the speaker button so that Charlotte could hear how ridiculous Bobby sounded.

"Listen, I know you're mad, baby, but you don't understand. I don't really love Connie, and then she went and got herself pregnant," Bobby pathetically explained. "Man, she and my mom and everybody else in the solar system started sweating me about marrying her."

"She got herself pregnant! She got herself pregnant! What? Did she steal your sperm while you were asleep and store it in a turkey baster? No, Bobby, *you* don't understand! And if you knew how to think with your top head instead of the bottom one . . . You know what? You're not even worth my minutes, not even the free weekend ones! If you ever call me again, I will file a harassment complaint against you. You got that? Now, get yourself ready for some of God's justice! Oh, by the way, congratulations!"

Click.

Timmi couldn't believe she'd just said that. Neither could Charlotte.

"Get ready for God's justice?" Charlotte asked, raising her eyebrows. "Where did that come from?"

"You know what? I was doing okay until that idiot called."

"And you're still doing okay. That was just something to catch you off guard."

"Well, it worked." Timmi started laughing and flinging suds at Charlotte. "I don't know why I told him to get ready for God's justice. That came from out of nowhere. I guess I really do believe God will handle it."

"If you leave it all to the Lord, He will take care of it. Bobby may have to hit rock bottom to get the message. He may be riding on a glory cloud now, but at some time in the future, he may or may not come and apologize to you, but you best believe he will have some trials. We all do. If his heart softens, he'll have some regrets about the way he did things." Charlotte placed the glasses in the cupboard.

"Forget him." There was a brief silence, then Timmi said, "I know this is Turtle Island and not Paradise Island, but what do people do around here for fun?" Timmi turned off her phone and placed it back in her pocket.

"I have no idea. I just came here to relax, or so I thought. Isn't it ironic?"

"What's that?" Timmi asked as she handed Charlotte the last dish from the sink.

"When I was at Truth in Love, they didn't want to use me in any capacity. No, I take that back. If you're a woman and a member at Truth in Love, they can use your services as an usher, a singer or to hand the pastor a glass of water. You can forget being trained in any other ministry. Now, I'm down here being used at a church that I don't even belong to. Of course, I won't be preaching here, but it's fulfilling to know that you're needed and your suggestions are helpful. It's funny how we make our own plans and then God shows you His."

"Do they allow women to preach where you're at now?" Timmi placed the silverware in the drawer.

"They do," Charlotte walked over to the wall where the telephone was mounted and picked up the receiver. "I'm going to call my Aunt Francine. Maybe they've heard something by now."

"Go ahead. I'll be up front. I want to find out more about the Albright murder."

Charlotte pulled out her grandmother's address book from the cabinet drawer and dialed the number to Francine's mother's house. After the third ring, a woman with a husky voice answered.

"Hello, this is Francine's niece, Charlotte. Is she there?"

"Yes, she's right here. Hold on," the woman said.

After about a millisecond of muffled background noises, Francine picked up the receiver and said "hello." Before she could say anything else, Charlotte blurted out, "Aunt Francine, this is Charlotte. How are you guys doing? Did I catch you at a bad time?"

"No. It's good to hear your voice, Charlotte. How is everybody there?"

"We're all fine. I was just calling to see if you've heard anything yet and how things were going with your family."

"So far, so good with my family here, but as far as my daughters are concerned, I really can't go into it over the phone."

"Why? What's wrong? Has something happened?"

"No . . . it's just that . . . things have gotten really confusing. The detective is in the Bahamas as we speak, so we should have more information soon. Tina and this man, John, shouldn't be too hard to find. The problem is that the detective is being given the runaround as to their whereabouts. He found the church where John is supposedly pastoring, but he described the congregation as being very closed-mouthed. We still believe Terry is in Atlanta. Charles is in Atlanta now talking to some of their friends from college and hoping to find Terry or find out something."

"I'm sure he'll find out something. We just have to keep praying, Aunt Francine. Don't give up hope."

"I'm trying not to. I just can't get rid of this feeling that something awful is about to happen."

Feeling Francine's pain, Charlotte said, "I wish I could do something to help."

"There's nothing you can do but pray, and I appreciate that. This is not your fault. Anyway, Charles and I will be back after he returns from Atlanta. Hopefully we'll know more by then. Mattie told me that one of your friends is there visiting. That's nice."

"Yes, Timmi. She's got a little drama of her own going on, but she'll be okay. Everybody is going through something."

"I guess so. Charlotte, I don't mean to rush you off the phone, but my mother needs to call and verify her dental appointment for next week."

"Sure. Instead of me taking my lazy butt upstairs to use my cell, I'm using up Grandma's long distance services, so I need to get off the phone anyway. Take care and we'll see you on Sunday."

After Charlotte hung up the receiver, she made her way toward the front door. She was startled to see Maggie Johnson standing at the front door peering through the screen. After Charlotte invited Maggie to come inside, Maggie held up one of the flyers in her hand and expressed her interest in auditioning for the praise and worship team. Charlotte explained to her that it was for the church members only and apologized that it wasn't made clear on the flyer.

Charlotte managed to smooth things over by telling Maggie that the invitation to come to church on Sundays was always open, and if she accepted Jesus Christ as her Lord and Savior and joined the church, she could look into joining the choir or any other ministry there.

Maggie thanked Charlotte for the clarification as they walked toward the door. Timmi was reading something on her laptop as Charlotte waved goodbye to Maggie, who then got inside John Edward's car.

"Who is that guy?" Timmi asked without looking up.

"That's Miss Sista's son, John Edward. I'll be back out in a minute. I want to take a peek at some of these donated clothes in here just in case some of them need washing."

"Roger that," Timmi said as she continued reading. Moments later, the door opened again. This time Charlotte returned dragging an old card table and a large plastic bag filled with clothes. She sat down and unfolded the legs of the table and started rummaging through the bag to sort and separate the items.

"Did you find out anything from your aunt?" Timmi asked, briefly glancing at a child's shirt that Charlotte was examining.

"Not really. I think she's got some kind of information, but she wouldn't say. She did say that Uncle Charles is in Atlanta searching for some of Tina and Terry's friends." Charlotte looked up and saw Sista approaching them.

"What did Maggie Johnson want?" Sista asked, sounding short of breath.

"She had some questions about the choir. Why do you ask?" Charlotte responded.

"I know how that gal is, and I was wonderin' what she was up to." Sista looked over at Timmi. "What kinda work you do, Lynn?"

"It's Timmi, and I am an attorney," Timmi answered, trying not to appear annoyed.

"I hope you ain't no crooked lawyer like these we got 'round here."

"I hope not too. At least I try not to be." Timmi chuckled.

Sista retied her scarf firmly on her head and said, "Charlotte, Mattie Mae called me from over Mamie's house. She sent me over for her bottle of camphor oil."

"Do you know where she keeps it, Miss Sista?" Charlotte asked.

"Chile, I don't know. Check in the medicine cabinet in her bathroom. It might be in there."

Charlotte pushed aside the bag of clothes and went inside to find the camphor oil. Sista waited until she was convinced that Charlotte had reached the top of the stairs to pounce on Timmi. "How come you ain't married yet? I know you ain't, 'cause Mattie Mae told me so."

"The reason why I'm not married is because I attract vermin," Timmi firmly answered.

"You got people down South anywhere?"

"No. My family is originally from Washington."

"Shucks, everybody is from down South somewhere. The only reason why colored folk are up North is because of that Underground Railroad. Then too, during my time, I've seen folk get railroaded out of town because they had to run from the white man over some foolishness. I guess you think us country folk don't know much." Sista remained at the foot of the steps waiting for Timmi to respond.

"No, I wouldn't say that at all. People are the same everywhere you go. That's why I don't pry into their business." Timmi hoped that Sista would get the hint about being so nosey. "I find that I learn more about people by being quiet and listening. People always have a way of proving how much they know. I do respect the wisdom of people from your generation, no matter where they live." In just that short period of time, Timmi and Sista had sized each other up and had formed their opinions of one another. Charlotte returned with the bottle of camphor oil just in time to catch a mischievous grin on Sista's face.

"Miss Sista, what did you think Maggie wanted when she came over?" Charlotte asked as she handed the bottle to her.

"I figured she came over here to get some clothes from you befo' we set 'em out tomorrow. It wouldn't be nothin' for her to come over here wit' some sad story just so she can pick out the best clothes."

"No, she didn't do that at all. As a matter of fact, she asked about singing in the choir," Charlotte reassured her.

Sista pouted and said, "I still don't believe her. Anyhow, I better go befo' Mattie Mae call over here to see what's takin' me so long. I'll see y'all later." Sista walked down the lane whistling a nursery rhyme.

"We'll see you later, Miss Sista," Charlotte said.

"She's a funny little lady. Full of spit and vinegar." Timmi laughed as she went back to her reading.

"She's a mess all right, that's for sure, but you have to overlook her sometimes."

"She's harmless. Getting back to your aunt, I wonder what they found out about your cousins," Timmi said, frowning.

"I don't know. We'll just have to wait and see. The detective she hired insinuated that Reverend Holiday's congregation was acting strange."

"Really? What a mess. What's the deal on Terry?"

"The consensus is that she's in Atlanta. I don't have a good feeling about any of this myself."

"You're just worrying for nothing. Look at it this way: Tina eloped. She wasn't kidnapped. I know it sounds like a hasty decision and maybe even bad judgment on her part. It was still her choice. Terry, on the other hand, well, I don't know what Terry is doing, but she'll probably show up soon claiming that she was entitled to travel without having to report to anyone. And you know what? She would be right. They *are* grown women, you know. To be honest, I really don't see what the big fuss is about. So stop worrying."

"I'm not worrying, and you don't understand. Remember earlier when we were talking about how God speaks to you? Even Aunt Francine is sensing something is wrong, and I don't believe it's just mother's wit, either. I've prayed and prayed for them, but I don't have any peace yet. I know that God is in control, but it's like I can smell death in the air."

"Death! Girl, I hope not. I'm sorry if I come off sounding harsh, but you're the one who is a Christian. I just don't want you or your family making this into something bigger than what it really is. Where is your faith?"

"Ouch! That hurts." Charlotte ceased folding a pair of child's corduroy pants.

"What hurts?" Timmi asked, checking to see if Charlotte had physically hurt herself on something.

"Pointing out my lack of faith after I just said that God is in control. Bad Christian!" Charlotte answered while slapping her wrist as an act of self-chastisement.

The sound of Timmi typing away on her laptop could be heard. "You're crazy. Got it!" Timmi exclaimed, throwing her hands up in the air.

"Got what?" Charlotte got up and peeked over Timmi's shoulders.

"Some detailed information on the Albright murder. Girl, you know I got the hook-up!" Timmi answered, smiling up at Charlotte. "Let's see how that intuition of yours saved you and Jeff."

31

Charlotte had completely forgotten about Yolanda's arrest and pulled her chair next to Timmi so that she could read along with her. Timmi had discovered a rather dark story reported by a best-selling tabloid. The two of them slowly began reading the tragic tale of thirty-three-year-old Melinda Hawkins Albright, the second oldest daughter of George and Venus Hawkins, who were successful African-American publishers of a major urban magazine.

Although the privileged and pampered Melinda Hawkins attended the very best private and Ivy League schools in the country, she was known to get buck wild and unfocused. Thanks to nepotism, Melinda had worked for her parents' magazine as a photographer, handling all of the choice assignments photographing African-American celebrities. That was how she met her husband, Harold Albright, a scrawny, average-looking wannabe manager of an obnoxious wannabe rap star who was related to a well-known film star.

Melinda met Harold on a photo shoot, and they married three months later, much to the chagrin of George and Venus. Many insiders felt that Melinda married Harold to spite her parents, describing it as another one of her rebellions.

It was Melinda's oldest sister, Joyce, who found her lifeless body in her unlocked home back in late February. When questioned by the police, Harold Albright provided them with an airtight alibi. He was out of town on business promoting his protégé's sexually explicit CD. Melinda's family still pointed their accusing fingers at Harold, and the police finally got a break two months after the murder when a neighbor who had left her house for a trip to Europe on the morning of the murder returned back home and discovered that Melinda had been killed.

The neighbor soon telephoned the police because she remembered something that seemed odd to her. She told them that she recalled seeing a tan-colored florist's truck parked in the Albrights' driveway that particular morning. Although flowers were delivered in the neighborhood all the time, she thought it odd that a florist truck was out delivering flowers so early in the morning. The police thanked the neighbor for her tip. Eventually, they found out that Harold had ordered a bouquet of flowers for his wife from a Mom and Pop florist shop the day before her death, and the only driver of the florist shop was an employee named Bruce Yates . . . Yolanda Yates's cousin and Brenda Yates Baxter's nineteen-year-old son.

Both Harold Albright and Yolanda told police that Bruce had been hired to kill Melinda, but each accused the other of doing the hiring. Bruce was instructed to quit his job at the florist shop, claiming to go into a family business venture, and to leave town immediately. However, Bruce chose to hang around a little longer to show off some of the spoils purchased from blood money. He didn't quit his job at the florist shop until two months later.

When the police questioned Bruce's former employers, the couple noted that Bruce had access to the delivery truck at any time. They trusted him. On his last day of employment, Bruce came by to pick up his final paycheck driving a brand new BMW and wearing designer clothes. The owners knew that Bruce certainly could not have afforded such on the salary they paid him, and when they asked him about his sudden prosperity, Bruce said that his good fortune was compensation for services rendered.

After that interview with Bruce's former employers, another month had passed before the police could locate Bruce for questioning. When they did, Bruce folded like a deck of cards. He quickly gave up Harold Albright and his cousin, Yolanda, for the brutal murder of Melinda Albright, and even though Bruce betrayed his cousin, he stopped short of revealing her whereabouts. Bruce also admitted that Harold and Yolanda did have an affair, but felt that it was one-sided. Bruce felt certain that Harold was only using them, but he didn't care so long as he got paid the $50,000 promised to him. Yolanda, however, had her heart set on becoming the next Mrs. Harold Albright.

Charlotte and Timmi stopped reading the story after hearing Mattie Mae and Miss Sista talking. Mattie Mae and Sista were just a few yards away discussing Mamie's condition. Apparently, Mamie's problem, aside from a slight case of senility, was frugality.

"Mamie's chi'ren really need to come down here and see about her," Mattie Mae said as she landed on the top step.

"You know her chi'ren just waitin' for her to die, Mattie Mae. Mamie *can* do a little better than what she doin' for herself, but she too stingy to even buy butter. Talkin' about it cost too much money. Shucks, everythin' cost too much money if you ask me. She needs to stop usin' so much lard. I bet if you strike a match near Mamie you'd have a grease fire." Sista stopped to roll up her suntan knee-highs.

"But Mamie does have a good heart. She tries to help people out whenever she can." Mattie Mae chuckled at Sista, who was tying a double knot in her stockings to keep them from sliding down her legs. Mattie Mae and Sista were so busy complaining about Mamie that they didn't even acknowledge Charlotte and Timmi before going inside the house.

Charlotte went back to sorting the children's clothes. "That's an awful story about the Albright murder. I wonder why it took them so long to catch up with Harold."

Timmi stopped reading and replied, "I think Bruce quit his job around April or May. The article doesn't say when the police tracked down the florist shop, but Bruce had already quit by the time the cops talked to the owners. Wait a minute. Here it goes. They arrested Harold around the end of May. Punk!"

"That's right. I forgot. Does it say when they arrested Bruce?" Charlotte held up a child-sized T-shirt riddled with holes. "Now, who gave this away expecting somebody to want this for their child?"

Timmi turned her head to see what Charlotte was talking about. "That's a shame. It would have been quicker for them to throw it in the trash than to send it as a donation. People are something else." Timmi shook her head. "Okay, Bruce was just arrested three weeks ago. It says here that he was staying with one of his sisters in Jersey. He was stopped for a traffic violation, and Jersey police called D.C. police, and the rest is history, as they say. Hold up. Hold up. It also says here that the police led Bruce away kicking and screaming like a two-year-old."

* * *

A full moon was shining brightly through the window just as Timmi was about to settle down on the bed. She found it amusing to be in the bed so early, and to her, midnight was early. Except for the constant chirping of crickets, it was eerily quiet. Timmi rolled over on her stomach and picked up the Bible on the nightstand and sat up in bed.

"Might as well start at the beginning," she said to herself as she turned to the Book of Genesis. Timmi closed her eyes and prayed. "God, help me to understand what I'm about to read. I believe that you do exist, and I ask you to forgive me of my sins. I want to experience your presence like Charlotte does. If you're really real like that, then I want to know you for myself. Amen."

When Timmi read Genesis 1:26, she wanted to know who God was talking about when He said, "Let us make man in *our* image . . ." She looked up at the ceiling and asked out loud, "Who is us? Father and Son? Is this the first mention of Jesus?" She found herself wondering who Cain had married. "Could it be that there were other people on earth besides Adam and Eve? After all, it is written that God had put a mark on Cain so that others would not harm him. What others? Who were these people?" she asked.

Timmi remembered hearing stories about who begat who, but couldn't keep up with the names or even pronounce half of them, which made the Bible even less interesting to her. Now she was interested. "He sure was quick to point his finger at Eve just because she took the first bite. How convenient! It's funny how men have this same habit even to this day. Adam didn't have to eat any of it. Where was Adam at anyway when Eve was out there socializing with a serpent?" she fumed. For the first time in her life, Timmi found the stories in Genesis to be fascinating, but she was too sleepy to delve into Exodus.

After reading the entire Book of Genesis and fussing and talking out loud like some folks do to the movie theatre screen, Timmi closed the Bible, placed it back on the nightstand, turned off the lamp, fluffed up two pillows, and placed them underneath her head. Soon, Timmi began to dream. In the dream, she was standing before a sliding glass door looking outside. On the outside were rows and rows of opened graves. She saw no one in the dream, but she could hear a voice say repeatedly, "Jesus is coming back. Jesus is coming back. The dead will rise."

Then she saw herself sitting on the floor in a small room. Standing before her was her father's mother, who had been deceased for several years, and looking very different from how Timmi remembered her. In fact, she appeared to be an illumination. In life, Grandma Ruth was a big and tall woman, but in the dream she was short and thin and Timmi could see straight through her. Grandma Ruth smiled at Timmi, and her silhouette faded away as Timmi drifted off to sleep.

32

A Friday had finally arrived. Everyone in the Morley household was getting ready for the day's events. Edmund had already gone out to pick up the van loaned to the church by one of the deacons, and even though Lilly volunteered to prepare the food, Mattie Mae insisted on making the red velvet cakes and had been up since 5:00 AM doing so. Timmi had been up since 6:00 AM or "o'dark:30," as she liked to call it. Timmi wanted to go back to sleep, but Mattie Mae's red velvet cakes kept calling her name. Charlotte was also up and in her room, writing out a thank you message to be incorporated on flyers for people who had donated clothing.

A large crowd was expected at the church, especially since all clothing would be sold dirt cheap. Dinners would be sold on the church grounds. The meals-on-wheels would be delivered free to the elderly, with all proceeds from the sales going toward an emergency loan fund set up for people in need, regardless of whether or not they were church members.

Mattie Mae had warned Charlotte and Jeff to expect some opposition. Not everyone was in agreement with the day's planned activities or the suggestions for reorganizing the church. She advised them to ignore any derogatory remarks they might overhear. Mattie Mae told them of a comment that Sista overheard between two people talking about Jeff and Charlotte. According to Sista, two female members of Greener Pastures were in Piggly Wiggly complaining about Jeff and Charlotte not being members of the church or even residents of Turtle Island, and accused them of trying to take over.

They didn't know that Sista was standing in line one aisle over. Sista got out of line, went over behind them and asked what had *they*, two pillars of the church, done for their church or the community. Then one of the uptight, uppity women foolishly decided to answer Sista by pointing out that she taught Sunday school faithfully. That was a mistake.

"You teach Sunday school!" Sista backfired. Everybody in the store turned around to see what was going on. Sista then told the Sunday school teacher, "You been *teachin'* folk for one whole year 'bout Moses pleadin' with Pharaoh to let God's people go. When you gonna tell everybody that Moses got the people out? Shucks, Jesus done come since then!"

Nonetheless, Charlotte and Jeff were prayed up and wearing their full armor.

The weather could not have been more perfect for outdoor activities. Charlotte and Mattie Mae picked up Sista in Edmund's truck, while Jeff and Timmi rode together to the church. Lilly and Mary had already set up their food booth near the front, and there were about six men going back and forth carrying tables and chairs from the church fellowship hall. Once Jeff parked his vehicle, he immediately claimed one of the tables, taping signs along the edges to alert folks that it was the table for job applicants. Timmi stood nearby hanging up balloons on a shade tree. During her morning prayer, Charlotte had thanked God for Jeff because he willingly rolled up his sleeves and worked hard for the community.

Maggie Johnson and her six rambunctious boys, Dozier, Dylan, David, Dexter, Derrick, and Damian, passed by Timmi, who was still hanging up the balloons. The youngest son ran back, pulled something out of his pocket and stuck it in one of the balloons. POW! Timmi jumped as if she heard gunshots.

"Look at that, Mattie Mae," Sista said while helping Mattie Mae set the clothes on the table. "I should have known Maggie would come out early and make sho' she got some clothes for them little mannish demons of hers. And do you think she spanked that bad-behind Damian for bustin' that balloon? No home trainin' at all!"

"About how old is little Damian?" Mattie Mae asked.

"Little Damian ain't but six."

Mattie Mae started laughing. "They might be bad, but they still precious."

"Precious my foot! There ain't nothin' precious about them little demons, and to make it worse, they got Cora *and* Otis's blood and alcohol mixed in 'em!" Sista turned around to get another stack of clothes and saw Nellie Moss walking toward the church carrying a large shopping bag.

"Don't say one word, Sista," Mattie Mae sternly warned.

"I ain't sayin' a word," Sista mumbled.

Nellie looked around and waved to everyone except Sista. Sista grumbled as she watched Nellie head straight toward Lilly.

"I gotta say this," Sista said. "Why is it that Nellie acts as if she ain't never seen food befo'?"

"You know she come from a large family. It was so many of them growing up, they had to fight for somethin' to eat. I guess if you grew up not knowin' where or when you gonna get yo' next meal, that kind of sticks wit' you. Nellie is just used to fightin' to get hers," Mattie Mae said.

"I wonder what she's up to," Sista questioned.

"None of our business, that's what," Mattie Mae said. "Why she gotta be up to somethin'?"

" 'Cause I know she is."

"Folk might surprise you one day, Sista."

"Not Nellie."

Edmund pulled up with a van loaded with people from the Cabbage Patch area. Joe Green and Bubba Watkins were driving closely behind in their pickup trucks carrying excited children. The last two passengers to file out of the van were Eric and Sherman. Sherman wore a sweat-trapping polyester shirt with polyester knit pants and fake alligator shoes. Charlotte and Timmi overheard Eric scold Sherman for putting butter in his hair when he could have borrowed some oil sheen from him.

Sherman had so much butter in his hair, he had attracted a swarm of bees, flies, and gnats. Charlotte knew that Sherman was out to impress the ladies, and she felt sorry for him. All of a sudden, it seemed as if half of Turtle Island had arrived all at once.

Charlotte looked around at the tables to find that all of the volunteers were present and ready to work. She closed her eyes, hoping for a successful afternoon, only to have a vision of her cousins Tina and Terry standing in her grandparents' living room.

Timmi walked over to Charlotte, looked over in the direction where Eric and Sherman were standing and said, "Did you see Turtle Island's most eligible bachelors over there?"

"Be nice, Timmi. You really were rude to them yesterday."

"I know, I know. I was wrong, and I felt bad after I realized how I sounded. But listen. Before it gets hectic around here, I want to tell you about my dream last night."

"What was it?" Charlotte asked, still thinking about the vision she'd just had.

"I dreamed I was looking outside and there were all these empty graves, a lot of them, and I heard this voice say Jesus is coming back and the dead will rise. What do you think it means?"

"Probably just that, because He is coming back, although you can have Him now if you accept Him. You see that? God spoke to you in a dream. The empty graves were probably an illustration of what you heard: 'the dead will rise.' Wow! That's pretty deep. We should go ahead and get started."

Charlotte went to her table, which was the sign-up table for auditions. Roy, the choir director, was already seated. Roy admittedly resented Charlotte's suggestion of organizing a praise and worship team at first. He confessed to Mattie Mae that it was because he had once submitted this very same suggestion to the board members only to have it rejected.

Mattie Mae assured Roy that Charlotte was only an advisor and had no intentions of moving to Turtle Island and taking over his position as choir director. Meanwhile, Eric was at the job applicant table giving Jeff the once over. Timmi watched as Eric struggled with filling out his application, and she was convinced that he had a reading problem.

"Do you need any help?" Timmi offered.

"Naw, I got it," he replied dryly.

"Please don't be afraid to ask for help if you need it. All of these jobs will pay more than what I'm sure you're making now, and I don't want you to miss your chance of obtaining a better job because you're stuck on a question. Here, let me help you." Timmi reached out for Eric's application.

"I don't want yo' husband to get mad at you for helpin' me," Eric said in a low voice as he looked at Jeff.

"He's not my husband." Timmi smiled at Eric's farfetched assumption. "He's my friend's cousin. Believe it or not, we're all out here just trying to help each other."

Eric pointed to the second line on the sheet and sheepishly asked, "What's this word right here?"

Timmi felt sad after seeing the word in question. He couldn't read the word *address*. Suddenly, Eric threw the paper down and stated that he didn't have a way to get to Clark for the job even if he was hired.

Timmi wouldn't hear of it. She knew an excuse when she heard one. "I tell you what. The position you're applying for is a mechanic. I take it that you are a mechanic at the service station, right?"

Eric nodded.

"As a mechanic," she continued, "the only thing you have to worry about is repairing things, not filling out applications all day. Let me help you with this, and more than likely you could ride with someone from around here who will also get a job at the plant. First, you've got to get past this hurdle and fill out the application. You give me the information and I'll write it in, but you have to sign it. We'll request for day shift as first choice. That way you can go to night school and finish your education if you'd like."

"Thanks."

"Not a problem." Timmi got up from her seat and gave Eric a hug for encouragement.

"Can I ask you something?" Eric asked.

"Sure."

"What kinda work you do?"

"I'm a lawyer."

After witnessing Timmi's heartwarming act of kindness, Charlotte told the Lord thank you and then asked God what the vision of Tina and Terry was all about. While she did not hear an answer from the Lord, she did hear Sista accusing a child of stealing.

"Why you feel like you gotta steal, and we givin' the clothes away?" Sista shouted.

"I ain't tryin' to steal nothin' from you!" the young child yelled.

Sista placed her hands on her hips and started to chastise the child. "Girl, you must think I'm a fool. And who do you think you talkin' to? I ain't yo' equal. I seen yo' mama and yo' sister over at Bessie's table, and I seen her wit' you at Jessie Mae's table. Twice! The clothes might be free, but there is a limit! Annie! Annie, get yo'-self over here right now!" Sista called out to the child's mother.

"Hey, Miss Sista. What's wrong now?" Annie asked innocently. Annie, who looked to be in her early thirties, sashayed over to Sista in a halter top that was no match for gravity, and a pair of low riders that just could not, would not, contain her overlapping belly.

"You know exactly what's wrong! Sendin' that chile over here to get more clothes! You ought to be ashamed of yo'self, Annie Richardson!"

"No, I didn't. Come here, LaDiamond!" Annie said, pinching her daughter on the arm.

"Annie, I looked right at you. Don't let these cataracts fool you. I can see. I know times are hard, but you know the rules: one stack per chile."

Annie rolled her eyes at Sista and pulled her daughter away from the table.

"A pig has got more manners than Annie and them chi'ren of hers. They think they so slick. All she doin' is teachin' 'em to have light fingers," Sista fumed. Off in the distance, Annie gathered all nine of her dirty children and pleaded with Lilly for a discount on the dinners.

It didn't take long for the clothes to be gone or for the food to practically sell out. In fact, the food had dwindled down to a few pieces of chicken, a pint of potato salad, and two slices of pecan pie. People who apparently came just to complain lingered around to continue criticizing.

"I don't see why they couldn't sell the clothes for more money. Some of these folks around here know they can afford to pay more than five dollars for clothes. They ain't that broke. And why didn't they ask Sammy from Friendship to come over and preach on Sunday?" one church member said.

"Half of these people won't be coming to a service anyway, and I hope they don't expect me to help out the next time they do somethin' like this," the other member said.

"You ain't help out *this* time, so I don't know whatcha complainin' for." Sista had interrupted. "People need somebody who can explain the Bible to them, not skip all over it and make up stuff." Sista knew that these two particular members were staunch supporters of Reverend Holiday, and that Sammy, who was an assistant pastor at Friendship Church, was also a relative of one of the women talking.

"I don't need nobody explainin' the Bible to me. I know the scriptures for myself!" one of the women said.

"What? Jesus wept?" Sista said and stomped off. Sista sauntered over to Mattie Mae, handing her a plate from Lilly's stand as the two church members whispered behind her back. As soon as Sista sat down, she noticed her son helping Mamie get out of the car.

"Looks like Mamie brought somethin'," Sista said, nudging Mattie Mae in her ribs. Mattie Mae nudged Sista back and got up to help John Edward assist Ms. Mamie to the table.

"Whatcha got there, Mamie?" Mattie Mae asked. "You feelin' better today?"

"Oh, I feel a whole heap better. I baked a walnut cake this mornin'. I thought it might help y'all feed this crowd."

John Edward shrugged his shoulders as he handed Mattie Mae the burnt bundt cake.

"Ain't no tellin' what Mamie done put in that cake thinkin' it's walnuts," Sista mumbled to herself.

"Mama, do you know if Mary is still here?" John Edward asked Sista, pinching her on the cheeks and looking around for his girlfriend.

Sista slapped his hand away. "She should be over there somewhere wit' Lilly. Check inside the chutch if you don't see her."

"Looks like y'all had a good turnout," Mamie observed. "Everything goin' good?"

"Everything went along fine, Mamie. I think most of Turtle Island showed up too," Mattie Mae stated. "They had a lot of people in the job line and a lot of people signin' up to sing in the choir." Mattie Mae scanned the crowd and saw that Charlotte and Roy had already gone inside to get ready for the auditions. Surprisingly, most people hung around to hear the auditions because of gratitude, and promised to come back on Sunday for service.

"Looks like most folk done gone inside. Let's go on in. Mamie, I'll help you up," Mattie Mae said. The three women strolled inside the packed church and took their seats as the musicians warmed up.

33

It took several minutes for Charlotte and Roy to decide on one more hymn to practice. They finally selected "Amazing Grace" to start with, but there were three people who were so out of tune that one would think they were not only tone deaf, but deaf period. Thus, the process of elimination had begun without great difficulty. One surprise of the evening came from a young man named Goliath James, who was short in stature, but had the voice of a giant. The other surprise came from Sherman, who was one of the best tenors Charlotte had ever heard.

Charlotte wanted to hear him sing solo and Roy agreed. Although Sherman chose a somewhat secular piece to show off his vocal talent, Charlotte was still convinced that he would make a perfect praise and worship leader, if his heart were right. Sherman admitted that he was not an active member, but said nothing of his salvation. He would have to understand that the church needed not only someone who could sing, but someone who knew what they were singing about. A pretty voice was not enough to be an addition to a choir.

Charlotte watched as everyone applauded and honored Sherman with a very deserving standing ovation. She had to talk to him. Since she would be leaving Turtle Island soon, Charlotte hoped that she and Roy could pull together something quickly. As soon as everyone finished singing, Charlotte motioned for Sherman to join her outside to talk.

"Man, I was killin' in there!" Sherman said, bursting with excitement.

"Yeah, you killed. Sherman you really were good, and personally, I think you would be a very good—"

"A very good what?" Sherman asked defensively, sensing a "but" coming.

Witnessing the disappointment settling on Sherman's face, Charlotte could feel her heart sink right along with his. "Sherman, it's one thing to be talented, but it's another to be anointed."

"Anointed?"

"Understand that I'm not the choir director. I'm only here to help, but one of the things I know the church is looking for, especially if you're going to lead a song, is someone who is filled with the Holy Spirit. You have to be able to take a song to another level when you lead. You can't just sing a song and not know the meaning behind it. You knew the words to 'Amazing Grace,' but do you really feel like a wretch that was saved? If you're a praise and worship leader, you have to be able to help lead the congregation to this next level. Do you understand what I'm saying?"

"Not really. I mean, look at how the people acted. I took them to another level."

"I'm afraid some of that was emotion. You said that you weren't an active member. How often do you come to church? More importantly, have you accepted Jesus Christ as your Lord and Savior?"

Without blinking, Sherman stared blankly at Charlotte and said, "I ain't gonna lie to ya. I admit I come to church about four times a year, and most of the times it's 'cause my mama nags me. I know Jesus is God and all that, but I want to get myself together first. Anyway, if I'm in the choir, then that means I'll be in church every Sunday."

"First of all, Sherman, *you* can't get yourself together. Only God can. Secondly, if you are not committed to God, what would be your real reason for showing up every Sunday? You must sing to glorify the Lord, not to receive praises from people."

"God knows my heart," Sherman said with a tinge of despair.

"God does know your heart. In fact, God knows your heart better than you do. Believe me. I'm not trying to discourage you. I just want you to know the truth."

"Okay."

Charlotte smiled, not totally convinced that Sherman did understand. "Please come to church Sunday. It won't be preaching as usual. Maybe you'll get some answers to things that are on your heart. Come on, let's go back inside."

A slightly disappointed Sherman followed Charlotte back inside the church with his head hung low. Charlotte watched as Sherman rejoined his friend, Eric, and she prayed that Sherman would accept Christ in his life and fully understand what she was trying to convey to him.

She noticed a small group of people forming a circle around Jeff and went over to investigate. Charlotte overheard one person ask Jeff what qualified him to teach and he politely explained that he had a background in Hebraic studies, attended theological school, and that the Holy Spirit, along with life itself, were his qualifications.

Roy approached Charlotte liked a messenger delivering an urgent message and told her that Sherman promised him he would come to Sunday services. Sherman had confessed to him his lack of interest and trust in the church and said he had found church to be rather boring in the past. Roy showed Charlotte a list of the members he had chosen for the young adult choir and those chosen for the praise and worship team, and she concurred with his selections. As people began leaving the sanctuary, many spoke about how they were anxious about the upcoming Sunday services.

Now it was time to complete another task: the dirty task of cleaning up. Thankfully, there were a handful of volunteers present for that job. Charlotte hadn't realized how much time had gone by until the reddish orange sun started to set. The day had gone by so quickly. Charlotte looked for the keys to the truck. She thought about how Timmi seemed to be transforming during her short visit.

Sista announced that she would ride home with her son, John Edward. Charlotte noticed that Edmund had already left the church grounds with a vanload of people to take home, and Mattie Mae was complaining of being tired and anxious to get home. Charlotte's mind then drifted back to Sherman as she opened the driver side door of Edmund's truck.

"I can't believe I'm saying this, but I actually had a nice time today," Timmi said as she climbed in the truck, sliding to the middle so that Mattie Mae could sit on the end.

"Everything did turn out nicely, didn't it? Not that you can't ride wit' us, but why aren't you ridin' wit' Jeff, Timmi?" Mattie Mae asked, hoping for sparks to fly between the two.

"No reason, Miss Mattie," Timmi answered, fully aware of Mattie Mae's curiosity.

"Glad to have your company. I just thought you and Jeff were hittin' it off, that's all."

Charlotte looked over at Timmi, raising her eyebrows and grinning from ear to ear.

"Don't look at me like that," Timmi said, rolling her eyes. Charlotte smiled.

No one spoke of what they had been thinking during the ride home. None of them knew that they all were wondering about Tina and Terry. Mattie Mae was so tired that she went straight to bed once she got inside the house. Timmi decided to watch a baseball game on television with Jeff and Edmund. Charlotte opted for a nice, invigorating shower and then to catch up on writing in her journal. She didn't want to forget about the vision she had of Tina and Terry, although she did not have a clue what it meant.

Charlotte went to her bathroom to prepare for her nightly ritual of showering with her favorite sugar scrub, only this night she decided to also treat herself to a much-needed oatmeal facial. The hot summer sun had not been kind to her oily skin. Charlotte thanked God for saving the rain until after the outdoor activities were over as she listened to yet another heavy downpour.

Charlotte stood under the showerhead with the water running full blast and scrubbed off the day's stress. She thought about how even though Reverend Holiday had left a holy mess behind, it looked as if the crooked path he created was about to get straightened out. Now all Greener Pastures needed was an upstanding, anointed minister. Charlotte prayed that Tina and Terry would be found and her Uncle Charles would be delivered.

Charlotte could hear her grandfather, Timmi, and Jeff

protesting from downstairs about an umpire's call as she pulled back the covers on her bed. They could have it. Although she was an avid sports fan, she was too exhausted to do anything but go to sleep. Today's entry into her journal would have to wait until tomorrow. The last thing Charlotte heard as she stretched out on the bed was a loud clap of thunder.

34

Flustered and rushing to be on time for the final day of rehearsal, Charlotte nearly burned her favorite silk blouse with the hot iron. Thankfully, Jeff waited patiently since he was taking her to church. Jeff and Charlotte arrived at Greener Pastures just a tad bit late and found only Roy, Goliath, and Stella Gibson present. Goliath waved at Charlotte while he picked up pieces of paper that people had either carelessly left or purposely dropped on the floor. Stella sat alone in the choir stand with her arms folded and wearing a serious pout. Stella was a beautiful young woman in her mid-twenties, fairly dark in complexion, with deep piercing eyes and the voice of an angel.

"What's wrong with her?" Charlotte asked Roy as she greeted him with a hug.

"Who? Stella? She's just upset, but she'll get over it. I told her that I wanted Goliath to sing the lead on 'Near the Cross.' Trust me. We're better off when she's quiet. If Stella is not singing, she's giving the latest update on the

'Calvin Chronicles' and you don't want to hear it. Believe that!"

"The what? The 'Calvin Chronicles'?" Charlotte's eyebrows furrowed.

Roy laughed. "Calvin is Stella's boyfriend, and she can go on and on 'til the break of dawn about Calvin. We could be over here talking about the moon exploding and Stella will find some kind of way to bring Calvin into the conversation. It's unbelievable."

"It sounds like she wants people to think that her life with Calvin is more than what it really is."

"You mean she tells lies. Everybody knows Calvin hardly pays that girl any attention."

"Roy, where are you from? I can tell you're not from here." Charlotte noticed that Roy did not speak broken English or with a Southern drawl.

"Hampton, Virginia! So, don't hate."

"There's no hateration here, man." Charlotte laughed. "What brings you here?"

"This is my family's church. I had just finished college, and my uncle knew I was looking for work as a musician, so he told me about the church needing a choir director. Their last director had moved back to his hometown. So here I am. I've only been here for five months, and it has been a real challenge, let me tell you."

"I'm sure it has been." Charlotte looked at Stella, who was still sporting a mile-long pout.

Charlotte summoned the newly formed praise and worship team to the front and informed the group that she would lead them in song since this was their first rehearsal. She suggested that whoever was to become the leader should be someone who was willing to share their testimony and be a motivator.

Charlotte wanted everyone to be clear that a praise and worship leader should be a gifted singer and leader.

By the time Charlotte finished her speech, the musicians had finished warming up on their instruments, and in that moment of brief silence, Charlotte heard in her spirit the name Goliath. She didn't know what to make of it, but was sure that in due time she would find out.

After Roy led the group in prayer, he signaled for Charlotte and the musicians to begin. Charlotte and the praise and worship team marched across the pulpit with raised hands, clapping and shouting "hallelujah!" She asked an invisible congregation to stand on their feet and help them praise the Lord, and reminded this pretend audience that Psalm 100:4 says that we are to enter His gates with thanksgiving and that if we did not praise the Lord, the rocks would cry out in our place.

"I don't care what you're going through," Charlotte shouted. "There is always someone out there who's going through something worse than you. Be grateful. No matter what you've lost, God has got something better for you." Charlotte then led the group in the first of four songs they would be singing. One great blessing was the fact that all of the musicians were very skilled and could also play by ear. This was a plus because they were unable to find sheet music for one particular song.

The rehearsal had been so anointed that the entire young adult choir was on their feet and some were even running down the aisles. As soon as the praise and worship team were through, Goliath timidly asked Charlotte if he could have a try at leading. Charlotte looked over at Roy, who said that it was more than fine with him.

Goliath humbly gave his heartfelt story of having suffered cruel teasing and crushing rejection since childhood. Being small in stature, he spoke on how he never seemed to click with anyone or fit into anything. Raised by his grandmother, he grew up listening to gospel hymns, which served as a solace for him. Every day he would sing along with each record his grandmother played on her old RCA stereo. During those years, his voice continued to develop. It wasn't long before Goliath recognized that God had given him a unique gift, and now he found a place that he could fit in, where he felt comfortable—the choir.

Goliath went on to say, "I know y'all can't understand *my* pain, but I know all of you know what pain is." He then broke into song, singing "Because of Who You Are" with the musicians playing with perfect precision. The atmosphere was so emotionally charged that Charlotte had not noticed Jeff sitting in the back watching the ushering in and the work of the Holy Spirit. She thought he had left.

When the song was over, Goliath was so overwhelmed by the warm reception and embraces he received, that he could hardly contain himself. As Charlotte took a seat in one of the deacon chairs to wait for her turn to hug Goliath, she saw Jeff walking toward her.

"That was something else," Jeff remarked.

"It sure was." Charlotte could feel perspiration under her arms and wanted to kick herself for wearing her silk blouse on such a warm morning. *I hope this blouse isn't soaking wet by the time I leave here,* she said to herself. Focusing back on Jeff, she said, "I don't know if the choir has enough energy to rehearse their songs after that."

"I know what you mean. Do you have a minute?"

"Sure, what's up?"

Jeff directed Charlotte to a pew so that they could talk in private. "I want you to look over my notes for tomorrow. Tell me what you think, or if you can think of something that I should add," Jeff said.

Charlotte sat next to Jeff as he handed her a notebook. After taking her time to read them, Charlotte nodded her head in approval.

"It looks good to me. The only other thing I can think of is that you might want to ask for a show of hands of how many people did not accept Christ because they think Christians live a boring life or because they think too many church folk are hypocrites," Charlotte added.

"Good point." Jeff jotted down what Charlotte said and excused himself to talk to Goliath. Soon afterwards, Jeff returned to tell Charlotte that he needed to go to Clark to drop off the job applications before the plant closed and then he would drive her back home. Although she would have loved to stick around to hear the choir rehearse, Charlotte was satisfied with the praise and worship team's rehearsal and knew that Roy was more than capable of handling his task. Before she left, Charlotte finally got her chance to kiss a blushing Goliath on his already rosy cheek.

"That was inspiring, Goliath," Charlotte said. Still blushing, Goliath thanked Charlotte before joining the rest of the choir. Charlotte looked back as she was leaving to see that even Stella's attitude had now changed. Apparently, Goliath's testimony and singing was used as a ministering tool to get Stella's mind off of herself.

Jeff backed out of the gravel-laden parking lot and headed toward Mattie Mae's house to drop off Charlotte. Standing near the edge of the driveway were Mattie Mae, Sista, and Timmi.

"I hope Miss Sista didn't wear out Timmi's nerves," Jeff said, laughing.

Charlotte chuckled as well. "Timmi can hold her own. You see she's still standing. I'll see you later, Jeff. Drive carefully."

Jeff pulled over to the side and checked his rearview mirror for any oncoming cars as Charlotte got out and waved goodbye. Jeff waved back and drove off. Charlotte walked over to the women, who stood there waiting for her.

"How was rehearsal?" Timmi asked.

"Awesome! I'm sorry I didn't wake you up to come with me, but I thought that you might have wanted to sleep a little longer."

"I did. I've been getting up early every morning since kindergarten, and I can't remember the last time I've gotten a chance to sleep in late. Anyway, it gave me a chance to get reacquainted with your grandmother and *real* acquainted with Miss Sista," Timmi said, winking her eye at Charlotte.

"What are you guys doing out here anyway?" Charlotte asked.

Sista immediately jumped at the chance to answer the question. "I was right in the middle of pressin' out this here shirt to wear for a funeral they havin' at Piney Grove today," Sista said.

Charlotte was stunned. Sista stood before her looking utterly ridiculous in a pink, orange, and yellow floral print blouse and a green-and-blue plaid skirt. Her bony knees revealed a pair of legs cloaked in suntan-colored knee-highs that were held up by thin rubber bands. And to top it all off, Sista wore a pair of black running shoes with extra-long white shoelaces.

Sista held up her wrinkled blue-and-white striped shirt and continued her saga. "I was just a-pressin' this shirt and I noticed the wrinkles weren't comin' out. I went and got some water to put in the iron, thinkin' it could use some steam, never thinkin' to check and see if the iron was hot. I went and laid the iron on the shirt and all the water spilled out on it. Look at all these brown spots! I came over here to use Mattie Mae's iron, thinkin' somethin' wrong wit' my iron. On the way over here I remembered leavin' my radio on at the house, but I didn't remember hearin' it when I left. That's when I saw Satan down the road. She was askin' Mattie Mae if her power was out."

"Satan?" Charlotte asked, looking confused. Charlotte noticed from the corner of her eye that Timmi also seemed confused.

"Yeah, you know her as Nellie. I know she goin' to the funeral today if ain't nobody there but her and the casket," Sista said.

Mattie Mae rolled her eyes and shook her head at Sista.

"The lights didn't go out at the church?" Sista asked.

"They were still on when we left the church."

"They just went out 'bout ten minutes ago," Mattie Mae said, looking quite serious. "I was on the phone wit' Edmund and he said that Mary was tryin' to find Joe. She said the ambulance came and took Lilly to the hospital. Lilly was flourin' some chicken and said she was havin' chest pains. Then she just fell out on the floor. I sho' hope it ain't nothin' serious. The lights kept flickerin' in and out while I was on the phone wit' Edmund, and then the phone just went dead."

"Oh, wow! So you don't know if Ms. Lilly is all right?" Charlotte asked.

"We don't know," Mattie Mae and Sista said at the same time.

"Do you know where Granddaddy was?" Charlotte asked.

"No, the phone went out befo' we got a chance to really talk, but I think he might have been at the feed store. I don't like my telephone. Every time you lose power the phone goes out."

"Why don't we go inside the house? The electricity may be back on. If it's not, we can use my cell phone," Charlotte suggested. "Besides, we're standing out here roasting in this sun."

Sista pardoned herself to go home in case the electricity was back on, so that she could finish getting ready for the funeral. Charlotte, Mattie Mae, and Timmi started toward the house when they heard Edmund's truck approaching. They moved to the side to let a speeding Edmund pass. As they got near him, Mattie Mae could tell by the look on her husband's face as he got out of the truck that something was terribly wrong. Edmund was shaking so badly that it was a wonder he made it home safely at all.

"Edmund, say somethin', why don't you? Is it Lilly? What happened?" Mattie Mae asked frantically.

"I'll get you a glass of water, Mr. Edmund," Timmi said, racing toward the house.

Edmund leaned against the truck while Mattie Mae and Charlotte repeatedly asked him what was wrong.

35

"Mattie . . . Joe is dead," Edmund said.

Mattie Mae screamed. "Joe? What Joe? What are you talkin' about? You just called and said they rushed Lilly to the hospital."

"I know, I know." Edmund kept shaking his head.

Grabbing Edmund by the arm, Charlotte said, "Granddaddy, let us help you onto the porch so you can sit down."

Timmi had returned with a glass of cold water and helped Charlotte assist a grief-stricken Edmund to the front porch. Walking like a zombie, Mattie Mae followed closely behind. Mattie Mae sat beside her husband while Charlotte and Timmi stood by waiting for him to explain what had happened.

A heartbroken Mattie Mae placed her hand in Edmund's hand and repeated, "Edmund, honey, what happened?"

"Me and Joe was at the feed store and somebody, I don't remember who it was, came in and said that the ambulance just carried Lilly off to the hospital. They said somethin' about her havin' chest pains. Joe ran outta the store befo' I could pay for the hog feed. By the time I got outside, he was already gone, and I couldn't have been no more than five minutes behind him, Mattie Mae."

Edmund's hand trembled as he carefully took a sip of water. "I had just turned on Highway Eight, hopin' to catch up wit' Joe, and then I saw his truck. He had to have been drivin' too fast, 'cause I don't see how else he could have smashed into that light pole like that."

Mattie Mae started rocking back and forth while Charlotte and Timmi both gasped. Charlotte figured that the fatal accident was the probable cause for the power outage. Suddenly, the sound of the television came back on, and Charlotte went inside to answer the ringing telephone. Timmi took the glass of water from Edmund for fear of him dropping it. She felt helpless as she watched Mattie Mae try to console her husband.

"Edmund, I can't believe this has happened. Are you sure Joe is dead?" Mattie Mae asked in disbelief.

"Mattie Mae, I know a dead person when I see one! I went up to the truck—"

"It's okay," Mattie Mae said, patting him gently on the back, not wanting Edmund to relive what he had just seen. "Was anybody else around?"

"People were already there when I got there. It happened right in front of Sam Miller's house, and somebody from the house called for an ambulance."

Mattie Mae was just about to ask about Lilly when Edmund seemingly read her mind.

"I came back here to get you. I thought we should go and check on Lilly. I guess Mary or somebody from the shop will call Shelley, if they hadn't already done so. I just don't know what to do." Edmund threw up his hands and leaned back in the chair.

Timmi was the first to see Charlotte come back outside, and she could tell that more bad news was imminent. Mattie Mae was too busy trying to be strong for her husband to notice Charlotte. She and Edmund had been friends with Joe and Lilly Green for many years, even though the Greens were a slightly younger couple. Mattie Mae looked up and saw Charlotte standing beside her.

"Who was that on the phone?" Mattie Mae asked Charlotte.

"Miss Sista," Charlotte answered solemnly.

Mattie Mae took her arms from around Edmund's shoulders and directed her attention toward Charlotte. "Sista called to tell us about Joe?" Mattie Mae asked.

With dread, Charlotte answered, "No, ma'am, not really. Miss Sista heard about his death, and she wanted to be sure that you knew already. I told her that you did." Charlotte and Timmi looked at each other and could literally feel Edmund and Mattie Mae's pain. Charlotte slowly announced, "Miss Sista said that Ms. Lilly just passed away."

Mattie Mae felt her heart pounding ever so fast as Edmund leaned forward and rested his head on her shoulder without uttering a sound.

"Miss Sista said that Ms. Lilly had a massive heart attack in the ambulance before she got inside the hospital. I am so sorry," Charlotte said.

Mattie Mae mumbled something about things happening in threes and the Lord knowing what's best. Mattie Mae suggested to Edmund that he go upstairs, lie down, and get some rest. She would take care of everything.

* * *

It had now been three hours since the shocking news of the sudden deaths of Joe and Lilly Green had rocked the community, and the Morley telephone had been ringing off the hook ever since. Edmund, who had lost his appetite, did manage to drink a full cup of tea before falling asleep. Charlotte and Timmi sat in the kitchen and waited for Mattie Mae to finish her conversation. Once Mattie Mae hung up the phone, she informed Charlotte and Timmi of what she knew and told them that, once again, they would be taking food over to another house of mourners and that Joe and Lilly's only child, Shelley, should be arriving from Atlanta within the next hour. Joe and Lilly's eldest child, Joseph, died from leukemia when he was ten years old.

According to witnesses, Joe had been speeding on the narrow stretch of highway and apparently lost control of his truck. The truck flipped over in a ditch and then rammed into a utility pole, where it rested in a crumpled heap. Sadly, the paramedics pronounced Joe, who suffered from a broken neck, dead at the scene. Joe never got the chance to see his wife, nor did Lilly survive long enough to learn of his death. The double funeral services would most certainly draw a huge crowd of mourners, blacks as well as whites.

Mattie Mae checked on the beef short ribs baking in the oven and enlisted the help of Charlotte and Timmi to peel and cut the red russet potatoes, bell peppers, and celery for a potato salad.

In an attempt to break such a somber atmosphere, Mattie Mae went on to tell them what Sista told her about the shenanigans that went on at Caleb's Funeral Home when they held homegoing service for Lucille's daughter. Sista said that half of Lucille's family was drunk, while the others dared to join Sasha in the grave. "Honorary family member" Nellie had been spotted and ceremoniously removed from the family lineup. Amazingly, and by the grace of God, Lucille had remained calm during the drama.

The soloist, Stella Gibson, who rushed over immediately after choir rehearsal, sang a song that lasted thirty minutes. Sista said that everyone was able to keep up with Stella at first because they all knew the song, but then Stella started adding verses. Sista said that Stella performed as if they were on television, so she turned around to see if there were any cameras. Furthermore, a he said/she said type of argument had erupted during the repast.

Someone mentioned they heard someone else say that one of Lucille's nephews was trying to slide the Rolex watch off of Sasha's wrist during the viewing. At this point, Sista decided that she had had enough and it was time for her to leave. That family was too violent even for her. Violence was just something that passed down the Johnson generation like blood flowing through veins. Even Lucille's and Cora's mother kept a pocketknife in her bra up until the time she died at age ninety.

Charlotte glanced apologetically at Timmi. Timmi didn't seem to mind her short visit being marred by such sadness. She sat there dutifully chopping celery and hanging on to every word that came from Mattie Mae's mouth. Perhaps it was because of Timmi's admiration of close-knit families and community involvement.

As Mattie Mae kneaded the dough for a batch of her mouth-watering sugar biscuits, she recalled Ms. Mamie's telephone request to stop by her house and pick up some chitlins she was making for the Green family.

"Mamie know good and well she ain't able to clean no chitlins. We'll just leave it in the car when we go over to Lilly's house." Mattie Mae managed to laugh for the first time since the deaths. "If I had the time, I'd put on a pot of catfish stew and some rice. Maybe I'll fix that tomorrow, or maybe some oxtails, 'cause I might not go to chutch tomorrow," Mattie Mae said, wiping away a tear. Charlotte and Timmi remained quiet.

"Hello, ladies," Jeff announced as he came into the kitchen.

Mattie Mae waved a flour-covered hand and Timmi gave a sad smile.

"I was beginning to worry about you. What took you so long?" Charlotte asked Jeff. Then Charlotte realized how much she sounded like a worried wife.

"I had one other thing to take care of, and then I ran by the store to pick up a few personal items. I heard about Joe and Lilly Green," Jeff said, looking at Mattie Mae. "Where is Uncle Edmund? I know how close he was to Mr. Green."

"Edmund is upstairs resting. He's a little shook up right now," Mattie Mae replied. "We know that God is in control. We just have to trust that he'll help us all through this. Busta called a little while ago and he kept sayin' how he just couldn't believe it."

"Did you get to the plant before they closed?" Timmi asked Jeff, purposely changing the subject to avoid a room full of sadness again.

"I did. Hopefully, they'll be calling people for interviews as soon as next week."

"That's good. I think I'll go check on Granddaddy," Charlotte said as she got up from the kitchen table. Mattie Mae instructed Charlotte to go ahead and wake Edmund from his nap. They needed to get ready to leave the house.

Charlotte climbed the stairs leading up to her grandparents' bedroom, trying to formulate some words of comfort and encouragement for her grandfather. She gently knocked on the door and then slowly opened it. Edmund was standing at the window, blankly staring out.

"Granddaddy, can I come in?" she asked.

"Come on in, Charlotte," Edmund said while reaching for his suspenders from the nightstand.

"I came to see if you were okay and to tell you that Grandma said we should be getting ready to leave soon."

"Just give me a minute to put my shoes on," Edmund said, his voice cracking.

"I can drive if you want me to," Charlotte offered.

"No, that's all right. Me and Busta will probably kill a hog for barbecue tomorrow to help feed. I know a lot of folk will be comin to town for this one."

"Yeah, Grandma said that my dad had called and said that he and Mama are coming. I think Aunt Willa and Aunt Mattie are coming too."

"More than likely. They got family spread out all over the place. Pass me my belt from off the dresser." Charlotte handed Edmund his black alligator belt that one of her cousins bought for him last Christmas.

"Well, I came up here to talk to you, but to be honest, I don't even know what to say."

"Just folk comin' together and helpin' out is word enough. I lost a good friend today. I lost two good friends, but Shelley lost a mother and a father at the same time. I'm an old man now, Charlotte. I done seen a lot of people come and go. Me and yo' grandmama was the babies in our families. We done buried both our parents and near 'bout buried all our sisters and brothers. We get happy when a baby is born, but when a person dies . . . that should remind us that we ain't here to stay forever. The decisions we make here on this earth are important, 'cause one of those decisions determine where we go when we die. Run along now befo' yo' grandmama get to hollerin' up here."

Charlotte felt like crying. This old man, whom she came upstairs to comfort, had done a reversal and spoke words of wisdom and comfort to her. Charlotte hugged Edmund tightly and kissed him on the cheek before leaving the room. Surely Edmund, who was so distraught mere hours ago, had received his comfort from God during his nap.

36

Edmund, Busta, and other neighbors were busy making homemade sausages for Shelley and her family. Jeff, Charlotte, Timmi, and Mattie Mae had just left Mamie's house to pick up her chitlin dish. Even though all the windows in the Hummer were rolled down, Jeff searched for the nearest trash can to throw out the foul-smelling piece of pork. After pulling over to the first Dumpster he saw, Charlotte jumped out and tossed the aluminum pan in.

The dusty air was cloudy and thick from dirt disturbed by farmers who were still plowing in the fields. The long driveway leading to Joe and Lilly Green's French country manor was lined with vehicles of all kinds, and the sight of Shelley's SUV indicated that she had arrived. Jeff, Charlotte, and Timmi started unloading the vehicle and quickly made their way to the sprawling red brick house. Sista greeted them as she passed by the trio, making her way toward Mattie Mae.

"Poor Shelley looks downright pitiful," Sista said.

"I guess so. Everything happened so fast. Where is she?"

"Inside the house," Sista answered as she and Mattie Mae pressed through the crowd of visitors.

The wreath on the front door was a solemn reminder that someone from Caleb's Funeral Home had been there. Some of the same faces that had been at Lucille's house were now at Joe and Lilly's home. Mattie Mae nodded at ole man Johnson as she passed by him in the foyer. Ole man Johnson, who was as blatantly nosey as Sista, stood at a podium flipping through the pages of the guest book, looking at the names. Mattie Mae noticed that dozens of sympathy cards had replaced the family photos that once graced the fireplace mantle.

Mattie Mae and Sista found Shelley, whose eyes were red and swollen from crying, in her late mother's gourmet kitchen trying to make sure everyone was being served. Wearing a pair of faded jeans and an oversized white shirt, Shelley could easily pass for a teenager.

"You know, when my girls were little," Sista said to Mattie Mae while looking at Shelley, "they hated when I used to braid their hair. I had to pop 'em on the hands all the time to get 'em to keep still. Now these girls grow up and pay all that money for somebody to do that to their heads."

"That's the style these young people wearin' these days. They call 'em twists or somethin' like that. You re-member Charlotte used to wear her hair like that," Mat-tie Mae stated.

"Twists! They look more like naps outta control if you ask me."

As soon as Shelley turned around from the stove, she spotted Mattie Mae in the doorway. Shelley walked over and literally collapsed in Mattie Mae's arms. "Ms. Mat-tie, I'm so glad to see you." Shelly started sobbing. "I don't know how I'm going to get through this."

Mattie Mae lifted up Shelley's chin and said, "The Lawd will help you through this, Shelley. You got yo' husband and yo' chi'ren, and ya got us."

Shelley lifted her head and dried her eyes with the cuff of her sleeve and said, "You know, Mommy and Dad weren't too crazy at first about me and Patrick getting married so soon after graduating from college. I'm glad we didn't listen to them, and eventually they were too. I don't know what I'd do without him or my sons."

Mattie Mae took Shelley's hand and led her away from the kitchen. "Come on, let's get outta here. People know how to fend for themselves."

Meanwhile, Sista stayed behind and went over to the kitchen island to check out the potluck. Standing beside her was one of Shelley's uppity sorority sisters, Felicia. She came with Shelley and her family from Atlanta to Turtle Island. Decked out in diamonds and expensive clothing, Felicia practically ordered people to sample her food, and made sure that no one took more than a spoonful of servings. Sista instantly peeped the snob's card.

"What is this?" Sista asked Felicia, lifting off the glass top of a casserole dish.

"*This* is called bubble and squeak. It's a British dish," Felicia said proudly. "And this over here is eggplant." Felicia pointed to a large blue-and-white casserole dish.

"Well, *this* right here looks like plain ole beef and cabbage to me, and *that* over there . . . Chile, don't nobody 'round here eat eggplant. That's for white folk," Sista said, skinning up her nose. "You got any okra, or better yet, some sweet peas in here? I know Johnny Mae brought some butter beans and okra here. That may be all she can cook, but Johnny Mae makes some good butter beans and okra."

Felicia made a loud hissing noise, slammed the tops back on the casserole bowls, and stormed out of the kitchen. Unhinged, Sista found a pot of Johnny Mae Baxter's butter beans and okra with seasoned pepper and fatback. She happily helped herself.

Everyone except for Edmund, who was still at Busta Watkins's house barbecuing, had returned home after an extremely draining day. Fortunately for Charlotte, all of the members of the praise and worship team were present at Joe and Lilly's house, saving her from making late-night phone calls. She had instructed the team to wear a solid bright-colored shirt or blouse with black pants or skirt for tomorrow's service. Charlotte had forgotten to give them this information at that morning's rehearsal. She had intended to purchase corsages from the local florist's shop for the women to wear, but with the deaths of Joe and Lilly Green, it had completely slipped her mind.

Jeff sat alone in the guest bedroom rewriting his opening speech to factor in some words of encouragement. He knew that many people did not understand why God would allow Shelley to experience such devastation, and he wasn't sure if he could properly explain it. The only thing he did know was that God held all the answers. Jeff said a short prayer, asking the Lord to give him the words to write, and then he turned on his laptop. He clicked on the icon to create a new document entitled "Greener Pastures" and typed:

Good morning, church. I ask that everyone please stand for prayer. Oh, Heavenly Father, thank you for waking us up this morning because of the mercy, grace and purpose that you have for each and every one of us. I thank you for the forgiveness that you have bestowed upon us. Thank you for being the supplier of our needs. Let your Holy Spirit flow in this place and in the hearts of the bereaved

Green and Johnson families. Now, Lord, as we prepare to worship you today, I ask for your manna for us all. Speak through me to them. Speak to them individually. This is our prayer, and we give thanks for your answer. Let the church come in agreement by saying amen.

Jeff then typed in a footnote as a reminder to refer to the Old Testament chapter of Isaiah 57: 1 and 2 as one possible explanation for untimely deaths.

Meanwhile, Mattie Mae was sound asleep in her room, and Charlotte and Timmi were downstairs in the living room having a little girl talk while Timmi rolled up Charlotte's hair. Soon afterwards, a very weary Edmund came through the front door, mumbled "goodnight," and went upstairs.

"I really feel sorry for your grandfather. He looks so sad," Timmi noted.

"I know. He never showed up at the Green's house. It's hard for me to believe that they are gone. I've known them for as long as I've known you. I remember hearing a rumor that Granddaddy and Mr. Joe were really half-brothers."

"Get out! You know, since you've said that, they did resemble each other. I only saw Mr. Green that one time at the clothes drive, but I remember thinking about how much they looked alike around the eyes. They even walked alike."

"They sure did. Granddaddy always denied the rumor, but Grandma said that she believed it was the truth. People said that my granddaddy's father used to hang around Mr. Joe's house before and after Mr. Joe was born, claiming that Mr. Joe's mother was all alone and needed help around the house. It's my understanding that Mr. Joe's mother never married. Boy, our ancestors sure did their dirt back in the day too."

"Tell me about it. I don't know what it was. Mr. Joe's mother needed help around the house, huh? Sounds to me like your great-grandfather helped himself to a little somethin'-somethin'. All I know is that the older generation dabbled in sin like everybody else, but they were a hypocritical, shame-based generation. This generation we have now! Whew! They thrive on shock value and will throw it in your face. What in God's name has happened to us? People are going to hell in a handbasket." Timmi combed out Charlotte's hair.

"Special delivery at that. Somewhere along the line, I guess people stopped keeping watch."

"What do you mean?" Timmi fastened a roller on a lock of Charlotte's freshly permed hair.

"Slowly but surely things have become more and more acceptable. Everybody winks at mess instead of praying about it."

Timmi reached for another hard plastic roller from Charlotte's bag and said, "Charlotte, I never told you this, but I really do admire you. Your faith was something that I never understood. You've been there for me through a lot of ups and downs, and you've had your share of heartache as well. But me, I held on to my neediness and looked to all the wrong people and things to medicate my pain. Each mistake I made caused just that much more grief in my life, and you just kept getting stronger."

"Timmi, you just don't know how many tears I've shed when I was alone. Putting on a happy face when you feel like you're dying inside can be hard work. Trust me, it's not always that easy believing that God is going to come through for you, especially when you go through something for a long time. Process, it's all a part of process."

"Process?"

"Process, girl. Sometimes, and this is just my belief, but sometimes I think that while some of the things we go through do hurt us personally, we can't take it personally."

"That's a lie! I take things personally—very personally, and I have a right to do so."

"No, I'm serious, Timmi. Your situation with Bobby may really be your opportunity to help someone who may go through the same thing. You can't counsel anybody on anything you don't know about. You may help prevent someone from going through the same thing because you know the signs to look for. Remember when we were in high school and this boy was in that car wreck and lost one of his arms? Oh, I can't think of his name. You know who I'm talking about, right?"

"Yeah," Timmi said, scratching her head. "It's right on the tip of my tongue. . . . Carl Shepherd! I think he opened up some kind of center."

"That's right, Carl Shepherd. The Carl Shepherd Rehabilitation Center. It's a rehab for amputees."

"That's a high price to pay to help somebody—losing your arm." Timmi sprayed Charlotte's hair with some spritz.

"It is, but it's not as high a price as hanging on a cross with your entrails hanging out and people mocking you."

"Jesus!"

"Exactly. Jesus. When you get a chance, read the Old Testament Book of Job. That man lost everything within the blink of an eye almost, but in the end he was restored with double. And the story of Joseph tells of how he was betrayed by his own jealous brothers. Joseph spent years in prison, but God raised him up, and his brothers, the same people who betrayed him, ended up needing him to survive. It takes God to help you help anyone who betrays you."

"Girl, it would have to take God or me being high out of my mind on crack to help *anybody* who stabbed me in my back. I must say I'm impressed with your Bible knowledge. Then again, being an ordained minister, you *should* know the Bible. Are you planning on having your own church one day?"

Charlotte laughed. "I don't think so, but you never know. I know that I'm called to minister. Right now, I'm just going with the flow."

"When do you plan to go back home?" Timmi asked, smoothing out the ends of Charlotte's hair and wrapping it around a roller.

"I'll stay another week to attend the funeral. My parents are coming down for it, so maybe I'll go back with them. If I were still working at the design store, I probably wouldn't be down here now."

"Why do you say that?"

"Because Mrs. Cavendish acted like she didn't want me to leave her sight to go to the bathroom, let alone take a vacation. I know she owns the store, but I was handling the bulk of her clients. I was out there hustling while she stayed in the store talking tea and crumpets over the phone with her friends back in England. Half of the clients were next to impossible to please, while the other half thought that not only was I there to decorate their homes, but I was supposed to clean them too! Girl, there was this one client, a black female mind you, and you could tell that she wasn't used to anything, but she married a man who was. All she did was brag. Brag and boast, boast and brag. She even bragged about how much her dog cost *and* how much she paid for his little Louis Vuitton carrier bag."

"I didn't know that they made designer bags for dogs." Timmi laughed.

"That pampered mutt had more designer items than most human beings."

"I never knew you felt like Ms. Cavendish had been taking you for granted."

"Not only that. I don't even know how to explain it. I just knew my time there was over."

"So, you don't plan to go back there to work?"

"No, bless God. I thought about doing some writing. Maybe I can get the idea sold on my pastor and put a production together using our drama ministry."

"Sounds good to me. Go for it."

"I don't know. We'll see."

After Timmi snapped the last roller into place on Charlotte's hair, she sprayed her hair once more with spritz. "I've been meaning to ask you who was that lady Miss Sista was snapping at when we were over at the Green family home."

Charlotte thought for a minute, trying to remember the incident and then said, "Oh, I know who you're talking about. That was Nellie. The woman Miss Sista had referred to as Satan," Charlotte said. "Every time Miss Sista sees Nellie with a piece of chicken she thinks it's one of her yard birds."

Noticing the puzzled look on Timmi's face as she got up from the floor, Charlotte went on to further explain. "Nellie's husband, Otis, is the town's alleged chicken thief. Or at least, Sista suspects him of stealing her chickens, I should say."

Timmi doubled over with laughter. "What? They don't have KFC here?" Timmi asked.

"You know what? They don't, come to think of it. I wouldn't be surprised if Miss Sista starts keeping her chickens in the house."

"That's too funny. Maybe she *should* keep her chickens

on lock down. Oh yeah, I also peeped out what's her name, Shelley's friend from Atlanta. Old girl was strutting around there like she was blue-blooded royalty."

"Felicia. Yeah, I saw that. Well, you know some people you just have to overlook."

"Some people don't want to be overlooked. Felicia was telling that lady Nellie how bad fried foods were for your health, and Nellie's response to her was that she didn't care if she died with a greasy piece of pork chop still hanging from her lip; she had to die from something and it might as well be from something that tasted good. Then this Nellie person and Miss Sista, who were fussing at each other earlier, turned around and tag-teamed the girl! It was hilarious. Miss Sista told Miss Nellie not to pay the girl any attention because she was just trying to find somebody to eat her eggplant. Girl, these folk around here are funny to me."

"They are," Charlotte said. "I don't remember seeing Felicia. Where was I during all of that?"

"She wasn't over there then."

Charlotte looked at her watch and said, "Girl, it's one o'clock in the morning. I need to get in the bed. Timmi, I really hate to see you leave tomorrow."

Timmi followed Charlotte upstairs and said, "You say that like you're not coming back to D.C. We'll see each other soon. I'm even thinking about visiting your church again."

"I know, but your visit was so short, and as for the church, you know the doors are always open. You can keep visiting as much as you want. We'll just call you an honorary visitor until you join."

Timmi rolled her eyes and said, "I want you to know that I had a good time in spite of all this tragedy. I really feel sorry for Shelley, losing both of her parents like that. But you know . . . it really felt good to be around people who are real. The way people come together in time of need . . . that's what it's all about. I've not been interested in going out for a drink and socializing since I've been here. All is well, Charlotte. I just hate that I can't pack up Miss Sista and take her back with me. She would be a good luck charm in the courtroom." Timmi chuckled. As she opened her bedroom door, she was instantly met by what felt like steam.

"My goodness! My room feels like a sauna," Timmi said.

"Check your vents. I bet Grandma accidentally closed it. I'll turn up the air conditioner anyway. It is rather warm tonight. I'll see you in the morning."

"See you in the morning," Timmi responded as Charlotte went back downstairs to check out the thermostat.

37

Charlotte lifted her head from the pillow to find all of her hard green plastic rollers on the floor near the head of her bed. She vaguely remembered snatching them out of her head so that she could rest comfortably. It was now nine o'clock in the morning. Charlotte got up and went to the bathroom to wash her face and brush her teeth. As she stood at the sink deciding on wearing her red ankle-length dress and a pair of black Nine West pumps, she could hear Jeff walking across the plank floors in the bedroom next to hers.

Charlotte stood in the bathtub and adjusted the shower cap around her head for full coverage. She then allowed the water pellets to beat against her body, giving the same soothing effects as the hands of a skilled masseuse. Charlotte poured a few drops of lime and coconut body wash onto a sponge, lathered up her body, and started singing in the shower.

"Good morning," Jeff announced to Mattie Mae and Edmund as he entered the kitchen.

"Morning, Jeff," Edmund replied, dipping his biscuit in syrup with one hand and pulling out the chair next to him for Jeff with his other.

"Sit down and have some breakfast," Mattie Mae said as she came forward, placing a few scoops of grits on the plate set before Jeff.

Spread out on the table, as if the Morleys were giving a banquet, were hefty servings of bacon, sausage patties, slices of liver pudding, various fruits, biscuits, French toast, scrambled eggs, and boiled eggs. Jeff tucked the corner end of a napkin in the collar of his white starched shirt. After spreading the napkin out over his chest, he placed another napkin in his lap.

"Good morning. I hope everybody slept well last night," Timmi said as she entered the kitchen, looking quite cute in a gray satin dress that hugged every curve of her figure-eight body.

"Good morning," Mattie Mae, Edmund, and Jeff responded back. Mattie Mae, who was already seated, told Timmi to help herself to some breakfast and asked if she knew whether Charlotte was up.

"I heard her moving around in her room," Timmi answered as she fixed herself a bowl of grits and butter. Seconds later, Charlotte appeared and joined her family. After everyone finished their meal, Jeff led them all in prayer and ended it with a request for the safe return of Charles, Francine, Tina, and Terry.

Jeff placed Timmi's luggage in his vehicle while Charlotte and Timmi took their seats inside. Mattie Mae, who decided to go to church after all, wrote out a note for Charles and Francine, stating that she and Edmund would be at Joe and Lilly's house following church service, and taped it on the screen door. She then got in the truck with her husband, and they trailed behind Jeff.

From his rearview mirror, Jeff noticed that Edmund had stopped at the edge of Miss Sista's lane to pick her up.

At Greener Pastures, the church parking lot was filled with cars, forcing Jeff and Edmund to park behind the church. As Charlotte and Timmi got out, they both waved at Sista, who was wearing a lime green hat, a forest green suit, pea green shoes, and carrying a mint green handbag.

"I don't mean any harm," Timmi whispered to Charlotte as they went inside the church, "but that ensemble Miss Sista is wearing is really speaking."

"Yes. Volumes! But you gotta love her," Charlotte said.

Charlotte went on to the back where all the singers were waiting, while Timmi, Edmund, Mattie Mae, and Sista searched for seats out front. Jeff went to take a seat in one of the burgundy leather armchairs in the pulpit next to Jesse Franklin, a theological student. After Roy said a prayer with the singers and musicians, they all marched out to take their places in the choir stand. Charlotte couldn't help noticing how happy Goliath looked, and she felt happy for him.

From her position in the choir stand, Charlotte studied the quiet congregation. Apparently, her suggestion that the ushers remind the congregation to keep quiet when entering the Lord's house had paid off. They were as quiet as church mice. In Charlotte's opinion, showing reverence for the Lord and respect for people who might want to pray in peace was important, and a matter of order. The members of Greener Pastures had a habit of chatting loudly before service started, as if they were at a party.

Jeff slowly got up from his seat and walked over to the Lucite podium. After he finished his introductory speech and opening prayer, he beckoned for the praise and worship team to come forward. While some of the members were a little reluctant at first to join in, most of the people eagerly participated in praise and worship. Everyone in the sanctuary participated by clapping their hands, nodding their heads, or patting their feet—everyone except for one person.

Mother Christine Hadley, who was about eighty-eight years old, sat with her arms folded and lips poked out, mainly because no one made her the center of attention as they usually did on Sunday mornings. This Sunday, Mother Hadley was being upstaged by a much higher and greater power.

After Charlotte led the team in a powerful worship service, Goliath led the choir with his touching version of the song, "It's Good to Know Jesus." Not a dry eye was in the house, not even Mother Hadley's. The shouting and crying was almost to the point of being chaotic. Once everyone had settled down, Jeff came back to the podium and proclaimed the goodness of God.

"People, we have so much to be thankful for. The Word of God says that the suffering we go through is only a light affliction! After we've suffered for a little while . . . OH GLORY! Brother Goliath, come over here and join me, please. I want everyone present to hear your latest testimony," Jeff said.

I wonder what's going on, Charlotte thought as she watched Goliath take the microphone from Jeff.

Goliath held the microphone to his mouth and started weeping and jumping. After unashamedly displaying his emotions for a minute, Goliath finally spoke through tears of joy and said, "I don't know how to thank God or Brother Jeff. What no one knows is that after rehearsal yesterday, Mr. Coates, I mean Jeff, got my address from Roy, and when Jeff came back from Clark, he came to my house and had me to sing. While I was singing, he made a demo and downloaded it to a friend of his in Nashville.

This friend of his happens to be the President of Redeemer Records. The President from Redeemer Records called me this morning, just when I was getting ready to leave the house to come here, and asked me if I would be interested in a contract deal and if I could come up there to Nashville to meet with him. I'm leaving tomorrow to sign as a gospel artist. Glory! Hallelujah!" Goliath shouted and handed the microphone back to Jeff. Goliath raised his clenched fists in the air and started jumping up and down.

By this time, more than half of the congregation stood on their feet, rejoicing with Goliath. Charlotte had to restrain herself from running over to Goliath, picking him up, and squeezing him like a roll of Charmin. Jeff high-fived Goliath and waited for Goliath to return to his seat in the choir stand before speaking. Jeff paced back and forth across the pulpit until everyone was seated.

"First, let me say to you, church, thank you for allowing me to speak to you today. It is an honor to be used by God for such a time as this. But how many of you know that God can use anybody for whatever He wants? If He can use a donkey to speak, He can use anybody! If He can use a virgin girl to give birth to His Son, He can use anybody! If He can use a prostitute to help two of His chosen people, He can use anybody!" Jeff shouted as his analogies were met with echoes of approval.

"God can use anybody, so don't ever look down on a person because of what *you* think. God can use anybody. Be careful of who you reject because God has a tendency to raise up those very ones you've rejected. I don't know who that was for; that wasn't part of *my* planned speech," Jeff continued. "Like myself, how many people here today are visitors? Please stand. I want to ask that the ushers pass out some books for you, and we hope that these books will bless and enrich your lives."

Most of the visitors were some of the people who

resided in the Cabbage Patch area. Charlotte looked for Sherman and was disappointed that she didn't see him. She did, however, see his friend, Eric, sitting behind Timmi. Charlotte figured that Eric came as a token of gratitude for Timmi's help in filling out his job application. The choir had begun singing another selection, and the ushers were busy passing out the collection plates for tithes and offerings.

Charlotte opened her purse and looked for the twenty-dollar bill she had tucked away in her change purse. After having found the crumpled bill, she placed it in the plate and quickly passed the plate on to the person in the next row. After the choir ended their song, Jeff returned to the podium, and Charlotte closed her eyes for a brief second.

As if watching a television program, Charlotte saw a quick flash of a woman wearing a yellow spaghetti-strap top, and she recognized the woman as either Tina or Terry. Although they were identical twins, there was one way of telling them apart: Tina had a large black mole on her left wrist. *If only I had seen her wrist*, Charlotte thought.

Jeff stood at the podium, confident that he had heard clearly from the Lord about the five areas to cover. He cleared his throat and spoke into the microphone. "I plan to be very brief this morning. There are five things I want to talk to you about, the first being your concerns about the tragedy that occurred yesterday. Some of you know how to trust God during difficult times, yet others may not. The deaths of Joe and Lilly Green came as a shock to the family and to the whole community. They were good people. I did not know them that well, but I do know a scripture. The Book of Isaiah, chapter 57, verses 1 and 2, says, 'The righteous pass away, the godly often die before their time and no one seems to care or wonder why.

No one seems to understand that God is protecting him or her from the evil to come. For the godly that die will rest in peace.'

"We live in perilous times. The quickness and the way that Joe and Lilly Green left baffled most of us, but God says our thoughts are not like His thoughts, and our ways are not like His ways. In God's mind, Joe and Lilly had served their purpose here on earth. Only He sees the big picture. So for those of us who remain here, we still have work to do, and I implore you to earnestly seek Him and find out what that work is. That is, if you don't already know. Not to worry. He will place it in your heart if you don't know.

"Too many of us spend our days making a living, but not living. We're fighting and scratching to keep food on the table and a roof over our heads. We need food and we need a roof, but is your life fulfilling and rewarding? You may be working on a job that is frustrating, but if you are a mother, your real job is to help birth something into your child or children.

"Take Goliath's grandmother, Ms. Bessie James, for instance. She was the only one willing to raise her grandson. She told me that she struggled financially, but she raised him in an atmosphere filled with love and the sounds of gospel music and the Word of the Lord. That atmosphere has propelled Goliath into his purpose. Now he is on his way to becoming a gospel artist who will reach millions of people.

"No, God's ways and thoughts are not like ours. Although the family and friends of Joe and Lilly Green are grieving right now, the Lord promised us a comforter— His Holy Spirit. The second topic that I want to address is that of disappointment. In the Book of Jeremiah, chapter 29, verses 11 through 13, it says: 'I alone know the plans I have for you, plans to bring you prosperity and not disaster, plans to bring about the future you hope for. Then when you call to Me and you will come and pray to Me and I will answer you. You will seek Me and you will find Me because you will seek Me with all your heart.'

"Let us think about that for a minute." Jeff paused to take a sip of water.

Satisfied that he, by way of the Holy Spirit, seemed to have captured the congregation's attention, Jeff continued. "All of us have been disappointed and discouraged by one thing or another, but take heart. Life's circumstances are tailor-made to keep us on our knees. They are designed to teach us patience and trust. You will learn to patiently wait on the Lord to fix it, or wait for Him to lead you in another direction. Pay attention to your life. I started out in real estate law, then I started a real estate development company, and now the Lord is leading me to write a book on operating a successful business using Biblical principals. We can make our own plans, but He orders our steps. Now I'm combining two topics here: pride and approval."

The congregation responded by saying, "Amen."

Jeff took another sip of water and wondered if he would still hear the "Amens" once he was done with this particular subject.

Jeff held the microphone to his mouth again and said, "On the matter of approval, you can no longer say that our young people are the only ones who try to fit in with the crowd. You can no longer say that it is only our young people who say yes to everything because they don't want to be rejected. People my age and even older, amen, are just as guilty. Too many of us are too concerned with image and reputation; image and reputation according to the world. But what does it profit a man to gain the whole world and lose his soul? What good does it do for Nee-Nee to marry little Johnny, the thuggish drug dealer, so that she can have material riches, but behind closed doors and fake smiles she lives in fear and misery? Nee-Nee sits at home afraid that one of Johnny's equally thuggish rivals will come in and kill her and her family. Nee-Nee sits at home afraid that Johnny himself, when he's not out with one of his women, may come home high and beat her up like she was a punching bag again. But Nee-Nee married Johnny because she can be seen with the bling-bling . . . black eyes, bruises, and all.

"What does it profit Leroy to marry Kiki, who is the most beautiful thing he's ever wrapped his arms around? At home, she can't cook or clean, but Kiki can cuss like a sailor and blow through his money like a hurricane. Again, I ask. What does it profit a man?"

The thunderous shouts and applause did not distract Jeff. "You can go after people, places, and things if you want to, folks, but if you don't go after God, that image and approval you strived so hard to attain can bring you heartache. Go after God, and He will bring you good things, things that have no sorrow attached to them. I'm just going to touch on pride a little because just as a color may come in different shades, so does the spirit of pride. Pride is not only walking around thinking that you are above everyone else; pride is what you have when you can't admit that you are wrong or when you won't say you're sorry. Pride is when you say no to help, knowing that you need it so desperately.

"And folks, you can't tell a prideful person anything. They're not teachable. Prideful people resent advice or ideas, even though they know deep inside their hearts that the advice or idea they heard was good, sound advice or a great idea. Often, you will hear these same people give away the very same advice or idea you gave them, and act as if *they* were the ones who came up with it.

"Oh Lord, I wish I had the time! I hope that I'm invited back to talk on this more, but I want to get on to the next topic. But let me leave you with this concerning pride: Pride comes before a fall. Have you wondered how a person can come back years later to say sorry? They fell. When you fall flat on your back, you look up. When you look up, you see the face of God. When you see the face of God, you see why you fell."

Everyone stood up clapping and shouting. Jeff went on to say, "Next, and I'm not spending a lot of time on this topic either . . . it's very simple: Occupy until He comes, for His return draws nigh. Seek Him. Find out what His will is for your life and do it. Accept Him as your Lord and Savior. We all must leave this place one day. You may not even live as long as Joe and Lilly Green did, and your life could be snuffed out just as quickly. My friends, I really don't think you want to hear Him say He never knew you.

"The last thing that I want to speak on is soul ties. Soul ties are very real, people. I believe one of the main reasons why the Lord forbids fornication is because it births soul ties. If you think about it, women are the ones who have the most difficult time getting over a break-up. Now, I don't want to offend anyone . . . no, let me back that up. I *do* want to offend you. Sometimes offense is a small price to pay if it can save somebody's life.

"I'm really saying this to the single women here. I want you to think about the fact that men are depositors and women are receivers. When you give away your bodies to every joker that comes along and shows you some attention, or even worse, *uses you*, you connected your spirit, your soul, to his. Sex is *not* just sex. It is spirit to spirit. It is a soul tie. And the reason why break-ups are so difficult to get over is because he . . . or they . . . broke their connection with you. Your flesh and spirit had become accustomed to theirs, and he severed the tie. Oh, I know I'm stepping on some toes in here, but you know what the sad thing is? The sad thing is that some of you know that I'm talking to you.

"You know that I'm stepping on your toes, and you will leave this place today, shake off the pain in your toe, and will stub it again because you've got to have a man in your life. Heal first. Wait on God to bring the right man in your life. Too many of you are being the man in your so-called relationships. Are you that desperate? If you are, let me tell you a little secret. We men can be stupid about many things, but we have radar when it comes to the different types of women. Don't fool yourself. If you're the needy type, you will constantly attract brothers that will take advantage of you. He sees the signal you give off even if you don't see it.

"I had no intentions of staying on this matter so long, but I'm not in charge here. Somebody needed to hear this. If it's any comfort to you, I want you to know that divorce and death is another way of breaking soul ties, and it hurts just the same. However, do not tie your soul up with someone illegally. Do you understand what I'm saying? And ladies, if you have children by a man who is no longer with you, don't let him nickel and dime you. Again, single ladies, quit being so anxious trying to prove what a great catch you are.

"If he's the man for you, he will recognize you as a good find. Ladies, he may be a so-called *good* man, but sometimes a man could be something else in disguise. A man is no good to you if he can't see . . . spiritually. A man is no good if he lacks integrity and honesty. If you see that he loves his mama, that's fine, but you still have to dig a little deeper than that to know what he's really about. And men, there is nothing like a spiritually discerning woman. She can see things that you can't, and *that's* a sister who's got your back. I sincerely hope somebody here was helped today."

38

Charlotte waited while Timmi thanked Mattie Mae and Edmund for their hospitality and promised to come back for another visit. Jeff had barely stepped down from the pulpit before the congregation had surrounded him to shake his hand, while Jesse Franklin escorted ten people who had given their lives to Christ during the altar call to the back. Out of the corner of her eye, Charlotte could see Eric leaving. She squeezed in between two rather large women standing in the center aisle and ran to catch up with Eric.

"Eric, Eric! Remember me? It is Eric, right?" Charlotte asked.

Eric turned around to see who was trying to get his attention. "Wassup?" Eric asked, flashing a big grin.

"I'm glad you came," Charlotte said. "Did you enjoy the service?"

"You know what? I did enjoy it. I liked that part when the preacher was talkin' about Leroy and Kiki. That was funny, but that was the truth. And Goliath . . . man, I can remember when people 'round here used to pick on that little dude. Now look at 'im. He fixin' to blow up."

Charlotte chuckled and said, "I pray so. To God be the glory. Listen. Where's your friend, Sherman?"

Eric looked down, shrugged his shoulders and said, "In jail."

Charlotte was surprised. "In jail! What's he doing in jail?"

Eric stepped aside to let an elderly couple pass by, and Charlotte could see the look of frustration on his face. "Man, that boy . . . I don't know. He came by my crib last night and wanted me to ride wit' him to the club. I said naw, I wanted to get up early and come here. I asked him if he was plannin' on goin' to church, but when he said he was gonna get his head bad, you know, get his drink on . . . I knew that meant he was gonna have a hang-over." Eric bit his lip. "Sherman is my boy and all, but sometimes he can do some dumb stuff. Now, I admit we both dropped outta school, but at least I will work. Sherman won't half work. He can sing just as good as Goliath can, and that coulda been him gettin' paid. Instead, he sittin' in jail 'cause he owes child support."

"Child support?" Charlotte asked.

"Child support. Man, Sherman got three kids, and he won't take care of near-a one of 'em. He keep makin' these babies and won't work. I told him he better chill on that. They snatched him right outta the club last night."

"Wow, that's messed up. Well, did he even fill out one of the job applications yesterday?"

"Nope. He don't wanna work."

"I hope you get the job, Eric. Listen, I've got to run. You take care of yourself, and tell Sherman that I asked about him and will be praying for him," Charlotte said as she saw Jeff and Timmi coming.

"Okay, I'll see ya later. Tell your friend I said thanks for helpin' me wit' the job application," Eric said as he walked out of the church.

Charlotte assured him that she would pass the message on.

Jeff tapped Charlotte lightly on the shoulder and informed her that her grandparents had already left with Sista riding shotgun. She followed Jeff and Timmi through the back door of the church to his vehicle. Jeff turned on the engine, shifted the gear in drive, and whirled around to the front of the church.

Except for a small cluster of members gathered around the front steps, the church grounds were virtually empty. The trio waved to the few as Jeff pulled off. Jeff turned on his windshield wipers, squirting water to wash away unwanted deposits left by birds that had apparently feasted on some berries.

"I'm so happy for Goliath," Charlotte said, powdering her shiny nose.

"I am too. What you did was really nice, Jeff," Timmi echoed in agreement from the back passenger seat.

"Goliath is a living testimony of what God can do in your life. My buddy really liked his voice, and he's real anxious to get the ball rolling," Jeff said, slamming on the brakes. This time a doe darted out in front of them and stood in the middle of the road for a second and stared at them as if they were crazy before crossing over. Then suddenly, a large buck with antlers that seemed to reach the heavens leaped across the road, causing Charlotte to gasp and Timmi to scream.

"Whew! That was close," Charlotte said, fanning herself with her hand.

"I know, and we're not far from Old Bay Bridge, either, so let's hope nothing jumps out of the water while we're on the bridge." Jeff laughed.

"What?" Timmi yelled in a panic. "What is in the water?"

"Nothing, girl, relax," Charlotte said, looking back at Timmi to see if she was all right.

"If you say so. I thought maybe they had some kind of folklore legend or something going on around here. You know, like the Loch Ness monster or Big Foot or something. Give me the two-legged beasts I have to work with anytime," Timmi said, still sounding uneasy.

Charlotte did not dare tell Timmi about the alligators that were known to inhabit the area. Jeff was just thankful that they didn't get hurt.

"Hey, listen to this," Timmi stated. "I forgot to tell you two, or at least I forgot to tell Miss Sista, that when she was kneeling at the altar during prayer, she forgot to take the price stickers off the soles of her shoes." Timmi nudged Charlotte in her back. "Girl, I tried to stop laughing and keep my eyes closed, but I just couldn't. What made it so bad, the price stickers were large! They were so big that they nearly covered the entire bottom of her shoes."

Jeff and Charlotte struggled to muffle their laughter, but they could not contain it.

As Jeff neared the airport terminal entrance, he was slowed down by heavy traffic. He turned on the radio just in time to catch the end of a late breaking news report. Apparently, a Boeing 747 aircraft that departed from Atlanta had just crashed into the Atlantic Ocean. Immediately, Charlotte remembered her vision of a vast body of water and felt a cold chill go down her spine as she watched helicopters fly over their heads.

"Oh my God!" Charlotte shouted.

"Oh my God is right," Jeff stated.

"You don't understand, Jeff. A few days ago I had a vision. I actually saw what looked like an ocean filled with debris and faces of people, only they had no features," Charlotte explained. "I had no idea this would happen."

"Really? You saw this?" Jeff asked, but Charlotte didn't answer. "I imagine half of these people are relatives seeking information. Let me see if these people know a little more about what happened."

Jeff turned off the air conditioner and rolled down his window. However, the people in the car to his left had their windows up and he couldn't get their attention. Jeff didn't want to be rude and disruptive by blowing his horn, so he just changed the radio station in hopes of finding another news report.

Within seconds, a reporter came on the air and stated, "Again, this just in. Atlantic Airlines, flight number 321, crashed into the Atlantic Ocean about forty-five minutes ago and approximately fifty miles from the coast. Most of the people on flight 321 were passengers who left the Bahamas some time this morning on another aircraft from another airline. The passengers had arrived at Atlanta's Hartsfield Airport about two hours ago, and the doomed flight 321 was a connecting flight headed for Charleston, South Carolina. It is not known why the aircraft bypassed the city and flew over the Atlantic Ocean. Speculation so far is that perhaps the pilot knew of some sort of problem and wanted to avoid any disaster on land involving a populated area. This is, however, only speculation.

"We've already received confirmation that it was *not* a terrorist related incident. Eyewitnesses say they saw the airplane take a steep dive into the ocean, and then there was an explosion. A great ball of fire is how one eyewitness described it. So far, local authorities are doubtful there are any survivors. Reportedly, the sky was perfectly clear . . ."

Jeff turned off the radio. Charlotte looked back at

Timmi and said, "I think that was insensitive of that reporter to make that comment about it being a 'doomed'
flight. It's bad enough that people are finding out that
their loved ones are gone. Comments like that are like
pouring salt in a wound. There has been so much death
around here lately."

"I agree," Timmi said.

Charlotte said a quick prayer before saying goodbye to
her friend. "Father, you are our God, our protector, and
we need you. I thank you for your traveling mercies. You
brought us here safely, and we continue to believe you
for our protection on the highways and airways. Father, I
ask that you arrest my friend Timmi in the spirit right
now with your peace. And Lord, as you know, loss of
lives has just occurred here. I lift up the grieving families
and friends to you for comfort. Confusion is all around,
and I ask for your peace in this situation. These things I
ask and thank you for in Jesus' name. Amen."

Jeff stopped by the curb long enough to hand Timmi
her luggage and give a goodbye hug. Charlotte also gave
her friend a warm hug before driving away with Jeff.

When Timmi got to the front entrance of United Airlines, she noticed through the glass doors scores of people frantically rushing to and fro down a narrow corridor.
They were being led by men and women dressed in navy
blue-and-gray uniforms and carrying walkie-talkies. Airport personnel were busy trying to calm down the waves
of mass hysteria. Numerous flights had been either cancelled or delayed. Dozens of passengers were standing
around crying.

Surprisingly, the United Airlines check-in line was rel-
atively short, and Timmi's flight had not been cancelled.
In fact, once Timmi approached the counter, she was told
by the clerk that her flight should be taking off as scheduled. The clerk also tearfully informed her that the ma-

jority of the people who were listed on Atlantic Airlines flight 321 were family members who were in the Bahamas for a family reunion.

After Timmi checked in her luggage, she headed toward Gate 11. She was a little apprehensive about getting on the airplane. On the way to the gate, she observed the various newsstands, restaurants, and shops. They were crowded with people watching the news on nearby television sets. Finally, she reached Gate 11 and stopped to join a group of folks gathered around a wall-mounted television. She watched in horror as teams of rescue workers and recovery crews darted about frantically trying to find and help victims.

Timmi decided that the news was too disturbing to watch and went to grab a seat. Shortly afterwards, the announcement was made for all first class passengers of United Airlines flight 411 to begin boarding. Timmi showed her boarding pass to the attendant and proceeded onto the airplane.

Meanwhile, Jeff and Charlotte were about to yield onto the highway. "This past week has really been a challenging one," Jeff reflected. "But God is still good and in control."

"I know," Charlotte responded. "Not to change the subject on how good God is, but I was wondering how many people were on that airplane."

"A hundred and forty-eight passengers according to the news report, and I don't think that includes the crew members," Jeff said.

"Lord! Just think . . . most of them were family members lost at sea. Whole families gone in a matter of minutes."

Jeff and Charlotte remained silent during the entire ride to his home. The fate of flight 321 had cast a spiritually thick, dark cloud on an otherwise sunny day. Charlotte searched her purse for the keys to her grandfather's car as Jeff pulled into the garage. After he unlocked the door to the house and disarmed the alarm system, he looked back to see Charlotte opening the driver side door of Edmund's car and tossing her purse in the front passenger seat.

"You're leaving now?" Jeff asked.

"Yes. My aunt and uncle may be at the house by now, and I'm kind of anxious to find out what information they have on Tina and Terry," Charlotte said.

"Sure. Well, let me come over there and give my little cousin a big hug," Jeff said.

"Jeff," she said, extending her arms, "I can't thank you enough for everything you've done."

"Thank me for what?" Jeff said then released her from his arms. "It's all good. Plus, I liked spending time with you and your friend and helping out the church. I'm serious about you and Timmi coming back for a visit any time you feel the need. My doors are always open."

"Thank you, Jeff. I'll keep that in mind."

"Drive carefully, Charlotte."

"I will," Charlotte said, gingerly pressing down on the gas pedal.

She glanced over at Brenda's vacant house while backing out of the driveway, and wondered how Yolanda was doing. The security guard waved at Charlotte as he opened the gate to allow her to exit. She then turned on the radio and scanned for a gospel station as soon as she got on the highway. The host of The Sunday Show on 81.5 FM was on the air talking about the airline disaster. She asked that the listening audience be in prayer for the families who lost loved ones.

Charlotte noticed that the drivers traveling in the opposite direction were driving with their headlights on.

Perhaps they were unaware of this fact, or this could have very will been an act to honor the deceased passengers of flight 321. Charlotte turned up the volume of the car radio and listened to the announcer mention Low Country Church on the Rock's upcoming Men's Day program, followed by announcing who the guest singers were for Mt. Hebron's summer concert, and the date for The Daughters of Esther fashion show.

After a long string of commercials, the announcer came back on the air to give an open invitation for auditions for The Tribe of Judah Singers, and to announce the cancellation of The Jethro Leadership Conference. By the time Charlotte had crossed over Old Bay Bridge, she realized that The Sunday Show was nothing more than a steady stream of church announcements and words from several sponsors. She turned off the radio.

As Charlotte made a right turn on to Lipscombe Road, she noticed huge amounts of debris in the street. Tree limbs, twigs, and leaves showed strong evidence that Turtle Island had been hit by either a storm or a strong gust of wind while she was in Charleston. Driving along the barren stretch of Lipscombe Road, Charlotte began to realize how she had been surrounded by so many unexpected twists and turns during her vacation and how God used her in these situations. Whether or not Maggie took the advice on how to treat her Aunt Lucille was on her. As far as Charlotte was concerned, she did her part.

And then there was the Lord's leading in a divine connection. She met her cousin, Jeff, and together they partnered in implementing ideas and improvements for the community and the church. The Lord even used Jeff to help Goliath get discovered by a record mogul. If Jeff had never heard Goliath's voice, the door to the recording industry would probably still be closed to Goliath. God was about to change Goliath from being a social outcast to a giant in the kingdom of God. Even convincing Timmi to come down South was a small miracle. Charlotte could tell by Timmi's demeanor during her visit that God was doing a work in her.

The stories of gratitude Charlotte heard at church about the elderly who received meals from the meals-on-wheels outreach program brought great joy to her. A few of the people had absolutely nothing to eat at home and their next Social Security checks weren't due for another week or two. Edmund, Joe Green, Busta Watkins, and a few others had come out of their pockets to put money in these people's hands. The plight of the Cabbage Patch elderly residents made Edmund vow to meet with the trustees of the church to come up with a way to help the senior citizens supplement their incomes.

If they could convince the members of the church to commit to paying their tithes, perhaps they would have a hefty surplus to help meet the needs of these people. Most of those who were over eighty years of age had been staunch supporters of Greener Pastures in the beginning years and used the money they earned from working in the fields and cleaning white folks' houses to help build the church. Yes, the thought of being used by God made Charlotte feel honored. She felt useful. She felt at peace knowing that she found her calling in organizing help ministries.

When Charlotte arrived at her grandparents' house, she saw Charles's black Mercedes parked outside the Morley residence. Charlotte felt a sense of dread. As she parked behind the Mercedes, she could hear loud, tormented wailing coming from inside the house, confirmation that something dreadful indeed had happened.

Charlotte ran into the house and found a distraught Francine kneeling at the sofa, screaming at the top of her lungs. Black mascara ran down her cheeks. Mattie Mae was standing over Francine, clutching her chest and humming an old gospel tune. Just as Charlotte was about to ask what was going on, she heard light footsteps coming from the dining room. She smelled the familiar scent of sandalwood and jasmine that lingered throughout the house only a week ago.

Out of the corner of her eye, Charlotte saw a bright yellow color. Standing in the entrance between the dining room and living room was a woman wearing a canary yellow spaghetti-strap tank top and a pair of white shorts. But it was the young woman's left wrist that commanded Charlotte's complete attention. It was Tina.

39

"Tina! I am so glad to see that you're all right, but will somebody please tell me what is going on?" Charlotte didn't know what to think.

Tina walked over to Charlotte and took her by the hand. "Charlotte, come in the kitchen with me, please," Tina said softly. Confused, Charlotte followed Tina, looking over her shoulder at her distraught aunt and grandmother and absorbing the wetness from Tina's sweaty palms.

Mattie Mae and Francine gave no indication that they were even aware of Charlotte's presence. Once inside the kitchen, Charlotte was all too eager for answers. "Tina, where have you been? Where is your husband? What in God's name is going on?"

Tina said nothing as she waited for Sista, who was in the kitchen wiping crumbs off the table, to leave the room.

"I'm fixin' to get outta the way," Sista said, throwing a tattered piece of paper towel in the garbage before leaving. Charlotte thought it odd that Sista voluntarily chose to leave the kitchen. Something had to be seriously wrong for Sista not to hang around to listen in on a conversation. Charlotte could feel her stomach twisting in knots. She waited.

"I didn't marry Reverend Holiday," Tina said bluntly. "Terry did."

Charlotte was speechless. Tina clasped Charlotte's hand tightly and said, "Charlotte, there is something else. I don't know if you've heard or not—"

Charlotte immediately felt a sharp pain in her stomach.

"A couple of hours ago, a plane crashed in the ocean. Terry and Reverend Holiday were on board." Tina's voice cracked.

All Charlotte could do was to stare at Tina in disbelief. She wanted to scream out, but her throat tightened. Hearing about yet another death was inconceivable, and this time, it was personal. Charlotte wanted to know if the family was sure that Terry and Reverend Holiday were on that airplane.

"We're positive," Tina told her. "Terry called me from the airport in the Bahamas just before they took off. She wanted me to know that they were coming on Atlantic Airlines flight 321." Tina's lips quivered.

"So what happened? I mean, I don't understand. We were told that it was *you* who married Reverend Holiday." Charlotte nearly shouted.

"Charlotte, all I can tell you is this: Terry and I have known John Holiday since college. At first, I thought he was a nice guy. But when Granddaddy told him off at dinner, I started having doubts about him. I was a little scared for Terry because I knew that they were eloping and they didn't want anybody to know. I didn't know that she pretended to be me until two days ago when this detective that my mom hired contacted me in Atlanta.

When he told me that Terry got married using my name, I got so angry. After he said that, I looked in my wallet for my Social Security card. It was gone, and so were a couple of my credit cards."

"Why did she feel she had to trade identities?" Charlotte asked, trying to make sense of it all.

"This may sound crazy, but in light of what the detective found out, I think she wanted to smear my name by having me linked to Reverend Holiday. He was about to be exposed along with some other people for being involved in some type of pyramid scheme bilking several churches out of millions of dollars," Tina said, looking Charlotte straight in the eye. "Terry blamed me and everybody else for what happened to her. Then, a few nights ago, Terry called me crying. Before she could say anything, I blasted into her. I didn't care why she was crying. I told her that if she didn't come back and straighten this mess out, I was going to have her arrested for identity theft."

Charlotte could not believe her ears. "How could she think she would get away with this?"

"I don't know."

Charlotte could now hear other voices besides Mattie Mae, Francine, and Sista coming from the living room. "So, did you find out why Terry was so upset?" Charlotte asked, still trying to process what she had learned so far.

"Terry said that John was beating her. They hadn't even been married a week, and he was beating on her . . . a preacher! When she told me that, I completely forgot about what she did to me and just redirected my anger toward him. Terry is—was still my sister. Anyway, Terry claimed she wanted to leave him and apologized for what she had done. I know it all sounds bizarre, but that was Terry. This family has no idea how messed up she was."

"*Bizarre* is not the word. Again, I don't understand. If she was leaving John, why was he on the airplane with her? My God! Was John in on this identity switch too?"

"Yeah, they were committing fraud against me, remember?"

Charlotte shook her head as she dabbed the corner of her eye with her index finger.

"But the reason why they boarded the plane together, I think, was probably because I had threatened to blow the whistle on them. I guess John thought he could come here and smooth-talk me into accepting some money, or maybe he wanted to beat me up too. Who knows? Anyway, he didn't know that Terry was going to leave him. Terry told him that I had forgiven them. She just wanted to return to the safe surroundings of her family before letting him know what her real plans were."

"Which were?"

"To leave him." Tina held her head down.

"I know this is a dumb question, Tina, but how are you feeling? You seem so calm to me."

"Well, I guess I'm in shock. I *know* I'm in shock."

"That's true. How can you not be? No wonder I kept hearing Terry's name."

"What do you mean you kept hearing Terry's name?" Tina frowned.

Charlotte wanted to kick herself for her careless slip of the tongue. The only way she could explain it would be to tell Tina that she heard Terry's name called in a dream, otherwise Tina would not understand. Besides, Charlotte was feeling uneasy around Tina. While it was true that Tina had just lost her only sibling, something still did not feel quite right.

Feeling somewhat guilty about not having bathed her visions more in prayer, Charlotte realized that she needed some quiet time before the Lord . . . and soon! But then

Charlotte got a check in her spirit. She felt a sense of peace as the Holy Spirit impressed upon her that while she was to pray, her prayers were not necessarily for intervention. He had given her visions as a means to prepare for things to come.

As Tina sat waiting for Charlotte's explanation regarding hearing Terry's name, Charlotte soon obliged her by saying, "It was just a dream. Listen, Tina, you must be exhausted. Why don't you go upstairs and get some rest?"

"I think I will do just that," Tina replied while looking at her watch.

Tina got up from her seat and hugged Charlotte. Charlotte went over to the cupboard to get a glass. She opened the refrigerator door and poured a small amount of fresh orange juice into the glass. Before taking her first sip, she asked the Lord for comfort and mercy for the family. After drinking her juice, Charlotte rinsed out the glass and placed it in the sink. She turned around and saw Sista standing behind her.

"Oh, Miss Sista! You startled me. How are they doing?" Charlotte asked.

"We finally talked Francine into goin' upstairs and gettin' some rest. I think she needs some nerve pills. A crowd of folk startin' to come in. Lawd have mercy. I ain't never seen nothin' like this," Sista said.

A weary-looking Mattie Mae came in the kitchen accompanied by Shelley's high maintenance friend, Felicia. Felicia was carrying a casserole dish, and Sista had a hunch that it was Felicia's leftover eggplant.

"What's that?" Sista asked sharply.

Felicia ignored the question as she placed the dish on the kitchen table and swiftly turned around to face Charlotte.

"I'm so sorry for your loss. I can't stay. I just wanted to drop this casserole off to help your family out. Shelley told me what a nice family this is, and now to have this happen." Felicia quickly left the room, leaving behind a heavy trail of her strong perfume.

"That heifer heard me talkin' to her," Sista said, lifting the lid off the casserole dish to see if her hunch was right.

"Leave it alone, Sista," Mattie Mae ordered as she sat down. "That gal got sense enough not to get in an argument, 'specially at a time like this."

"Grandma, you look so tired," Charlotte said as she went over to massage Mattie Mae's shoulders.

"Just get me some water, please, baby." Mattie Mae loosened the cap of a prescription bottle. "I came in here to take my pressure pill. I forgot to take one earlier today."

"Mattie Mae, why don't you stay in here and talk wit' Charlotte? I'll go around front and keep these folks company," Sista suggested as she started to leave the kitchen. Charlotte sat next to her grandmother and briefly held her hand before getting her a drink of water.

"Thanks, Sista. I think I will for a minute," Mattie Mae said. "I feel so helpless. I don't know how to help Charles and Francine . . . losin' their chile like that. Francine's nerves done shot to pieces."

"Maybe you should lie down too, Grandma," Charlotte suggested, handing Mattie Mae a glass of cold water. "Where is Granddaddy and Uncle Charles?"

Mattie Mae swallowed her pill. "At the airport. When I think about the fact that we might not even have a body to bury—"

"Grandma," Charlotte interrupted, "I really think you should get some rest. People will understand. Has anybody notified the rest of the family? Do I need to make any phone calls?"

"I had Sista call Willa Belle so that she can let everybody know what happened. Esau and Betty called right after Willa Belle called them. As much as this hurts, it just goes to show that none of us are here to stay."

"That's true, Grandma."

"It's just that Terry was so young." Mattie Mae sighed. "My mama used to say that there are just as many long graves as there is short ones."

"Come on, I'll go up front and sit with everybody. You go upstairs and try to get some rest. If anything happens, I'll let you know," Charlotte said, helping her grand-mother out of her seat.

Mattie Mae went upstairs after excusing herself to the guests sitting in the living room. Charlotte informed Sista, Deacon Brown, Ms. Mamie, Goliath, and his grand-mother that Mattie Mae was going to lie down for a minute, and everyone understood. Just as Charlotte was about to sit down, the telephone rang.

"Hello," Charlotte answered. "This is the Morley resi-dence."

"Hey, girl," the voice on the other end of the receiver said. "I made it home safe and sound, and it was sheer madness at Dulles too. Everybody is talking about—"

"Timmi," Charlotte interrupted. "Terry and Reverend Holiday were on flight 321."

"What? Your cousin Terry? Oh my God! I'm so sorry, Charlotte. Wait a minute. What were Reverend Holiday and *Terry* doing on that flight? I thought he was married to Tina."

"We did too, but Tina is here with us now. Timmi, I can't go into it right now and I apologize, but I'll try to call you back later. Are you going to be home?"

"Yeah, sure. Call me back whenever you get the chance. I don't care how late it is. Go do whatever it is you have to do, Charlotte."

"Thanks. I'll call you back. Bye." Charlotte hung up the phone and sat on the sofa next to Ms. Mamie, who was drifting in and out of sleep and reeked of Ben-Gay ointment. Sitting on the other side of Ms. Mamie was the ever-faithful Sista. Goliath's grandmother and Deacon Brown were seated in the loveseat chatting quietly. Goliath sat in Edmund's big leather recliner reading a Christian magazine.

"Charlotte, I don't think you've met Goliath's grandmother, Bessie James." Sista introduced the two women to each other.

"No, I haven't. It's nice to meet you, Miss Bessie. You have a very gifted grandson," Charlotte said as she went over to shake Bessie's hand. Bessie, who looked to be no more than sixty years old, beamed with pride at the mention of her grandson's talent.

"Glad to meet you too. I've heard a lot about you, young lady. I enjoyed yo' singin' so much today. Y'all done a beautiful job. Sho' did. I just wish we didn't have to meet like this, but the Lord knows what's best."

"Yes, ma'am, as difficult as it is for us to understand, the Lord does know what is best. Thank you for the compliment also. Oh, can I offer anyone a drink or something?" Charlotte said, her eyes scanning the room. Everyone declined her offer.

"Goliath has got a big day ahead of him, and he needs to get ready for his trip. We just stopped by for a quick second. Tell Mattie Mae that I'll stop back by here tomorrow," Bessie said as she and Goliath got up to leave.

Goliath approached Charlotte and said, "I want to thank you again for what you did for me, and I'll be praying for your family."

"Thank you, but it was God who orchestrated your blessing. It's a shame that Reverend Holiday died, but when you think about it, if he had not left the church, then I wouldn't have been inspired to ask Jeff to come speak, Jeff would not have heard you sing, and so forth and so on. What the devil meant for evil, the Lord turned it around and made something good out of it. I'm real happy for you, Goliath, and wish you the best."

"Thank you. You know, you're right, Charlotte," Goliath said as if he received a fresh revelation. "When it's your time, God will position you to be at the right place at the right time."

"Well, we're gonna run on too," Deacon Brown announced as he helped Ms. Mamie up from the chair.

Charlotte thanked each of them for dropping by as she walked them to the door, including Sista, who accepted Deacon Brown's offer to drive her home. There was an eerie calm in the air, and the house was as quiet as a tombstone. Charlotte sat alone in the living room waiting for Edmund and Charles to return.

She thought about how in just a short time, she witnessed tragedy after tragedy, while on the other hand, the community had renewed hope and opportunities.

Suddenly, Charlotte heard the name Terry again, and a chill traced down her spine. She felt that there was something about Tina that was not quite right, but she couldn't put her finger on it. Charlotte asked the Lord to show her what it was as she closed her eyes and prayed. During her prayer, in a still, small voice, she heard the word "deception."

40

Meanwhile, upstairs in the attic-turned-spare-bedroom was Terry, not Tina, standing in front of the tiny porthole window. She was drenched in sweat and rubbing the new rose tattoo on her left wrist, the only distinguishing mark between her and Tina. How clever she thought she had been in getting it. The tattoo was a last minute idea. Francine, despite not having been the most nurturing mother in the world, could, however, tell her daughters apart regardless of any tattoo. Luckily for Terry, Francine was too distraught to pay any attention to such detail.

However, Terry knew that first thing in the morning she would have to make a decision to either tell the truth or run away again. So far, she had been successful in avoiding Francine, who was too grief-stricken to see clearly. Terry had also been successful in telling half-truths to Charlotte. She did marry Reverend Holiday. She and Reverend Holiday were involved in a scam, and it was Tina who was floating dead in the ocean.

But what no one knew was that Terry had not called

Tina crying about being abused by Reverend Holiday. Rather, it was to plead with Tina not to press charges or testify against her. She had come prepared to tell the truth, if she had to, but she was better prepared to lie.

Prior to coming to Turtle Island, Terry had successfully brainwashed Tina into believing that their father had been molesting her over the years, an act that convinced Tina to move to Atlanta and alienate herself from her parents. Terry promised to let Tina know of her whereabouts, but not even Tina was aware of the fact that Reverend Holiday and Terry had been secretly dating and had eloped.

In Terry's warped mind, posing as Tina would be a safety measure. If anything went wrong with the money scam, it would be Tina who would take the fall as Mrs. Holiday, not her. Terry secretly hated Tina and her parents, and blamed them for not coming to her rescue by using their lung power to defend her when she was molested.

After being informed that her identity had been stolen, an angry Tina *did* fly to the Bahamas, along with the pesky detective who was about to expose the couple for fraud. Even though Tina was angry, she knew Terry needed help—psychological help. But Terry fled the island on an earlier flight the day before Tina and the detective could catch up with her.

Terry did not anticipate such an occurrence of disaster involving flight 321. Surprisingly, Reverend Holiday accompanied Tina and the detective back to the States to turn himself in to the authorities after the pair's confrontation. Terry, on the other hand, was holed up in a motel in Charleston, contemplating whether to exercise her power to run again or deal with her family and face criminal consequences, when she heard the news.

She rubbed her hand across the rose tattoo once more

thinking of Tina. She wanted to kick herself for not noti-
fying her parents of her whereabouts and nuptials. They
would not have liked it, but they certainly would not
have cause to hire a detective if she had made that phone
call.

Then there was the clerk with the uncanny memory
who worked at the license bureau. If it weren't for her in-
sistence when questioned by the detective that she did
not see a rose tattoo on Terry's wrist, no one would be the
wiser. Even when she married Reverend Holiday, Terry
had a sneaky suspicion that his house of cards would
soon fall. But she married him even though she didn't
love him. At least not in the conventional sense. She saw
her marital state as an escapism. A potentially wealthy
escapism. One thing was for sure: no amount of hatred
made her wish doom for Tina.

Terry admitted to herself that she made many mistakes
in carrying out this plot. Sadly, she did not recognize her
confusion nor knew anything of God's sovereignty. Now
somewhere deep in the crevices of her mind, Terry was
feeling a small amount of remorse and shame. Only a
small amount. Ignoring the still, small voice telling her to
repent, she opened her suitcase and took out a map of
the United States. She had made her decision.

Reader's Group Guide

1) Reverend Holiday caused a scandal by stealing money from the church and his girlfriend. However, what the enemy meant for harm, God can turn around and use for His glory. Can you think of situations where you saw Genesis 50:2 in your life?

2) Do you think Charlotte was getting spiritually fed at her former church, Truth in Love Tabernacle? If not, what were some of the possible hindrances going on that might have blocked true worship and spiritual breakthroughs?

3) Throughout Charlotte's life, she'd been given warnings through dreams and visions. Do you believe God still speaks to us today this way? If so, do you recognize warnings and practice intercession?

4) During the early stages of Charlotte's spiritual growth, she reached out to people for help in understanding. Have you ever experienced times when you shared something (your spiritual gifting, Holy Spirit encounters, etc.) with someone and discerned their envy, jealousy, or lack of understanding? Or has God sent you a mentor in this area?

5)   The scandal at the church set tongues wagging. Charlotte overheard a conversation wherein one person told another, "All the preacher wants is your money." Charlotte did not interject. Do you think she should have? If someone were to make such a comment to you, how would respond?

6)   The enemy has been after the seed (children) since the days of Moses. Molestation was one form he used against Terry. Can you name other ways used today against our children, and do you intercede on their behalf?

7)   Sista is a brash woman who is not afraid to speak her mind. A church member tried to console a mother who lost her drug addicted daughter by saying that the deceased child was in a much better place. Sista bluntly applied John 14:6 to the situation. Do you know many people who claim to believe there is a God, attend church on a regular basis, and yet tend to forget that Jesus Christ is the way to the Father?

8)   Jeff tried to help Charlotte's friend, Timmi, gain some spiritual understanding as to why there is poverty in the world and the benefits of suffering. Can you think of other situations where you can help someone see the big picture?

9)   How was Charlotte used during her visit on Turtle Island? Can you think of instances where your steps have been ordered by God and how He used you?

10) Greener Pastures demonstrated God's love outside the church walls by feeding the elderly, organizing a clothes drive, and setting up a financial fund to help low-income families. What are some other ways you think the church can help make a difference and/or influence our communities and industries?